BARRY B. LONGYEAR

SCIENCE FICTION'S ONLY
"TRIPLE CROWN" WINNER

Barry B. Longyear is the first writer ever to win
Science Fiction's top three awards in the same
year—the Hugo and the Nebula for his novella
ENEMY MINE, published in Berkley's MANI-
FEST DESTINY, and the John W. Campbell, Jr.
Award for Best New Writer of 1979. Turn the page
for the outstanding reviews of his acclaimed novels
of CIRCUS WORLD . . .

**Barry B. Longyear's fabulous
CIRCUS WORLD—**

"The further adventures of the interplanetary circus performers of Longyear's enchanting, delightful CITY OF BARABOO . . . Fast paced with a touch of wit and humor . . . fun reading!"

—*Concise Book Reviews*

"Longyear tells a consistently absorbing tale . . . never losing his wit, his eye for detail, or his skill at characterization. One may not finish the book believing Momus could exist, but one does very much *wish* it could!"

—*Booklist*

*Berkley books
by Barry B. Longyear*

CIRCUS WORLD
CITY OF BARABOO
ELEPHANT SONG
MANIFEST DESTINY

ELEPHANT SONG

BARRY B. LONGYEAR

BERKLEY BOOKS, NEW YORK

To Martin Fleishman, M.D.

ELEPHANT SONG

A Berkley Book / published by arrangement with
the author

PRINTING HISTORY
Berkley edition / April 1982

ISBN: 0-425-05167-6

THE ELEPHANT

The elephant's a beast, 'tis said,
That wears its tail upon its head;
And where the beastie's tail should be,
A wrinkled suit's all one can see.
It eats too much, its brain's too small
It takes up room from wall to wall;
Ears too big, and feet too flat,
Now, who could love a thing like that?

Yet, bullhands tell of circus rings
Surrounded by those smelly things.
Ballet girls would perch on top
While bullhands followed with a mop
And spade and barrow to haul away
The stuff the beasts et yesterday.
Bullhands speak of those squashed flat
By giants who are sorry that
Their keepers, friends, companions all
Must be scraped from off the wall.

Bullhands sing in tones adored
Of all of those who have been gored,
Or torn apart, or trampled down
By some bewrinkled, tusked clown.
It's sad to say but it's no act,
They love the beasts, and that's a fact.
And if you have but half a wit,
Can't find that 'pon which you sit,
Your back is strong, your mind is weak,
Your sense of smell is not at peak,
Then what they say, my friends, is true:
You can be a bullhand too.

The Admiralty Office of the Tenth Quadrant Federation announced today that the circus starship, *City of Baraboo,* enroute to the planet H'dgva in the Tenth Quadrant, failed to report in accordance with its flight plan four days ago. Ninth and Tenth Quadrant deep space radio searches detected neither distress calls nor automatic emergency beacon signals. Standard trade route sweeps have been begun.

The ship, housing the entire company of O'Hara's Greater Shows, the first of the interstellar circuses, is presumed to have been lost with all hands.

BILLBOARD, *May 29th, 2148, p.1.*

ONE

In the darkness above the atmosphere of the strange planet, ten smaller crafts detached themselves from a great ship, fired their entry burns, and fell toward the planet's surface. When the shuttles were little more than points of reflected light, the great ship seemed to wobble, then roll. For a moment the ship's movement seemed to stabilize, then its powerful engines gave a brief, blinding flash, the ship nosed over, and dived toward the planet.

A huge man with a bandaged head moaned and opened his eyes as he felt the reality around him shaking, then slamming to a devastating halt. He closed his eyes as pains that could melt steel shot through his head.

Noises. The smell of acid. The smell of smoke.

He drove awareness from his mind. There was so much to drive away. A dying ship, a dying show, a dying daughter—

"Get these two patched up, fast! I need them back on the radios."

"Are we down?"

"*Are we down, Mange? Hell yes we're down! Just put a dent in a goddamned mountain!*"

. . . so much to keep away: a dying show, a dying daughter, dying itself, the bulls—

He opened his eyes and stared blankly at the blur of rushing, screaming bodies. Someone had said something about the bulls—

"*Jesus, we're spread all over the place!*"

"*Fire control, down to the main carrousel! Pony? Pony Red, where are you?*"

Unintelligible crackles, words.

"*Get down to the main carrousel! The bulls and horses've broken loose and are shredding the place. Fire control, where'n the hell are you? Flame in the port carrousel!*"

The bulls. Something about the bulls. And fire.

He lifted an arm. Tingling numbness covering his body. Data began to enter the blank circuits of his mind. The bulls. Have to get to the bulls.

"*What about the atmospheric readings?*"

"*Screw 'em! If the air out there's no good, it doesn't matter much, does it? With that Hartford going in the port bay we don't have enough left in here to light a match. Open the damned vents and hit the fans!*"

"*That was some great landing, Fireball.*"

"*You try and deadstick in one of these bastards, punk! It's got the glide angle of a brick.*"

"*I said it was a good landing—*"

"*Where'n the hell are the others?*"

"*Try the radio, stupid—wait. What's that call?*"

"*It . . . it's the* Baraboo, *skipper. It's out of control. . . . It's diving into the atmosphere. . . . Signal's dead.*"

The voices. He pushed himself up from the couch and stumbled toward the voices. But now the control cabin was silent.

There was a breath of fresh air on his face, and he inhaled. He gulped at the air, and gulped again. His vision cleared a bit and he could make out the shuttle crew standing like statues before the control banks.

"You. Fireball. What is it?"

The command pilot of the Number Three car turned her head and looked at him. She seemed not to notice the blood dripping from her forehead. "The *Baraboo*. It . . . it just got exed. We got away just in time."

Fireball nodded at another crewmember. "Try and raise the other cars."

The crewmember stabbed at some buttons. "Any cars, this is Number Three. Where are you?" She listened, then tried again. "This is Number Three. Any cars, where are you?"

He rubbed his eyes, sat down on the edge of a couch, and looked at the shuttle's pilot. "Somebody said something about the bulls."

Fireball Hanah Sanagi squatted next to him. "Bullhook, it's hell down there. The outside hatch to the loading runs is jammed. The bulls are going crazy." The pilot stood and shouted toward the hands that stabbed at the communications bank. "What about fire control?"

"Forget it."

"Anything yet from the other cars?"

"Not yet."

Bullhook Willy got to his feet and supported himself against the couch's backrest as a crackle filled the compartment. "Hey! It's Number Ten! One, Four, Five, and Ten are within sight of each other near a big body of water." The crewmember talked rapidly into the communications system. "We're pretty bunged up. Came to a stop against a mountain. Heard anything from the others?"

He squinted his eyes against the light coming through the cockpit observation ports. Through them he could see bright sky, green trees hung with golden hair, a range of mountains.

More crackling. "Wait! I'm getting a strong signal from Number Six. Six can see Number Eight. Eight can't see Nine, but is getting a good signal. Number Two? Where are you, Number Two?" Silence. "Can anyone get a signal from Two? What about Seven?" Crackles, desperate calls, silence. "Okay, let's try and figure out how far we are from each other and in what relation."

On the couch rested a meter-long gold-tipped hook and goad. Bullhook Willy picked it up, turned, pulled himself through the compartment door, and headed down the dark companionway. The smell of it. Hot insulation, boiling hydraulic fluid, and overpowering every other odor, the smell of burning flesh.

The frantic calls from the control cabin were soon covered by the screams of the animals. He turned into the companionway leading to the huge cage of rotating tubes that held the elephants. An emergency light flashed in his face, then out of the darkness and smoke a voice yelled.

"Pony! Pony Red! It's Bullhook! The boss elephant man is here!"

Bullhook held his hand between the light and his eyes. "Waxy, you want to get that damn light out of my face."

The beam of light dropped as Bullhook supported himself by placing a hand against a bulkhead. The bulkhead was hot. Too hot. That was the smaller port carrousel containing half of the remaining Perches. Bullhook withdrew his hand. "Waxy, what about the horses?"

The dark shape holding the emergency light shook his head. "No good. Pony Red had to seal off the port carrousel to try and contain the fire. Doesn't look good. There's no fire in the starboard horse barn and in the main carrousel, but the smoke and lack of air is driving the nags and bulls crazy."

"There'll be air soon."

Another shape joined the one holding the lamp. "Mother Machree, but it's the hell of Hartford down there." The voice belonged to Pony Red Miira, boss animal man. "Waxy, why'd you put out the call?"

The one holding the lamp pointed at Bullhook. "The boss elephant man."

Pony Red moved next to Bullhook and placed a hand on the boss elephant man's shoulder. "Are you all right? The last time I saw you the back of your skull was caved in."

"I'm on my feet. We're down. We got to get the lead stock out of here. Why aren't the bay doors open?"

The boss animal man shook his head. "The last I heard from the crew back there, the doors were jammed. They can't get to the control that blows the damn doors off because of the bulls. Two of 'em are loose in the runs tearing up the place. Now we can't raise the aft crew at all."

Bullhook rubbed his eyes. "The carrousel. Can it still rotate?"

"Sure, but—"

"Get some lights on and move tube number one to the bottom, facing the doors. I'll get 'em open."

Pony Red shook Bullhook's shoulder. "You can't get through any of the tubes; especially number one. Six of the eight bulls in there have broken loose. We're trying now to get a crew around to open the doors from the outside."

Bullhook began to pull himself down the companionway.

"Dammit, Pony, if they won't open from the inside, they sure as hell can't be opened from the outside. Not in time. Just get tube number one facing the doors. I'll get through."

"Why number one?"

"Ming is in number one."

Bullhook walked between the two men and felt his way down the corridor until he reached the port to the main bay. He pulled himself through, ignored the elevator, and began working his way down the access ladder. Half of the way down nausea and dizziness washed over him as the pain in his head flashed lights before his eyes. He hung onto the ladder, resting his cheek against one of its cleated rungs. The smoke covered him like a hot blanket; the screams from the animals numbed his ears.

Crying. Just barely audible, there was crying among the screams. Lights went on in the access tube, turning the blackness into a dark gray pall. Bullhook Willy lowered himself another rung, then another, until he stood on the lower deck access compartment to the main carrousel. The air was a bit better. Fresh, cool air. He glanced to his left and could see the hazy outline of an open maintenance port. Through the man-sized doorway, he could see green grass. He turned from the ladder and lurched toward the closed doors that opened into the tubes as the rumble of the main carrousel turning vibrated the shuttle.

Before the doors, three figures knelt over a fourth. One of the kneeling figures stood and grabbed Bullhook. "What're you doin' here, Bullhook? You can hardly stand."

Bullhook forced his eyes to resolve the images before him. Packy Dern was holding him; Waco Whacko and Dot the Pot were kneeling over the still body of Haystack Harry. "What happened, Packy?"

The bullhand nodded toward Haystack. "Waco and I managed to pull him out of the number four tube. Too late." He looked back at Bullhook. "There's some others still in there."

"What about the rest of the bullhands?"

Packy shook his head. "God, I don't know. Most of 'em must be out of the shuttle by now."

Bullhook closed his eyes for a moment. "Waco. Get Dot out of here. Go through that open maintenance port."

The snake charmer looked over his shoulder at the boss elephant man. "What about you?"

Bullhook moved over and pulled Dot the Pot to her feet.

"Haystack's been exed, Dot. You have to get out of here."

Dot wiped the tears from her cheeks with the back of her hand. "I can't just leave him. Don't make me leave him."

"Packy and I'll take care of him. You go with Waco now. You're just in the way."

The snake charmer stood, held Dot's arm, and looked at Bullhook. "What about you?"

"I'll be along."

The snake charmer studied Bullhook with dark, narrowed eyes. "There aren't any heroes in the circus, Bullhook; just dead troupers and live ones."

"Get along, Waco." He placed a hand on the snake charmer's shoulder. "I'll be all right."

Waco spat on the deck and turned Dot the Pot toward the maintenance port. As the pair moved toward the opening, Bullhook pointed at the body. "Packy, grab Haystack and get out of here."

Packy Dern shook his head. "I heard the big cage turning, Bullhook. If you open those doors, it'll take about two seconds for this compartment to be full up with damned mad pachyderms."

The boss elephant man motioned with his bullhook toward the body. "Get Haystack and beat it. I have to get to the other end and open the main hatch."

"There's a crew outside working on it now."

"Packy, there's no time to work through from the outside. Now get moving."

"You can't make it!"

"Ming and I can." Bullhook pointed again at the body. "Now beat it."

Packy shook his head and lifted the dead bullhand's shoulders. "Maybe I can help."

Bullhook Willy stared at the closed doors to the main carrousel. "Beat it. And get that crew away from the doors."

Packy pulled Haystack's body away, and just before he reached the maintenance port, Bullhook called out. "Hey, Packy!"

"What?"

"Little Will. Take care of her. You know."

"Yeah. I know." The bullhand lowered Haystack's body through the port, then dropped himself through to the outside.

Bullhook Willy weaved before the closed doors, looking at the red square that needed to be pressed to open them. "Just hope to hell Ming is the first one out."

He reached out his left hand, slapped the red square, and stumbled to the right of the doors as they hissed open. There was no addition to the smoke, but the sound of the screaming bulls deafened him. A panic-driven elephant thundered through the open doorway, her shredded left ear dripping blood. It took only a split-second for Bullhook to recognize Cambo. As Cambo rumbled around the compartment looking for a pachyderm-sized exit, she was immediately followed by Queenie. Queenie's trunk was almost severed through.

Bullhook looked around the edge of the door and screamed. "Ming! Here, Ming! Goddammit, Ming, where are you?"

Down the length of the tube, three bulls were in the aisle on their sides either dead or dying. The remaining five bulls were loose and stampeding in the confined area.

"Ming! Dammit, Ming!" Bullhook sagged against the open door as his vision blurred. One of the five bulls paused, turned toward the forward end, then began walking toward the compartment. "Ming. That's it, baby. Right here."

Bullhook felt a thunderous whack across his shoulders, his face smashed against the bulkhead. He stopped himself from sagging to the deck, reached out, grabbed the rungs of an access ladder, and began pulling himself out of danger. Queenie rushed at him again and tried to pull him down, but she could not raise her wounded trunk. Just as he managed to pull himself above her, Queenie rammed the ladder and bulkhead.

Ming entered the compartment and bellowed. Bullhook called from his perch upon the ladder. "Ming! Over here, girl! Get Queenie away from the ladder! C'mon, Ming, you beautiful thing!"

Bullhook saw Ming look up at him. The sound she made was a blast of relief and joy.

"That's right, Ming. I'm here. Come on over and save old Bullhook's ass."

Ming lowered her head, tucked her trunk down, and charged at Queenie's side. The impact vibrated the entire compartment, almost causing Bullhook to lose his grip. Frightened by the attack, Queenie moved away from the ladder.

"Over here, Ming!" He smacked his bullhook against the bulkhead and Ming moved toward the ladder. The pachyderm presented her port side to the boss elephant man when she saw him whirl his bullhook in a circle. When she was close enough, Bullhook Willy leaped from the ladder and landed upon Ming's back. Painfully he pulled himself forward until he sat straddling the great beast's neck, the toes of his boots behind her ears.

"All right, babe! Let's get us the hell out of here!" He tapped Ming's right shoulder with his bullhook. "Shy, babe! Shy!"

The elephant turned to the right, and when she was facing the doors, Bullhook lowered himself until his right cheek was against the top of Ming's head. The stink of burned flesh filled his nostrils. "Let's go, babe! Mule up that damned machine! Go!"

Ming went through the doors and entered the number one tube of the main carousel, first at a fast walk, then at a trot. With screamed commands and taps with his bullhook, the boss elephant man steered Ming around the three dead elephants. With butts of her head, swats with her trunk, and goads with her tusks, Ming bulldozed the frightened elephants out of her path. One of the bulls attempted to fight back, and Bullhook felt a tusk enter the calf of his left leg. "Go, dammit! Go Ming!"

At the other end of the tube, the smoke was still thick. "Tut, babe. Park that thing until I can find the doorknob."

Ming stopped and the boss elephant man tried to clear his vision. "Great Boolabong, show me the doorknob. Show me." He shook his head, but the motion did more to increase the pain in his head than it did to clarify his vision. "Hell." He leaned to his right, reached down, and tapped the front of the elephant's shoulder.

"Give old Bullhook a kneel, babe. Let's go. Down, Ming."

As the elephant slowly knelt, Bullhook slid from her neck until his feet touched the hot deck plates. His left leg collapsed, and he crawled upon his hands and knees until he came to the aft tube doors. Pulling himself up, he felt for the door panel. Once he found it, he pounded it with his fist, causing the doors to hiss open. On the other side of the door, the two bulls that had broken loose from the number four tube were screaming and stampeding up and down the runs that led from the three carousel doors to the main hatch. The bulkhead panels above the port carousel door radiated orange heat. The remains of two human bodies smeared against the cleated surface of the runs explained why Pony Red Miira hadn't been able to raise the aft watch.

Bullhook pushed away from the bulkhead, collapsing upon the deck. He looked at the bull. Ming stood patiently awaiting further instructions. The boss elephant man thought he blacked out for a second, then was brought wide awake by the blinding pains that coursed through his leg, back, and head. The pains eased for a moment, and Bullhook called out. "Ming. I can't make it. Get that durante out and log me out of here!" He smacked his bullhook against the deck. "Ming, let's go!"

The pachyderm moved to her right until she faced the boss elephant man's prone figure. Then she reared up on her hind legs and screamed. Her front legs came down hard, and Bullhook knew what was in her mind. He knew because he had been there. "Ming! This is Bullhook, honey. Bullhook." The elephant snorted, rocking back and forth. "That was another crash, another time, another place. Years ago, babe. This is Bullhook, Ming." He held up his gold-tipped hook and goad. "Bullhook."

Ming stood still for a moment, then she lowered her head, lifted her trunk, and gently shoved her tusks beneath Bullhook's body. The boss elephant man held his gold tipped bullhook out so that it would not be out of the elephant's sight. "Remember me, Ming. You gore me and it's liable to ruin my whole day."

The elephant's trunk wrapped gently around Bullhook's waist as her head came up. "Okay, babe. Let's lead this parade out of here. Go, babe, go!"

Ming moved out toward the main hatch. The two bulls rampaging in the runs moved toward her. "Mile, babe! Get me to that damned switch box! Go!" Ming crossed the runs and stopped before the huge hatch door. The heavy metal door was warped from the impact against the bottom of the shuttle. Nothing short of blowing the thing off of its bolts would open it. "Shy, babe. Get me over! Shy!"

The elephant moved Bullhook to the right, and the boss elephant man reached out and flipped open the cover on the emergency switch. He pulled down the bright red handle inside and then blackened out as two hundred exploding bolts went off at the same time that a bull smashed into Ming's side. When he opened his eyes, his body was being shaken unmercifully as Ming stampeded through the open air and tall grass of the strange planet. Voices called after them, but Ming wasn't listening.

"Ming! Ming!" The elephant slowed to a trot, then to a walk. "Tut, babe! Put me down, honey."

The huge beast shuddered and then lowered her head, de-

positing the boss elephant man upon the grass. Her head lifted
and she stood, snorting and shaking her head. "Good girl. Good
girl."

The voices again. Louder. Feet running through the grass.
Bullhook opened his eyes and looked at the clear, blue sky.
Parade weather. Damn, but it's a beautiful day. Packy Dern's
face came into view as the bullhand knelt and quickly examined
the boss elephant man. Bullhook felt something placed beneath
his head and pressure being applied to his left leg. Other hands;
other faces. Waco, Dot the Pot, Madman, Pony Red, Moll . . .

Packy's face looked at him and smiled. "Whatcha been up
to, Bullhook?"

"A little this; a little that."

Bullhook felt a needle being poked into his arm. Packy
nodded. "Well, it sure looks like it was fun."

"You know what they say, Packy . . . life with the circus is
just one long uninterrupted dee-light."

*The blue sky grew black, Packy's face faded, and the sharp
jags and angles of pain smoothed into a calm night sea of slow
motions and soft sounds.*

*There was more touching against his body, dim voices, a
bullhand singing "Elephant Kindergarten" to her pachyderm.
That's Kim's voice. That's right, honey. The car crashed, I
don't know where in the hell we are, no one will ever find us,
don't know where our next meal is coming from, but calm
down. Some things are still the same. I'm still here, and mule
up still means trot. . . .*

*And life? It's the same as its always been: life with the
circus is just one long uninterrupted dee-light.*

Yowzuh! Yowzuh!

*Step right up and feast your little bug-eyes on the wonderous
monsters from the planet Earth! Peruse the ponderous pachyderms—*

*—That's what I said, sir, or madam, or thing, as the case
may be. Pachyderms—*

—'Cause that's what they're called, sonny.

*One quarter credit, a mere twenty-five percent of a one note
will admit you to feast your eyes, bulbs, sensors, or whatever
the hell it is you use—*

Beat it boy, you bother me.

Now, folks, slither right up . . .

TWO

Waco Whacko, the snake charmer, turned away from Bull-hook Willy's body as Mange Ranger, the show's vet, ran up and began pushing his way through to the fallen bullhand. Waco headed back to the shuttle and climbed one of the ladders to one of the open emergency ports. The other bullhands were urging, coaxing, and cursing their pachyderms out of the main hatch. As he entered the port and headed for his quarters, he could feel the rumble of the main carrousel turning, bringing another tube of bulls in line with the hatch.

Entering his quarters, he sat upon a locker, the smoke still heavy in the air. He picked up a gray cardboard box and placed it upon his lap. He opened the box and looked at the five fist-sized blue eggs within it. A spot of moisture appeared upon one of the eggs, and Waco wiped the shell of the egg dry with a fingertip. Another droplet appeared and Waco lifted his hand and touched his cheek. Tears. The sickness. Again the sickness.

A voice came from the compartment door. "Everybody out!"

Waco's head turned and he saw Fireball Hanah Sanagi's face looking through the hatch.

"Waco, you have to get out. The only way we can control the fire is to smother it. We're sealing up the shuttle."

Waco nodded and Fireball's face disappeared. The snake charmer closed the box, but remained sitting upon the locker.

The sickness. God, the sickness.

Fifteen years before, Buns Bunyoro had brought it on. And now, Bullhook Willy. Waco remembered the Arcadia wintering grounds in a distant place called Florida. In another time, another place, another dimension.

Waco had been reading when someone knocked upon the door to his van. Waco opened the door to see the boss animal man, Pony Red Miira, standing on the lot.

"Waco, you know we went to pick up those two new bulls this morning. It was a mess. The freighter crew exed one bull and cut up the other one."

The snake charmer stared at the boss animal man, his face and heart frozen.

Pony Red looked down. "Buns got it. I'll be by later to gather up his things." The big man thrust his hands into his trouser pockets, turned, and walked toward the elephant barn. "Sorry."

Waco closed the van's door and returned to his reading.

Later that evening there was another knock upon the door. Waco looked at his book, realizing that he had been looking at the same page for over two hours. He put the book aside and opened the door. The new bullhand that Buns had taken under his wing, Bullhook Willy, climbed the steps and stood in the open doorway. "Buns got exed. Thought you'd want to know." Willy looked up at Waco.

"I heard." Waco nodded toward Bullhook's bandaged hand. "How's the mitt?"

"Okay. We had to winch that one bull out of the freighter. Caught my hand between the cable and deck. Bone Breaker fixed it up'n gave me something for the pain."

Waco cocked his head toward the interior of his van. "Come in if you want."

"I just wanted to say how sorry I am."

Waco dropped into an easy chair and clasped his hands together. "Don't be sorry on my account, Bullhook."

Willy sat down in a chair facing the snake charmer. "He was your friend, wasn't he?"

"That's what he called himself." The snake charmer's deep black eyes studied Willy. "I have no friends—no *human* friends."

Willy looked down and shook his head. "Why'd you live with him then? And for ten years?"

"He paid rent." The snake charmer reached out a hand and stroked a passing python. "His conversation was enjoyable." He sat back. "Do I sound a little cold to you?"

Willy slowly nodded. "That's the word: cold."

Waco closed his eyes and leaned his head against the chair's headrest. "I never let myself become friends with a human. The human is the only animal that ever disappoints me." He opened his eyes and looked at Willy. "I haven't had much contact with nonhuman intelligent aliens, but I imagine that they, too, will disappoint me. Buns went and committed suicide today, or the next thing to it. By doing so, I suppose you think he is some sort of hero. I don't. Although I do not include myself among them, there are those who have an affection for Buns. Buns cheated them. Buns is a cheat. He is a human and a cheat. I expected nothing more from him; I expect nothing more from any human."

Bullhook Willy sat quietly for a moment, and then he swung his bullhook from his left hand, stood and turned toward the door. "I better be getting back to the barn. I start trying to break in that bull tonight."

The snake charmer stood and walked Bullhook Willy to the door. As Willy reached the bottom step, Waco spoke. "What is the bull's name?"

"Ming."

"How old are you, Bullhook?"

"Eighteen."

"Do you think you can handle her?"

Willy shrugged, then ran the fingers of his good hand through his hair. "I don't know. That's not good, is it? Poison Jim used to say that you have to know you can do it. If you don't the bull can tell."

Waco nodded. "Animals can read humans a whole lot better than humans can read animals. Does Ming have you scared?"

Willy licked his lips, shrugged, then nodded. "Now she does. Out there on the airfield I didn't even think about it. There wasn't time to think. But ... since then I've had some time."

"Good. You keep thinking, Bullhook. It works the same with any animal. You think, watch, and study. You study Ming until you can read her—understand her. When you understand her, you'll know what she wants, what she needs, and what you have to do. Once you understand her, you won't be scared. Don't make your move until then."

Willy rubbed his chin, then dropped his hand to his side. "Waco, did you know Poison Jim? You two talk a lot alike."

Waco shook his head. "Just to talk to years ago when he was with O'Hara's. But all animal men know the same things. The ones who don't either wind up dead or killing their animals."

Willy nodded and turned toward the barn. "Thanks, Waco."

"Bullhook?"

Willy turned and looked back at the snake charmer. "Yeah?"

"If you want you can move out of the barn and stay here."

Willy's eyebrows went up. "What for?"

"Ten credits a week."

Willy shrugged. "Why not? I'll go get my kit."

"Not tonight." The snake charmer half-turned back into his van. "Tomorrow. Move in tomorrow. Tonight...tonight I have some thinking to do." Waco went inside, closing the door behind him.

And then there came the sickness. Waco had cried and swore to the universe that he would never again love.

And now Bullhook Willy was broken and gasping upon the surface of a planet that didn't even appear in any of the star charts. And the sickness was again upon the snake charmer.

In the box upon his lap were the eggs of five of the twenty Ssendissian snake telepaths that Waco had brought to the show. The eggs were all that remained of the Ssendissians. And the eggs were conscious, feeling their own special sickness for their dead parents.

Waco stood and left the compartment. When he again stood upon the planet's soil, he looked at the huge lake that began far down the slope from the wrecked shuttle. Beyond the lake was a forest, or swamp. But no humans; nothing to love.

He began walking toward the shore.

THREE

On the evening of that first day, across the huge lake, into the thin edge of the swamp just visible beyond it, the sun was setting. Packy Dern sat on the dew-weighted grass with his arms wrapped around his knees. The few clouds in the sky were black-red edged with gold placed against a sky as scarlet as blood. And, lordy, there had been plenty of blood.

He closed his eyes and held his head down for a moment. "Hell, yes." He lifted his head and looked at the near shore of the lake. The vee-shaped trough cut by the menagerie shuttle's belly began there. It ended in the trees far to his left. To the right of the trough were rock-capped hills. To the left was a ravine cut by the exiting waters of the lake as they flowed downhill toward the south. Considering the alternatives, Fireball had made a great landing.

A practical landing, too.

Bullhook Willy and the thirty-two other troupers who had died had been laid out in the short stretch of trough a hundred yards from the shore. There weren't any dozers or shovels with which to dig graves. And after the bodies were arranged at the bottom of the trough, all those who weren't injured gathered on the two sides. The boss animal man had stared at the bodies for an instant and then began kicking clods of dirt and grass into the cut. The two hundred and twenty-six troupers standing with him then became animated. With feet, hands, sticks and tears they covered the dead.

Packy shook the image from his mind. Without looking at it, he picked up the mahogany-handled, gold-tipped bullhook that was on the grass next to his own steel and rubber affair. With the warmth of the fine wood against his rough hands, he remembered. Poison Jim Bolger used to carry that hook before his trunk was put on the lot. Poison Jim was a lush, and nobody wants a bulland with a nose like a fire alarm in control of tons of pachyderm.

So he was fired and the bullhand was swallowed up by that strange, cruel universe that existed outside the lot. Then, fifteen years later, the gold-tipped bullhook returned. It was in the hands of a skinny, eighteen-year-old Johnny-come-lately named Willy Kole. The kid never let that bullhook out of his sight. That's why they called him Bullhook Willy. And only ten years later, Pony Red made Bullhook boss elephant man even though there were other hands older and carrying more years with the bulls. No one ever questioned the boss animal man's decision, because the bullhands knew Bullhook Willy, and Bullhook Willy knew which end of a bull the tail was on.

"Hell." Packy picked up his own bullhook, pushed himself to his feet, and brushed the seat of his trousers. He turned and moved up the gentle incline toward the *kraal*.

"Poison Jim would say 'Boy, I say, boy, hosses go in a corral. 'Zat look like a damn hoss, boy? 'Zat's a bull, boy, an' bulls go in a kraal.'"

And Bullhook Willy would laugh at his own story.

Packy halted at the crude fence the bullhands had constructed out of rocks and the trunks of trees uprooted by the landing of the Number Three car. The fence formed one side of a rough triangle. The second was formed by a sheer wall of stone that seemed to extend forever upwards. The third side was formed by a cliff.

"You don't have to worry about a bull walking off a cliff, boy. Bull's got more sense'n a man. Don't you, I say, don't you know nothin'?"

And Bullhook would laugh.

Packy reached the fence and climbed up the rocks and logs until he could look over the top. Ghostly beams of white light in the shadows below the reflected red of the rock wall testified that the show's vet, Mange Ranger, was still working on sewing together Queenie's trunk. Several hands were helping the vet work on the anesthetized pachyderm while two bullhands stood between the operation and the remaining bulls. Just in case.

Packy's bull, Robber, was contentedly yanking up and munching the grass of the compound. Thank the Boolabong for small favors. The grass was edible. Most of the hay and grain feed had been tossed out to lighten ship long before the *Baraboo* had burned.

Out of seventy-five bulls, thirty-four remained. Most of them had died in the parent ship's bad air, their carcasses tossed out to lighten ship. Nine had died when Number Three went down. Tomorrow would begin the job of hauling the dead bulls and the eighty dead horses from the port carrousel out of the shuttle to join the others in the big ditch. The one hundred and twenty-two surviving horses, Percherons and performing, were strung out at the edge of the trees below the *kraal*. One hundred and twenty-two horses remaining out of three hundred and fifty. None of the thousand or so other animals—big cats, camels, giraffes, apes, birds, snakes—none of them had made it down.

Near the edge of the cliff, her form motionless in the shadows, Ming stood away from the other bulls looking toward the darkness. Years before, it had been Ming on her side while Mange Ranger worked to sew up the cuts and the laser burns inflicted by some airfield yahoo at Port Paolito. That was in '27, fifteen years before O'Hara's Greater Shows took to the star road, in the elephant barn at the show's wintering grounds in Arcadia, Florida, North American Union.

Packy looked at Mange and his crew working on Queenie, but what he saw was that night so long ago. Mange had finished working on Ming, and Packy had agreed to sit up in the barn and keep watch. It was very late, and Ming struggled to her feet as the anesthetic wore off. She tested the chains on her feet, snorted, and then bellowed. She fought against her chains for a few minutes, then stood motionless except for her sides, heaving with each hard breath she took.

Packy had picked up an armload of hay and began walking toward Ming, but before he could offer the hay, Ming bellowed, stamped her feet, and began swinging her trunk. That trunk had taken out one bullhand, Buns Bunyoro, as Buns and the new kid, Bullhook Willy, tried to get the pachyderm out of the air-freighter's hold. Ming swung her trunk again and Packy threw the hay down upon the concrete floor of the elephant barn. "To hell with you, lady. I got a wife and a whiskey habit to consider." Packy returned to the stacked haybales and stretched out, waiting for the bull to settle down.

He dozed, then came awake as he sensed another presence in the barn. A number of the bullhands slept in the barn when they were tapped, and Packy prepared to resume his nap. Then he saw the new kid, Bullhook Willy, sitting in the hay a few feet away. His forearms rested upon his knees, the famous bullhook dangling from his right hand tapped steadily against his shoe. Directly across from Bullhook, Ming stood silently, staring back at him. The mountain of gray flesh was a living part of the shadows; then a glint from an eye, the gleam of a tusk. Each detectable motion from the elephant seemed to knot the kid's insides tighter and tighter.

Ming was the only bull without a bullhand; and the kid was the only bullhand short one pachyderm. But besides being a killer, that particular pachyderm was hurting, frightened, and angry. Packy wiped the sleep from his eyes, crawled across the haybales, and deposited himself next to Bullhook Willy.

"If you was smart, you'd wait 'till morning."

Willy turned his head. "Who's that?"

"It's me: Packy."

Willy looked back toward Ming. "If I was smart, Packy, I'd be in the treasury wagon."

"Bullhook, in the morning we can get her chained up on a cross and her head tethered down so she can't swing those tusks so wide. You need at least a couple of extra hands to bring that bull in line."

"Ming's already scared and confused, Packy. I want her to know that I'm the one she's supposed to mind." Willy looked up at the darkness. "It's quiet now and she's calm. I figure it's now or never." He looked back at Packy. "Ming is *mine*. She's got to know that."

"Buns was a good hand, Bullhook. And that pachyderm exed him."

A snort came from the shadows, then the clank of a leg testing the strength of a chain. Bullhook studied the shadows. He pointed his bullhook toward the animal. "If I don't get her to toe the line, she'll be meat for the cats."

Packy placed a hand on Bullhook's shoulder. "Ming is still scared. Wait until morning."

"No."

Packy removed his hand. "That joy juice Mange Ranger

shot in her rump's all wore off by now. She's hurtin'."

"She won't hurt any less in the morning."

Packy sighed and leaned back in the straw. "Bullhook, you and Buns have a lot in common."

"Thanks."

"Yessir, pig-headed, bull-happy, and dead."

Bullhook's head snapped toward the other bullhand. "Packy . . ."

"What?"

Bullhook took a deep breath, exhaled, then looked back toward Ming. "Like I said: if I was smart, I'd be in the treasury wagon." He looked back toward the shadows and pushed himself to his feet. "I got to go and see my elephant."

Packy sat up. "Talk to her. All the time; talk to her. Keep your voice quiet, but let 'er know you mean business."

"Right." Bullhook bent over, picked up a handful of hay, and stood.

"Remember, kid: all you have to do is chicken once and it's all over."

Bullhook nodded and walked from the straw onto the concrete in front of Ming's stall. "All right, girl. Easy now." Ming studied Willy, first with one eye, then the next. He stopped before her, just out of reach. "You don't hurt much now, girl. You're nothing but scared." He reached out the hay. "You haven't eaten for a long time, baby. Come on, now." He shook the hay.

Packy saw the elephant study the interior of the bull pen, then examine the scrap of flesh standing in front of her. No bullhand ever looked so small; nor any bull so large.

Ming reached out her trunk and took the offering. As she stuffed the hay into her mouth, she kept an eye on Bullhook. As she chewed, Bullhook Willy moved closer. Ming brought up her head, then lowered it. Willy reached out a hand and stroked Ming's trunk. The bull swung her trunk, caught Bullhook in his middle, and sent him tumbling across the floor.

Packy sighed and shook his head. "Are you still alive?"

The boy got up on one elbow, reached two fingers into his mouth, and withdrew a tooth. Bullhook Willy laughed. "Packy, I'll be damned if we don't have a dentist in the show now."

Willy pushed himself up from the floor, picked up his bullhook, and walked until he stood directly in front of Ming. He swatted her cheek with the bullhook and commanded: "No." He reached out a hand and stroked her trunk. "This is what we should be doing, babe. I don't want to hit you. But you have to behave. If we don't get along, you'll be cut up and fed to the cats. Let's go."

Ming again swung her trunk, bowling Bullhook across the floor and into a wall. Again, Packy shook his head. When the kid stood his face dripped red. He returned, stood before the pachyderm, wiped the blood on his sleeve, lifted his stick, and swatted her cheek with it. "No, babe. Don't do that."

The pachyderm stood quietly. Willy turned away then came back carrying another load of hay. Ming studied it, then reached out her trunk. She took the hay and allowed Bullhook to stroke her trunk as she ate. After stuffing in a load of hay, she slowly raised her trunk and wrapped it around Bullhook's shoulders, then his waist.

Packy got to his feet. A trunk around his waist, then the bull pulls you between its front legs, then it begins to work on you with the ivory. But this bull was not preparing for a gore job; she was sniffing her new master. The kid didn't tremble, and he kept his gold-tipped bullhook in plain view. Ming eyed the stick, then let her trunk drop to pick up some of the hay that was in front of her.

Bullhook Willy went back to get some more hay. As he stooped down, Packy let out his breath. "She's yours, Bullhook. She's all yours."

"Yeah." There was a glistening of tears on the kid's cheeks. "Yeah." Bullhook Willy picked up the hay and returned to his elephant.

But that was a lot of years ago.

And the first sunset was dying on a strange planet.

And Madman Mulligan was Ming's bullhand, now.

The survivors were setting up housekeeping in grass shacks and caves. Packy felt a chill, climbed down from the fence, and looked toward the rough long house that had been put up as a makeshift infirmary to house the injured. Somewhere in there, fighting for her life, was Little Will, Bullhook's twelve-year-old daughter. Footsteps came from the direction of the still-smoldering shuttle. It was Pony Red Miira, the boss animal man.

"Packy?"

"Yeah?"

"You're boss elephant man."

"I don't want the job, Pony."

"Who asked you?" Pony Red climbed the fence, went over

the top, down the other side, and continued toward the white lights. Mange was still working on Queenie.

Packy glanced at the final red of the sun against the sky, then looked down at the gold-tipped bullhook in his hands.

"Yessir, pig-headed, bull-happy, and dead."

He began walking toward the infirmary.

FOUR

Little Will held herself motionless in the dark. She knew
that all she had to do was to open her eyes, and the blackness
would go away. But then would come the hurt.

She smelled wood smoke, heard a fire's quiet crackle, then
noticed that someone was holding her left hand. The hand
holding hers was large, warm, and gentle. She cautiously rose
from the blackness, just a little, ready to recoil if the pain
returned. Her head ached, but that searing, shattering bolt of
agony that had always waited for her to open her eyes appeared
to be gone. She let more of that cotton of blackness drop from
her and opened her eyes to tiny slits.

Above her were poles and thatch. They seemed to move in
the flickering yellow light. She turned her head slightly to the
left. A shadow hovered over her; a shadow and half a face.
The face was familiar. Wispy gray hair, long face. She opened
her eyes the rest of the way and tried to call out to the man
with her thoughts.

The man's eyes were closed, his face relaxed. Little Will
tried to project her thought into the man's mind as Nhissia had
trained her to do. She frowned as the thought refused to form.
She tried harder, and then gasped as the pain returned. She

gripped the man's hand as she covered herself with the blackness.

In her dream she looked for another face; another man. The one who had deserted her. So long ago. Long before she could speak.

In the brightly lit hotel room, she sat on the big man's knee, his arms around her resting on the edge of the table, his large hands holding four cards. She looked into his sad face, then turned to see the man on the other side of the table. He was dark and was also holding four cards. His face was also sad. "Your draw, Bullhook."

The large man reached forward, picked up a card from a stack of cards, looked at it, then tossed it upon the table.

The dark man frowned as he drew a card. The dark man put the new card into his hand and hesitated.

"Throw anything you want, Waco. Anything at all."

The dark man raised his eyebrows without looking away from his cards. "You sound awfully smug for a man with bull plop for brains."

"Sticks and stones, Waco. C'mon."

The dark man touched first one card, a second, then pulled out and discarded a third. "Chew on that, Bullhook."

The big man put down his cards next to the dark one's discard. "Ain't they pretty? How many did I catch you with?"

The dark one tossed his cards on the table. "I'm over. That's game."

The big man wrapped his arms around her and jiggled her on his knee. "How about that, Little Will? Your old man just wipped the drawers off that hose merchant over there."

She giggled.

The dark one gathered up the cards. "Another game?"

The big man shook his head. "I can't. I have to go soon."

"Do you think you'll have much trouble rounding up the bulls?"

The big man shrugged. "Can't tell, yet. Eco-Watch doesn't want to let anything off of Earth—officially."

The dark one leaned back in his chair. "Unofficially?"

"Money talks. I'm supposed to come up with around two hundred bulls. I'll probably be away for two, three months." He mussed up her hair. "I sure hate to go right after you and me found each other." He kissed her cheek, then looked back at the dark one. "Waco, how come she doesn't talk? I thought kids this age could say at least a few words."

"It takes some kids longer than others."

The big man shook his head. "I wonder if it's that genetic thing. From the war. There was a problem."

"Bullhook, it takes some kids longer than others. Don't go looking for trouble." The dark one nodded his head toward the hotel room's outside glass wall. "What were you doing out in the cold cruel for the past two years?"

"Wandered around. I saw a couple of planets; Mendik and Ourylim. Handled some animals there." He pushed a lock of black hair from the little girl's eyes, then he looked back at the dark one. "I went back to the foster camp—except it's not a foster camp anymore. You remember the place I told you about?"

The dark one nodded. "I remember."

"Old Doctor Mentz is dead. The camp is just a regular school. Atabi is the school district superintendent. I talked to him." The big man shook his head. "He's a lot different than I remembered."

"Did you ever find what you were looking for, Bullhook?"

The big man studied her, and then hugged her again. "I think so." He looked back at the dark one. "How come you came back to the show, Waco? Ssendiss sounded like snake heaven."

The dark one laughed, then sipped at a cup of herb tea. "Bullhook, I was a flop as a teacher. My course on Earth snakes bored my students stiff. The trouble with telepaths is that they have some rather startling ways to let you know that they're bored. I can tell you that the novelty of juvenile telepathic pranksters wears off quickly."

The big man bounced her on his knee. "How did you get your act together?"

"The ones I have with me are adults. They know better than to mess with someone's mind. In between classes I guess I prattled to them about the circus. The circus they found interesting. When Mr. John put out the call for the star show, I decided to see what I could put together. What I have with me, Bullhook, is almost the entire faculty of the Surissa—the school where I was teaching."

"When do I get to meet them?"

The dark one shrugged. "They should be up soon. Ssendissians sleep about fifty percent of the time. Are you sure you can't stick around a little longer?"

The big man shook his head. "Me and my crew have to be at Eastern Regional in half an hour to catch the Burma shuttle." He lifted her and placed her on the floor. The door to the hotel room opened, and she saw her mother standing in the doorway.

Kristina looked at the big man. "I see you two found each other. How've you been, Willy?"

Bullhook stood up. "Fine. You're looking good, Kris."

"No thanks to you."

The big man looked down. "I had that coming."

Kristina snorted out a laugh. "That and a lot more, you bastard. Two and a half years without a damned word."

The big man turned to the dark one. "I got to be going, Waco." He looked at Kristina, then averted his glance and walked around her, leaving the room.

The dark one drummed his fingertips on the table top, but remained silent. Kristina looked at him. "Waco, can you look after Wilhelmina for another hour or so? I have a few things to iron out about the delivery of my new cat."

The dark one shrugged. "No problem."

Kristina looked at the dark one for a moment. "Do you think I'm too rough on Willy?"

"It's none of my business."

Kristina nodded. "You're damned right." She turned and left, closing the door behind her.

Little Will sat on the room's carpet and she watched as the dark one got up to brew another cup of tea. Through the open bedroom door came a long, gray serpent. It halted in the doorway and studied her. She crawled toward the serpent. When she was within arm's length, she reached out a hand and touched its warm skin. She looked up at the triangular head weaving on that slender gray body.

"You are pretty."

The head of the serpent weaved down until it was at the same level as Little Will's head. The serpent's eyes were violet; the pupils cat-like. *"To me do you speak?"*

She stroked the serpent again. *"You are pretty. So very pretty."*

The serpent reared up, examined the little girl, then again brought down its head. *"Thank you. I think you are pretty, too."*

She giggled and hid her face in her hands. *"Oh, I'm not pretty. Kristina says I am a horror."*

The serpent looked at the dark one. The dark one was absorbed in brewing his tea. The serpent looked back at the little girl. *"Who is Kristina?"*

"She's my mommy."

The serpent's head rocked up and down. *"She is your mother."* The serpent hissed. *"Who is your father?"*

She held her hands on her cheeks. *"I think it is the man who just left. He looks very sad to me."*

"I am not surprised."

Little Will frowned. *"I do not understand."*

The serpent reared up again. *"I meant nothing."* The serpent's head turned toward the dark one. The dark one turned toward the serpent, then picked up his fresh cup of tea. He nodded at the serpent, then left the room. The serpent turned back to face the little girl. *"What is your name?"*

"Mommy calls me Wilhelmina. Everyone else calls me Little Will."

The serpent's head bobbed up and down. *"I am called Hassih, Little Will. Would you like to be friends?"*

Little Will clapped her hands. *"Oh yes! Oh yes!"*

The serpent's head bobbed again. *"Then we shall be friends, Little Will. Watch as I tie myself into a knot."*

Little Will clapped her hands and opened her mouth to a silent laugh.

. . . and the dream faded as the smell of smoke returned.

Little Will did not see; she did not hear. But she felt the man's presence next to her. And there was another. They talked.

"I got the gang working on beefing up the *kraal*. All the dead stock is out of Number Three. Christ, what a mess." Silence. "Pony, some of the troupers're talking like we ought to cut up and preserve the meat."

A longer silence. "Put 'em in the trench, Packy. We've found enough edible stuff to get by. We're not eating our damned animals!" Silence. "Hell, Packy, we've been covered in crap before, but this . . ."

More silence.

"I don't have no answers, Pony. Except we do like always: don't think about it—"

"—And just move on to the next stand, Packy? Just where is that next stand? And when in blood-eyed damnation is the city going to kick us off *this* lot?!"

Little Will opened her eyes to narrow slits. It was night

again. Packy Dern was still sitting on the platform to her left. Pony Red Miira's huge form stood between the two platforms. He was rubbing his eyes. He lowered his hand and jabbed Packy's shoulder. "Look, you. Keep your trap shut about this. I just need a little sleep. Haven't slept since . . ."

"This ain't my first May, Pony."

The boss animal man looked to his right, then to his left. In the light from a fire, Little Will could see that Pony's eyes were dark circled, his leather-brown face deeply lined. "There's an empty spot." He turned his head back toward Packy. "Fireball hasn't had any luck with the radios. Her knob twirlers can talk to the other cars, but no subspace commo. I just can't understand how Arnheim managed to sabotage every single stinking radio in the show."

"The guy had a head full of bedbugs. What's to explain? They got hold of Number Two yet?"

The boss animal man slowly shook his head. "They finally got a fix on Number Seven. Kuumic says that he's in the middle of some damned desert." He rubbed the back of his neck. "I'm for some sleep."

"Pony?"

"What?"

"What's the name of this planet? Just in case someone should ask?"

The boss animal man stared off into the darkness for a long time. "Funny. Back on the *Baraboo* when the route book man was running that damned fool name-the-planet contest, I had more important things on my mind. Never did find out what name won. A name seems a lot more important now." He looked down at the boss elephant man. "What did you pick?"

"Nowhere."

"That stinks."

"What did you pick?"

"Philadelphia." Pony Red shrugged and let his hands fall to his sides. "I thought it was funny."

"Go get some sleep."

As the boss animal man turned and stumbled off into the darkness, Packy looked down at Little Will. His long, sorrowfulface frowned for an instant, then smiled. "I'll be—" He turned away and whispered loudly. "Mange! Mange! Come here."

Another shadow rushed up and stopped. "For crissakes, Packy, will you pipe down?"

"I whispered."

"Like a foghorn you whispered." The shadow nodded toward Little Will. "What is it?"

"She's awake. Her eyes are open."

Mange moved to the right, bent over, and placed a warm hand against Little Will's face. The hand quickly moved down her left arm and held her wrist. "Little Will?"

She opened her mouth and tried to speak. Pain; white, stunning pain. The shadows and yellows blended together, swam, and faded as she felt herself falling end-over-end into a universe where pain was not allowed.

It was a beautiful universe. All of it lights, laughter, and glitter. It was a straw house on a hard lot and a warm evening. It was the windjammers playing "The Governor's Waltz" while seventy-five bulls turned, hind-ended, and kootched in unison. It was thousands of cheering voices, and they all cheered for her. Covered in spangles, she sat astride Ming's neck in the spectacular. Her father would steal an instant and look up at her.

She would always sneak a peek during the Lion Lady's performance. Center ring, the spots all turned toward her mother and the cats, the crowd hushed, applauding, gasping, cheering. No matter where they played, however alien the planet or its people, this universe stayed the same. It was like the dog who buried a bone beneath the treasury wagon and then at the next stand, on another planet, went beneath the treasury wagon to dig it up again. Once she saw her father sneaking a peek at the Lion Lady's act, and from then on, they watched together.

On the *City of Baraboo* between planets, the universe was huge gray pets, Goofy Joe gossiping, Mootch Movill telling funny stories; clowns, canvasmen, tackspitters, bullhands, hostlers, and a white-bearded giant that everyone called "Mr. John."

But the universe had some special moments. Little Will watched porter Pickle Nose Porse set up the table, champagne and glasses in the exercise run next to the main carrousel in shuttle Number Three. Bullhook Willy was sitting on a haybale with his arm around Kristina, and both of them were talking to Pony Red. She walked through the crowd of handlers, medics, and animal act performers until she stood next to Bullhook. *"Daddy, is it all right if I go see the bulls?"*

Bullhook looked down at her. "Just for a little while. You don't want to miss the line-crossing ceremony."

"*I won't.*" She stood on her toes and kissed him, then turned and kissed Kristina. "*I'll be right back, Mommy.*"

The Lion Lady kissed Little Will. "All right, but don't get your clothes dirty. I want you pretty for the ceremony."

"*Yes, Mommy.*" She turned and ran through the crowd. She waved as she saw Waco and his twenty Ssendissians. When she reached the port to the main carrousel, she stepped in and walked to the center of the great rotatable tube. Within the large tube were more tubes, each one independantly rotatable, and each one containing ten or more elephants. She climbed the ladder and catwalk and entered one of the tubes. Inside the smells of elephant and hay were strong. In their separate stalls, the bulls contentedly munched their rations. Seated on a bucket in front of Robber's stall was Packy Dern. "*Hi, Packy!*"

The bullhand jumped, turned around, then shook his head. "You shouldn't ought to sneak up on a man that way, Little Will. Give a fellow time to get used to you yelling at his eardrums from the inside."

Little Will held her hands behind her. "*I'm sorry.*"

Packy waved a hand. "It's all right." He resumed his seat on the bucket. "Are you gonna try and talk to Reg again?"

She nodded. "*Some day I bet I can talk to the bulls. I get a feeling from Reg. She's really trying to say something.*"

Packy shrugged and looked up at Robber. "I been talking to Robber a lot of years, now. I think she understands."

"*How come you aren't with everybody else?*"

He looked at the little girl. "Big moment coming up, Little Will. We're going to be the very first starshow to cross the quadrant line. Important occasion." He nodded, then looked back at Robber. "At a time like this, I can't think of anyone I'd rather be with."

"*I'm going to see Reg.*"

Packy nodded. "Good luck."

Little Will walked around the bucket and headed toward the back of the tube. When she got to Reg's stall, she looked up at the great pachyderm. "*Reg? Reg? Do you hear me, Reg?*"

The bull turned her head, then reached out her trunk and caressed Little Will. The trunk moved back to its hay.

"*Oh, please, Reg! Say something to me. Please.*"

The bull continued eating.

Little Will moved in next to the bull, reached up, and stroked the animal's cheek. *"Nhissia says that touching helps mind-talk with people. Can you hear me now, Reg?"*

The bull stopped eating. She stood motionless, then Little Will closed her eyes and felt a flood of warmth; an ocean of love. It covered her. *"Oh, Reg! Oh, Reg! You talked to me! I love you, Reg. And you love me."* Little Will felt a tremble beneath her feet. She opened her eyes and looked toward Packy.

The bullhand was standing, looking toward the entrance to the tube. "What in the hell was that?"

The deck pulled out from beneath Little Will's feet, and she saw Packy being knocked to his knees just before her head struck the deck. *"Daddy! Daddy! Mommy! Oh, it hurts!"* She looked up, her vision blurred with tears, and saw Reg's enormous foot swinging toward her.

And the universe is all laughter, bright colors, and cotton candy. And it's mud, broken bones, fights with rubes, pain, endless hard work, frustration, poisoned animals, crooked governments. It's wind-blown ice shredding the main top on a dark night; it's maimed, crippled, and dead friends; it's the Lion Lady putting a gun to her head an instant after killing her cats; it's Bullhook Willy broken and bleeding on the grass of an unknown planet; it's a little girl, hurt, alone, and afraid.

The universe is what it's always been: one long uninterrupted dee-light.

"Little Will? Little Will? It's me, Packy."

She opened her eyes. The light said that it was morning. There were no feelings. If you don't feel you don't hurt. The little girl's stare remained fixed for a moment upon the thatched roof above. She turned her head to her left and saw Packy Dern sitting on the platform next to her own. Little Will closed her eyes.

"Little Will. Now that Bullhook's gone, I'm going to take care of you." Packy's voice broke. "Bullhook . . . he asked me to take care of you. Is that all right?"

A stone does not love; a stone does not suffer loss; a stone does not hurt. Lucky stone.

Packy took her hand in both of his. "We'll be okay together, Little Will. You'll see." He reached to his side and placed something in Little Will's hand. She opened her eyes as she lifted the object. It was her father's golden-tipped bullhook.

No one loves a stone; no one cares if a stone suffers; no one hurts for the sake of a stone. Poor stone.

Little Will clutched the bullhook to her breast and cried.

Packy put his arms beneath her knees and shoulders, lifted her, and held her close. "We'll be okay together. You'll see."

FIVE

It seems that the winner of the name-the-planet contest was the late John J. O'Hara. Before he had died in the bad air of the *Baraboo*, the Governor had picked the name Momus, after the ancient Earth god of ridicule. And they called the planet Momus.

In the days that passed other things took on names. Car Number Three, the menagerie shuttle, looked out upon the body of water they called Table Lake. The waters came from the surrounding mountains that formed a huge basin they called the Great Muck Swamp. At the edge of the swamp, was the lake. At the southeast edge of the lake, its waters drained over rocky falls forming the headwaters of what they called the Fake Foot River.

The metal panels from the shuttle that formed the blades of the waterwheel were strangely shaped, roughly resembling the oversized fake feet some of the Joeys once wore. The waterwheel drove the stripped armature taken from the shuttle, upon which was speed-gear mounted the abrasive core blades taken from the port engine boring assembly. The blades could cut the almost indestructable metal that formed the shuttle's skin. To build a road, there must be tools. To have tools, there must be metal. To have metal, Number Three was devoured.

The road would stretch from the three cars north of Number Three, through the mountains, south past Table Lake, to the four cars next to the sea. The northernmost car was run by Cross-eyed Mike Ikona, the boss porter. The southernmost car was run by the boss canvasman, Duckfoot Tarzak. Before it was constructed it was called the Ikona–Tarzak Road.

Fireball Hanah Sanagi, chief pilot of Number Three, sat upon a grassy hilltop and watched as her ship disappeared bit by bit. She looked down as she listened to the shriek of the core blades cutting teeth into saw blades, cutting cargo blocks into wedges, axes, and sledges. They were making shovel blades, dredges, parts for the scoop assembly the bulls would pull as they carved their way through the gap in the mountains to the north. A rivulet from the north edge of Table Lake fell and twisted its way through the gorge at the bottom of the gap. The sheer walls of the gorge meant putting in a climbing, twisting road to get above the walls. The scouts reported that there was a lot of digging to do to make it to what the troupers in the three northern cars were calling the Emerald Valley.

Southeast toward Tarzak, the expedition reported that it was mostly brush and trees to clear, bridges to throw across streams, bits of swamp to drain. The Fake Foot River did flow all of the way to Tarzak. It was not suitable for navigation except for very short stretches. Midway between Miira and Tarzak, the river cascaded down a great cliff. That would require some carving, too.

She looked up again and studied her ship. For eight years, ever since she abandoned her post at the Arnheim & Boon orbiting shipyard to help crew the *City of Baraboo*, Number Three had been all of home, mission, and her reason for existence. She winced as a large sheet of metal fell from beneath the port wing of the huge delta-shaped craft. She tried to blot out the cheers of the ones who had worked so tirelessly to detach that sheet of metal. The first saw blades were already in use bringing down trees, shaping the trees into planks, and the planks into wagons to be pulled by the Percherons. Number Three's wheelwrights had been busy. The wagons would roll on wooden wheels rimmed by strips of metal cut from Number Three's skin.

She stood, turned her back on Number Three, and looked across Table Lake at the green of the swamp and jungle beyond. They said that Waco Whacko had taken his box of eggs and

had walked out into the darkness. The water-filled footprints
the next morning pointed toward the lake. A search party had
followed the footsteps around the lake until the marks were
obscured by the underbrush and the darkness of the jungle's
overhanging cover.

She studied the jungle, wondering what had driven Wacō
into it; what Waco had found there. The scream of the core
blades cutting into hardened metal deafened her.

She heard footsteps in the grass behind her, but she did not
turn to see who it was. "Fireball?" The voice belonged to the
boss animal man.

"What do you want, Pony?"

"We need some help hacking apart the carrousels."

Fireball slowly shook her head. "Not me, Pony. You talk
to Hollywood; he's Number Three's engineer. He'll help you
shred that car down until there's nothing left but a memory."

Pony Red studied Fireball's back for a moment. "We could
use more help."

"Count me out." She turned and faced the boss animal man.
"Pony, I signed up with the show eight years ago to push the
menagerie shuttle. My job is over."

"We're in the cart, Fireball. And we've got to plug it
through—"

She looked back at the edge of the jungle. "I've seen this
show in bloody fights, smashed to pieces by the weather, in
jail, and every other which way." She held her hand to her
neck. "I am up to here watching reruns of this plucky little
troupe pulling its cookies out of the fire. If you want Number
Three hacked up, find yourself another girl."

The boss animal man reached out a hand and touched her
shoulder. Instantly the shoulder withdrew and Fireball began
walking rapidly toward the lake. Pony Red Miira yelled after
her, but his words were covered by the scream of the core
blades cutting metal.

She began running. Her speed increased as she reached the
hard sand of the lake shore. Faster and faster she ran along the
shore, driven by the sounds of screaming metal. There came
a moment when the harshness of her breaths, the pounding of
her heart, and the pains in her legs and gut blotted out everything. She splashed through the shallows that led to the Snake
Mountain Gap and continued on the other side, running. She
ran until the setting sun washed her face, and the blood pounding in her head blinded her.

Just about all of the shipyard gang that had crewed the *Baraboo* and its ten shuttles had burned in the atmosphere along with the starship. Sabotage. Devilishly clever, and designed to maroon the show in the middle of nowhere. Karl Arnheim, the former owner of the A&BCE shipyard, was pulled from one of the pod assemblies, his body burned to a crisp.

"Why?" Fireball screamed her question at the setting sun, then she collapsed upon the sand. "Why?" Her breaths came in short gasps as she ground her cheek into the coolness of the wet sand.

Night came, she opened her eyes, and pushed herself to a sitting position. Above her spread countless stars. Never to travel among them again; never to see the show, hear the crowd . . .

She struggled to her feet, almost pleased at the ache in her muscles. The still lake reflected the starlight, and it looked to Fireball as though she were standing on the edge of the universe. A thin band of darkness between the stars of the lake and the stars of the night sky told her that the jungle was near. She looked back toward the Number Three car, but could see only the yellow pinpricks of a half dozen campfires. She turned toward the band of darkness and resumed running along the edge of the universe. Before the sun made visible the details of the shore she had left, she wanted to be deep within the jungle.

At the edge of the jungle, great dark shapes noted the tiny creature running toward them. They turned and slithered off into the mud. The past few days had brought much to disturb the serenity of the swamp. It was none of their concern, and so they hissed quietly and moved toward the swamp's dark, steaming interior.

SIX

Packy Dern sat upon a rock outside the door of the sick shack. He was looking across the dusty way at one of the crude hootches that had been built. The particular hootch he had built had done worlds to convince him that his calling was pushing bull. Years before, his career as husband and father had convinced him of the same thing as wife and son hit the lot and jumped the gate to look for what they hoped would be saner surroundings. Packy kicked a small stone and clasped his hands. "Can't say I much blame 'em."

"Blame who?"

Packy looked around and saw Mange Ranger standing in the sick shack's doorway. "Nothin'." He looked back at his hootch. "How's it goin' in there, Mange?"

The veterinarian sat upon a stump and grinned. "I think we're going to do just fine. Everybody in there is on the mend and I just had my first good night's sleep since I don't know when."

Packy nodded once then bent over, picked up a stick, and began breaking it into tiny pieces. "Maybe we can go a couple days at a time now without burying someone."

"What was in your feed this morning, Packy?"

The boss elephant man tossed the remains of the stick on the ground. "Little Will. She just sits there in the hootch. Now that she can talk like everybody else, she don't talk at all. Even that think-talk. It's like livin' with a ghost, her sittin' around starin' at that damned bullhook."

Mange bent over, placed his elbows on his knees, and clasped his hands together. "She's lost, Packy. Her parents are dead. A lot of her friends are dead. The show is gone. Her whole world is different."

"For a man that sticks his arm up a bull's hind end for a living, Mange, you sure are talking up a shrink storm."

Mange looked toward Packy's hootch. "I make a better shrink that you do an architect."

Packy snorted. "That's no damned lie." He looked at the show's veterinarian. "Mange, what am I going to do with her?"

Mange thought upon it for a long time. He looked up at the boss elephant man. "Tell her about what she does for a living."

"You mean the show? The show's dead."

The veterinarian shook his head. "No. I don't mean the show. Tell her about the bulls and the bullhands." Mange pushed himself to his feet. "I'd better get back." He grinned. "I'm going to deliver a baby."

"A baby what?"

"A baby *human*, plopbrain. Our Saint Travers is about to increase our numbers by one."

Mange went back into the sick shack and Packy went back to staring at his hootch. He thought for a moment about Jewel Travers, Wild West equestrian, known to the show as "Saint." Her husband, Shorty was dead. "Yet life goes on." Packy stood and headed toward his hootch. "And on, and on, and on."

Gangs in the Emerald Valley and in Tarzak would connect their own cars with roads the best they could without bulls or horses, and would then begin cutting their ways toward the gangs working north and south from Miira. Pony Red Miira bossed the road gang working south toward Tarzak, while Packy Dern bossed the gang that worked its way through the shorter, but more treacherous, Snake Mountain Gap.

At night Packy Dern's gang would huddle around fires and talk about nothing—old show stories, idle speculations about the next day's work, anything but the fix they were in. Little Will would remain silent, watching. Ming was with the Snake Mountain gang, and it seemed that at any time Bullhook Willy might appear, swinging his gold-tipped bullhook, bellowing out his orders to the rest of the bullhands. Then she would see Madman Mulligan pushing Ming. Then she would look at the bullhook in her hands and softly cry.

The sun would rise, the gang would begin the next day's work, and Little Will would remain at the camp either staring at her bullhook or into the depths of the gorge. Thirty days into the cut, and Packy began bringing Little Will with him to work.

Little Will sat quietly in the back of the wagon watching the bullhands and hostlers work their animals. With harness, carefully planned avalanches, but more often with shovels and backs, the crew cut their way up the steep incline to get above the walls of the Gap. The boiling river at the bottom of the gorge made a constant background roar causing both bullhands and hostlers to shout their instructions to their animals. The noise the river made sounded like the crowd in the blues on a good night. The river was named The Push.

Packy Dern brought Robber to a stop next to the wagon. "Little Will?"

She remained motionless. "Yes?"

"Honey, you can't just sit around all the time. It's not good."

"I don't feel like doing anything." She looked down, shook her head, and sniffed. "Don't want to do anything."

She was talking now. But the fact registered on no one, including herself. She talked because the thoughts wouldn't talk for her. That's all she knew. No big deal.

Packy reached out a hand and gave Little Will's back an unacknowledged pat. He studied her for a moment, shook his head, then shouted, "Mile up, girl!" Robber lumbered forward where Packy turned her around to hitch her harness to a wagon recently filled with dirt and rock.

Little Will wiped her eyes with the backs of her hands and turned to see Stub Jacobs bringing Reg's wagonload of fill to the edge of the cliff that formed the gap wall. She saw him call Reg to a halt, then Stub went back to the wagon to watch as two men placed rocks behind the wheels. They waved as Stub and the bullhand called to Reg to back up. As the bull backed toward the cliff's edge, the front of the wagon rose causing the wagon to begin emptying its load.

She saw it before it happened. The rock disappearing in a cloud of dust, the wagon falling over the cliff—

"Wait!" Her tiny scream was drowned by the roar from The

Push. She began climbing up the side of the wagon. "Wait! Stop!" As the dirt and rock began falling down the face of the cliff, the rock behind the wagon's left wheel crumbled slewing the wagon around. Stub called to Reg, but the wagon's other wheel jumped the rock behind it and the wagon went over the cliff.

Reg dug in as the weight of the wagon pulled her toward the gap and Stub rushed behind her and began trying to free the harness from the wagon. One of the men threw Stub a knife, and in seconds the harness parted. The wagon fell and Stub Jacobs fell with it, his screams covered by the roar of the water. Reg stood alone on the edge of the cliff waiting for Stub to hand out the next order.

Work stopped and bullhands and hostlers gathered at the edge of the cliff and looked down. Little Will climbed down from the wagon and walked over to Reg. She stood in front of the bull, reached out a hand, and stroked her trunk. *"It's me, Reg. Do you remember me?"*

Reg gently wrapped her trunk around Little Will's shoulders. Little Will looked up at Reg's eyes. *"I have to go get something first, Reg."*

Little Will went back to the wagon and returned carrying a mahogany-handled, gold-tipped bullhook. She stood by Reg's left front leg. *"Let's go, Reg. There's work to do."*

She led the elephant away from the cliff and backed her up to the next wagon in line. Little Will looked back to see Packy staring at her. "Packy, I need someone to repair Reg's harness."

Packy continued staring at her, then he looked at those standing around at the edge of the cliff. Shiner Pete Adnelli nodded at Packy and moved off to repair the harness. The rest returned to their animals and shovels.

That night around the fire, they talked about Stub Jacobs. Not a spectacular human being; just another elephant tramp, which made him a spectacular human being in some circles.

Packy held Little Will and talked. "Honey, did you ever wonder why the show don't have big legends—super heroes— like Paul Bunyan or Pecos Pete?"

Little Will shook her head. "Who are they?"

"See, now. The loggers in the north end of the union used to storytell about a monster logger name of Paul Bunyan. He was so big that his footprints left lakes, and he could take his ax and fell a thousand trees at a time. Cowboys out in the west end of the union used to talk of Pecos Pete. Pete would wrassel rivers and windstorms and tame 'em. But, honey, loggin' and bein' a cowboy are small things next to bein' a trouper. The show is full of heroes, and it'd take one bungus imagination to come up with something like a Paul Bunyan for the circus."

Waxy Adnelli, boss harnessman, leaned forward and pointed across the fire at Little Will. "At the clem on Masstone I saw Stub Jacobs, along with Mr. John and your papa, wade into a mean bunch of soldiers with nothin' but tent stakes, and they flattened the lot of 'em."

Dot the Pot Drake nodded as she stared into the fire. "Bottle Bottom got killed in that clem." She looked up at Little Will. "He was the route book man before the show picked up that lumpy guy from the planet Pendiia, Warts." Dot tossed a tiny stick into the fire. "And now he's dead as a doornail."

The silence around the fire grew oppressive, and one by one they left the flames to find a private place to sleep. Little Will, still looking into the fire, leaned against Packy. "How come they don't talk like they used to? Back before the crash?"

Packy put his left arm around Little Will's shoulders. "Don't know if I can put it right, Little Will. Back before they were troupers. Now they're a road gang. It'd be all right if they could see the end of this season; but they can't. We're stuck, there's nothin' anybody can do about it, and it sticks in their throats. If they'd start cussin' Arnheim, makin' jokes, things'd be back to normal. But they don't want to talk about it. And as long as they don't talk about it, Arnheim has us whipped."

"Packy, isn't Karl Arnheim dead?"

The boss elephant man nodded his head. "And that's what's got 'em, Little Will. A trouper can fight anything. Anything but a damned ghost." He looked into her eyes, seeing the confusion there. "When you get a little older and begin collectin' your own stable of ghosts, you'll see what I'm talkin' about."

Little Will looked back at the flames. In them she could see shapes form—puzzle pieces. What they were pieces to, she couldn't see; she could see that not enough pieces were there. When Packy moved off to his bedroll, Little Will continued staring at the fire.

"I wish it could be like it was," she thought.

"Me too."

Little Will looked up across the fire, startled, to see another startled face looking back at her. It was Shiner Pete Adnelli, Waxy's son.

She tried her thoughts again. *"Shiner, was that you?"*

He nodded, his mouth gaping.

"Did you work with Waco and the Ssendissians?"

"A . . . a little." He held his hands to his head for a moment, then stood and walked away from the fire.

Little Will studied the flames for a long time, then stood and made her way to Packy's bedroll. She snuggled against the boss elephant man, and as she was dozing she let the thought escape. *"Goodnight Shiner."*

A troubled thought returned. *"Yeah. Goodnight."*

Little Will closed her eyes and let her dreams carry her back to the ship and her good friends the Ssendissians.

They were laying up on the planet Ahngar at the main spaceport near the Royal City of Almandiia. Hassih the Ssendissian was looped several times over Bullhook Willy's right shoulder and across his chest. Bullhook held Little Will's hand as the three of them watched the technicians and welders working on the main animal carrousel in shuttle Number Three. The Ssendissian turned from the work and looked at Bullhook. *"How many were killed when the meteor struck?"*

Bullhook shook his head. "Nineteen troupers and forty-nine animals—sixteen of them bulls. Four bullhands, nine from the shuttle crew, a pony punk, three hostlers, and two camel hands." Again he shook his head. "God, what a nightmare. The damage jammed the main carrousel and we couldn't rotate it to get the bulls out of the shuttle and into the ship. We had to cut them out. Those that weren't injured from the meteorite got it in the stampede."

Hassih looked back at the workers. *"It is such a pity. Can the bulls be replaced?"*

The big man turned and went down the gangway to the ground port, Little Will walking beside him. "We can get more bulls. We just can't replace the one's we lost. Big Mo got it, Go Go, Princess . . . "

Little Will pulled on the tip of the Sssendissian's tail. *"Hassih, please tell my daddy I'm sorry."*

They stepped down to the surface of the parking ramp and headed for their van. Hassih spoke to Bullhook. *"Little Will expresses her condolences."*

The big man looked down at the little girl and smiled. "I'm glad you're with me right now, baby. Very glad." He squeezed her hand and she squeezed back.

"Hassih, tell my daddy I love him."

The Ssendissian bobbed its head around. *"Your daughter expresses her affection."*

Bullhook Willy raised an eyebrow and looked at Hassih. "You know, Hassih old shoelace, I can't help but believe her words lost something in the translation." He opened the van door, Hassih slithered inside, and Little Will climbed in after. After closing the passenger door, Bullhook Willy walked around the front of the van and climbed into the driver's seat, closing his door behind him. He reached to energize the van's motor, then hesitated. He faced the Ssendissian. "Hassih, I don't understand this telepathy stuff. If Little Will can talk to you, and if you can talk to me, why can't *she* talk to me?"

"Bullhook, you cannot receive the same as she sends. It is much like the radios on the ships. She is sending on one frequency, but you can only receive on another. It is much more complicated than that, but that is why."

"And you can dial up and down both sending and receiving?"

"Roughly. But Little Will cannot. Perhaps she could with training. Perhaps you could be trained." Hassih swung its head around and studied Little Will. Then the Ssendissian looked at Bullhook. *"I will ask Nhissia. Nhissia is an expert in communications. My talents lie elsewhere."*

Bulhook Willy started up the van. "What did you do back at the old academy, Hassih?"

The Ssendissian looked through the windshield. *"My training is in the arts of killing and preparing the kill for consumption. I am told you call this home economics."*

The big man moved the van. As it approached the fences surrounding the field, he turned to the Ssendissian. "I would appreciate it if you would ask Nhissia if anything can be done."

Hassih's head bobbed up and down. The Ssendissian looked at Little Will, then turned its head toward Bullhook. *"Little Will expresses her discomfort."*

Willy sighed and shook his head. "Hassih, just tell me what she said—exactly."

Hassih cocked its head to one side, then looked back through the windshield. *"Little Will said: 'Tell my daddy that I have to go to the bathroom.'"*

•   •   •

It was a stand somewhere. Only one among many, but important. All stands are important.

The show's children crowded the dressing top donning their costumes for the most spectacular street parade ever put on by O'Hara's Greater Shows. The inhabitants of the planet, as well as their cities and their streets, were on a grand scale. The city of Tiomo was the first stand, and Tiomo's main street would dwarf any kind of human display—except the circus. O'Hara swore to fill the enormous avenue. All seventy-five bulls, the entire compliment of baggage and performing horses, all performers, every show and cage wagon, even the show's canvasmen and razorbacks found themselves costuming for the parade.

As her costuming and makeup were completed, Little Will gathered with the other show children under the watchful eye of Iron Jaw Jill, the show's ballet director. "Now you kids freeze. Mess up those spangles, and I'll see your bony little buns across a trunk!" She turned and disappeared into the crowd of ballet girls donning briefs and feathered headdresses. On a row of trunks off to the side, Clown Alley was touching up its last frizzy head and securing its last fake foot.

Little Will turned as she heard angry shouting. The show kids backed away from a scuffling pair of boys rolling on the wood shavings. They pounded and punched each other without mercy until Iron Jaw Jill pulled them apart. Even held apart, they swung in each other's direction at the empty air. "Hold your hosses! *Now!*" She shook the two until they stopped swinging. "Look at your costumes!"

Little Will stood on her toes to see who the boys were. The blond-haired one with the bloody nose was Mikey Dirak, the advance manager's son. The brown-haired one with the bloody nose was Pete Adnelli, Waxy the harnessman's son. Both of their costumes were in blood-covered tatters. Iron Jaw shook Mikey. "What's this about?"

He sniffed and wiped his nose with the back of his hand. "Nothin'. Pete just jumped me."

Iron Jaw looked at Pete. "Well?"

Pete tried to take another swing at Mikey, but was pulled out of range by Iron Jaw. "You liar!"

Iron Jaw shook Pete until he quieted. "Now, what do you have to say for yourself?"

Even flushed from fighting, Little Will could see the blush creeping into Pete's cheeks. "Mikey said something."

"What thing? Out with it!"

Pete mumbled.

Iron Jaw shook his shoulder again. "Speak up, young man!"

Pete pointed at Mikey. "He called . . . he called Little Will a name."

Iron Jaw looked at Mikey. "What name?"

"Nothin'!"

Pete lunged again at Mikey and succeeded in landing another punch on Mikey's nose. "Liar!"

Iron Jaw pulled Pete back. "Calm down, young man, or I'll drop your drawers and tan your hide right this minute!" She glowered at Pete until he stood motionless.

Pete looked from Mikey down to the wood shavings. "He said she was a dummy."

Iron Jaw's eyebrows went up. "What?"

Pete pointed at Mikey. "He called Little Will a dummy!"

Mikey grimaced. "I . . . I didn't mean nothin' by it. Everybody knows she can't talk!"

Little Will noticed some of the other children looking in her direction. Tears welled in her eyes, she hid her face and ran from the dressing top.

Later that evening in the Number Three car moving to the next stand, Little Will went through the port carrousel. Among the massive white Percheron horses, she found Pete Adnelli seated on a bucket, glumly polishing a mountain of harnesses. She walked up to him and stopped. He looked up at her, blushed, then looked back at his work. "Uh, hi." He glanced at the pile of brass-studded leather at his side. "Waxy wasn't too happy to hear about me missin' parade."

She squatted down and placed her hand on his. Pete's blush turned fire-red. He grinned. "It wasn't nothin'. He . . . just shouldn't of said that."

Little Will smiled, removed her hand, and pulled a halter from the mountain of leather. She dipped her fingertips in the clear, liquid polish and began rubbing it into the halter's leather.

Pete kept looking at his work, but he grinned.

Little Will watched as Waco Whacko, her father and the Ssendissian, Nhissia, sat silently. Bullhook Willy and Waco sat in chairs facing Nhissia, who was hanging from the cabin's light fixture.

"Well, Nhissia, you told Waco you might have figured out something new. Can Little Will talk to me now?"

Nhissia's head bobbed around, looking first at Little Will, then at Waco, then at Bullhook. *"Can you all tell what I am saying?"*

Waco nodded. "I heard."

Bullhook's eyebrows went up. "Yes." He turned to his daughter. "Did you hear that?"

She nodded, then looked up at Nhissia. *"I heard. We all heard at the same time, Nhissia."*

The Ssendissian's head bobbed up and down. *"It is as I suspected. I hoped that I could train myself to communicate with more than one human at a time. I have been trying out various combinations."* Nhissia looked at Bullhook. *"Waco and I have been working on this together. We didn't let you know because we didn't want to raise false hope."*

The big man looked at Waco. "Thank you." He looked at Nhissia. "Thank you both."

Little Will stood up. *"Can I talk to my daddy now?"* She looked at Bullhook, but he only frowned. Little Will pouted. *"Nhissia, I can't!"*

"Have patience, Little Will. I have only learned to do this with humans myself." Nhissia looked at Bullhook. *"I found that a number of the young humans on this ship have the same mind ability as Little Will's."*

Waco leaned toward Bullhook. "We checked it out with Bone Breaker's records. There are twenty-six kids with the show that have the same genetic peculiarity. Bone Breaker thinks it's the war. Anyway, nine of the kids have the ability to transmit communications, but never developed it because they can talk. The rest of us don't transmit simply because we don't have the ability. But all of us can receive." The snake charmer smiled at Nhissia. "So far Nhissia has trained two of the kids to transmit by mind, and one of the two can speak directly to me."

Little Will sat back down in her chair. *"Can you fix my mind to talk to others?"*

Nhissia looked from Little Will to the bullhand and the snake charmer. *"She asked if she can be trained."* The Ssendissian looked back at Little Will. *"I think so. It will take much work, but I think it can be done."*

Bullhook Willy Kole looked down at his daughter . . .

Little Will awakened, a hand shaking her shoulder. She turned and saw Packy's outline against the almost light of the new morning. "What is it, Packy?"

"You were havin' some dream. Thought I'd step in just in case the tigers had you cornered." The boss elephant man patted her shoulder. "Okay?"

Little Will nodded and they both snuggled into the bedroll. "Packy?"

"What, honey?"

"Packy, was my daddy a nice man?"

Packy remained motionless for a moment, then shrugged the shoulder he wasn't attempting to sleep upon. "He was an elephant tramp."

High praise from Packy Dern.

SEVEN

The gang working toward Tarzak had made it to the place where the Fake Foot River cascaded down a steep cliff; forty miles from Miira, the half-way point to Tarzak. As the gang moved farther south, the thinner became the trees; and logs and planks were needed to cross the streams. Pickle Nose Porse, Number Three's porter, had established a supply and timbering point midway between Number Three and the cliff.

The cliff extended right and left as far as could be seen. A harsh, steady wind blew from the *plateau* where Pony's gang stood, down the face of the cliff. The rock of the cliff wasn't the shale and crumbled ledge of the Snake Mountain Gap. The face of Blowdown Cliff was solid granite. After his bull, Bandit, had been killed in a fall down the cliff, bullhand Sergeant Spook Tieras established a tool sharpening and repair station at the drop in the river which became known as the Bandit Falls. The road down Blowdown Cliff would have to be chiseled.

In the Snake Mountain Gap, seven days work went sliding into The Push when a tremor near a fault in the gap's vicinity caused thousands of tons of rock and soil to loosen. No one was killed, but boss harnessman Waxy Adnelli's left arm was crushed. Waxy was carried back to the place that everyone now called Miira, where Mange Ranger managed to save the harnessman's life at the cost of his arm.

Several nights after Packy's crew had begun to repair the damage, canvasman Goofy Joe Napoli climbed the road into the camp near the peak of the Snake Mountains. There were greetings then everyone gathered around a fire to eat and hear the news that Goofy Joe brought. Since the only radios left working were in cars Ten and Four—both in Tarzak—the gang was eager to hear what Goofy had to say.

Packy nodded at the canvasman and asked the first question. "Goofy, have the radios in Tarzak picked up anything yet?"

Goofy Joe shook his head. "And they're not listening anymore, either. They want to save the juice they have left for when Number Ten takes off. They've got the remaining fuel from the other three cars loaded up in her. Leadfoot Sina's taking it up to try and find Number Two."

Dot the Pot leaned forward toward the fire. "When does it take off?"

"It should be gone by now. While they're looking for Number Two, Leadfoot's going to try a little mapping. There's a chance he can find a route to Number Seven. So far we have roads connecting all of the cars in Tarzak. We made the bridges out of the cars. No wood to speak of down there."

"What're you doing for houses?"

"Packy, we haven't had a drop of rain since we touched down. We're building houses out of sun-dried mud bricks. Roofs are the problem. We can thatch with the long grass we have down there, but we don't have any wood for roof poles."

Packy nodded. "Once we get the road through, we can get planks, logs, and poles to you." He pointed at Goofy Joe. "You tell Tarzak that in exchange for those planks and poles, we're going to need metal. Especially another set of those core blades. We grind with them, but both of ours from Number Three are about all wore out."

"When I was in Pony Red's camp, he said the same thing."

Little Will looked up at the canvasman. "Goofy, what's it like in Tarzak? How're they taking all this?"

Goofy looked around at the grim-faced circle of listeners. "It's about the same all over. We're in the cart and there's no question about it. It's like everybody needed to hit someone, but that someone isn't around."

Snaggletooth scratched his head, then held out his hands.

"What about Rat Man Jack, the route man? Won't he send out someone when we don't show up on time?"

Goofy shrugged. "Snaggletooth, do you know what a parsec is?"

"No."

"Leadfoot sort of explained it to me. It's one bullzonkus distance, I can tell you that. Take ten and multiply it by itself thirteen times, then multiply it some more. Got that?"

Snaggletooth shrugged.

"Never mind. It's a bunch. It's about fifty or so of those things between Ahngar and H'dgva in the Tenth Quadrant. That's in a straight line, which we didn't take. Now, we could've gone anywhere in between, see? And those searches have to be done at sublight speed to do any good. On top of that, we could have gone off course anywhere in between, which we did. Add to that the possiblity that we just might have blown up, and there's not going to be a lot of enthusiasm for spending the next several centuries searching for us."

The listeners sat quietly for awhile. Packy picked up a handful of pebbles and began flicking them one at a time into the fire. "Goofy, we're almost through the gap. Stretch Dirak's gang from the north is only a couple of miles away. Fisty Bill Ris's gang and Cross-eyed Mike Ikona have roads connecting all of the Emerald Valley cars. If Fatlip Louie will have the road cleared from Tarzak, then all we have left is Pony Red getting down that cliff."

Goofy nodded. "That sound's good to me."

Dot the Pot looked at Packy, then looked at Goofy Joe. "And then what, Goofy? What then? We'll have a road from Ikona to Tarzak, but we'll still be stuck on this damned little mudball."

"Don't really know." He held out his hands. "We'll have to get some kind of act together. There's still Number Seven to get to."

Dot snorted out a laugh. "Another damned road." She pushed herself to her feet and walked from the fire. One by one the others got up and went to put in some shut-eye before the next day's hard work.

Goofy Joe sat staring at the fire for a long time, then he stood and looked around at the night. Little Will was still at the fire. He looked down at her. "This is sure a happy bunch."

She smiled sympathetically. "Because of that fault, we lost a week's work. Where are you going now?"

"I thought I'd cross the mountain here and spread the gossip to the gangs up north."

"Goofy, it's dangerous to travel that way even when you have the light with you. At night you could kill yourself."

The canvasman rubbed a finger beneath his nose and then snorted as he let his hands drop to side. "I just don't want to hang around this bunch of sad sacks. I'm too easy to depress."

Little Will thought for a moment, then looked up again at the canvasman. "Goofy Joe, how long have you been with O'Hara's?"

The canvasman rubbed his chin and looked up at the stars. "Let's see. That was some after the war... must be about twenty-five—twenty-six years."

"You were there when my mother and father got married?"

"There?" Goofy Joe resumed his seat by the fire. "The world was there, Little Will. Little Joe, the show's chaplin, did the honors in the center ring. The boss elephant man marrying the Lion Lady. Mr. John gave away the bride, and Waco Whacko was Bullhook's best man." Goofy frowned. "I wonder where Waco is now. Anyway, that was an occasion. You should've been there... well, you know what I mean."

"Goofy, what happened to them? Why did they split up?"

The canvasman settled back upon his elbows. "The show's hard on a lot of marriages, Little Will. And you got to understand this thing between cats and bulls. They're natural enemies. You know that when a bull died it was usually cut up and fed to the cats."

Little Will nodded.

"Five tons of meat isn't to be sneezed at, prices being what they are... were. Anyway, after your parents got married, things were just fine until that stand in..." Goofy rubbed his chin. "That was in Richmond, North American Union." He nodded. "Damn, but that was one helluva night."

He sat up. "I guess you were only one or two years old then." The canvasman shook his head. "See, the Lion Lady's father, Humpy Ireland, he was a camel hand. Never did like the cats, old Humpy. But Kris wanted a cat act, and you'd have to know Kris before Richmond to know why she got everything she ever wanted. I never met anybody who was harder to say no to.

"Well, Humpy gave up his camel and became part of the Lion Lady's cat act." Goofy shook his head. "God, but Humpy was scared of those cats." He looked up at the stars. "The cats got Humpy in Richmond. Chewed him up so that there wasn't enough left to call spit. Kris stepped in and tried to stop it, but the cats were crazy and cut her up real bad. Took off half of her face."

Little Will gasped.

Goofy Joe held out his hands. "They fixed her up in the hospital, though. Remolded her face and sealed up her cuts like nothing happened. Both of them left the show then. A year later the Lion Lady was back with her act. We didn't see anything of Bullhook Willy until right before the *City of Baraboo* took to the star road. They must've separated in Richmond."

"But why?"

Goofy Joe stretched out next to the fire. "The most reliable gossip I heard was that Bullhook went crazy and tried to kill the cats. Those cats were more important to the Lion Lady than even her own life. I bet that's what happened, and Kris put Bullhook's trunk out on the lot."

The canvasman yawned and cradled his head against his arm. "That's why Kris killed herself, Little Will. The air on the *Baraboo* was bad, and her cats were suffering. I think one or two had already died. What I heard was that she killed the rest of them, then killed herself."

He lifted himself upon one elbow. "Hey, I shouldn't be talking this stuff. I'm sorry."

"I wanted you to, Goofy. I wanted to know."

The canvasman snorted and put his head back down upon his arm. He snorted again and closed his eyes. "Guess I'm about as cheery as the rest of this flipping funeral."

Little Will pushed herself to her feet, walked until she found Packy in the shadows, and cuddled in next to the boss elephant man.

"Mumph."

"Goodnight Packy."

"Mmph."

Little Will closed her eyes until the light from the fire sparkled and filled her vision. Bullhook Willy and the Lion Lady had been apart, but there had been a time.

Her mind called out a name: *"Pete. Are you awake?"*

"I'm awake."

"Pete, Nhissia once taught me how to share a memory. Can you do that?"

"I suppose so. What do I do?"

*"Just open your mind as far as you can; as though you were
listening as hard as you could."*

"Okay. I'm listening."

Little Will closed her eyes and brought back the beautiful
starship—deep inside.

*Most of the show's three thousand troupers were gathered
in the main practice arena of the* City of Baraboo. *Those who
manned the ship's stations listened to the intercom.* Little Will
sat in the crowded seats between Kristina and Bullhook. Little
Will watched as, in the center of the arena, John J. O'Hara
took a microphone from a propman and lifted it to his lips.

"The last two seasons were rough. Karl Arnheim had as
many as six shows dogging our tracks at one point." He lifted
a fist. "By damn, we met opposition with opposition and each
time walked away with victory!"

The troupers cheered.

O'Hara lowered his fist, then looked around the arena. "But
we left friends behind. Joliet Jake Sobie and Siren Sally Fong
died in the clem on Tuulurim. On the planet Morvah,
Arnheim's sabotage made us leave nine of the Irish Brigade
in hospitals and another four troupers in the ground. Blondie
MacDeer, Pieface Jack Goolahan, Tooter Tamazan, and Peyote
Pete Beartooth died there." The Governor rubbed his eyes, then
lowered his hand. "At the last stand, on Dyvaul, eleven
died. . . . You all know who they were."

Again he looked around the arena. "We obtained
victory . . . but the price. The price is too high." He held out
his arms. "All of us—we are entertainers. We are show people.
I am in the entertainment business. I am not going to spend
any more lives on Karl Arnheim."

The stands around the arena buzzed with chatter. O'Hara
waited for the troupers to quiet down. "Beginning next season,
I'm taking the show out of the Ninth Quadrant. O'Hara's
Greater Shows is going to open up the Tenth Quadrant to the
star circus." The stands were silent. O'Hara looked around the
arena, then continued. "We will be gone for a long time each
stretch. Five, maybe six years at a time. Each one of your has
to decide if you want to come along with the show, or leave
it when we lay up on Ahngar." He held the microphone to his
lips for a few moments longer, then lowered it. A propman
took the microphone from O'Hara's hand and the show's owner
walked slowly out of the arena.

As the troupers came down the stands in small groups, Kristina reached across Little Will and placed her hand on Bullhook's arm. "What about you, Willy? Are you staying with the show?"

He watched the troupers filing out of the practice arena, then shrugged. "What about you and Little Will?"

The Lion Lady smiled. "The cats stay with the show, and so do we."

"Then so do I."

Kristina looked down for a moment, then aimed her gaze at Willy. "I've been rough on you."

Bullhook nodded. "I don't blame you."

The Lion Lady glanced at Little Will, then back at Bullhook. "No. But I'm beginning to."

Little Will watched as the big man placed his hand on Kristina's hand. "Regal lady, can a humble bullhand interest you in a cup of coffee?"

Her mother laughed. "In sooth, Willy Kole, that's the best offer I've had all day."

Little Will smiled and looked around at the stands. *"Hassih? Hassih? Where are you?"*

"Little Will?" The Ssendissian's thought was weak. *"I am in my quarters with one of your cursed human colds. Are you well?"*

She looked at her parents holding hands, smiling at each other. *"My mommy and daddy love each other. Isn't that wonderful?"*

An almost audible telepathic sniff, then Hassih said: *"Life with a circus is one long uninterrupted dee-light."*

Little Will and Shiner Pete both laughed. She opened her eyes, stood, and walked around the sleeping bodies until she was next to the boss harnessman's son.

"Is it all right, Pete?"

"Sure."

She sat beside him and they held hands.

"Pete, what's going to happen to us? The show?"

The boy was silent for a moment. *"I asked Waxy that just before Mange cut off my dad's arm. Waxy said you can kill troupers and you can kill animals, but you can't kill the show."* Pete squeezed her hand. *"You can't kill the show."*

They watched the fire until they both drifted off to sleep.

EIGHT

In the Snake Mountain Gap, when the gangs working north and south met, that night a celebration was held. The attempt at merriment was lubricated by a brew that the Emerald Valley folks made out of the sweet sap from angelhair trees that came in several grades ranging from sweet wine to varnish remover.

As both gangs gathered around fires and drank, Goofy Joe made his way into the camp from the south. Shortly after, the gangs learned that boss animal man Pony Red Miira had been killed south of the Tieras station in a fall down Blowdown Cliff.

Little Will and Shiner Pete left their fire and grim companions and walked the gap road in the darkness toward the Emerald Valley. When they reached the downslope, they saw below them the fire lights of the town of Dirak. Beyond that were the lights of Ris; and far away against the soft blackness of a huge mountain were the faint flickerings of the lights of Ikona. Below them, from the direction of Dirak, came the metallic wail of a tin flute. That would be Dublin Dan, a bannerman with Stretch Dirak's advance.

Singing joined the sounds of the flute. The night air and distance blurred the words, but Little Will recognized the song

about the killer elephant, Black Diamond. Bullhook Willy had
taught her the song about the outlaw bull and how it was
tortured to death, committing all future bullhands to seek revenge upon an extinct organization called the Texas Rangers.

It was a mournful song, and Shiner Pete spoke out loud.
"Someone from the Emerald Valley gang must've gone ahead
and told 'em about Pony Red."

Little Will put her arm around Shiner's waist and leaned her
head against his shoulder. *"I feel a thought in your mind."*

Shiner Pete nodded. *"I was just remembering on the ship
after the sabotage had been discovered and the air was running
short. They were going to kill the animals to conserve air, but
Pony sealed off Number Three and refused to open the hatch
until Mr. John agreed to try and save them."* He looked down
at her. *"That was after you were hurt."* He looked back at the
lights of Dirak. *"If it wasn't for Pony, there wouldn't be bulls
or horses on Momus."*

Little Will wiped the tears from her cheeks and turned away
from the lights. *"Let's go back. I don't want to go any farther."*

Shiner Pete turned, placed his arm around Little Will's
shoulders, and they both walked the dark road toward where
the road gangs were sorting through their own thoughts.

When they reached their bedrolls, only a few troupers still
sat around the fires, drinking. Shiner Pete fell into a troubled
sleep, but Little Will continued staring at one of the fires.

She was watching the same fire as the dawnlight came upon
the camp, gray and chilly. Packy Dern, Stretch Dirak, Fisty
Bill Ris, and Goofy Joe still sat around the fire. Stretch Dirak
looked at the gathering evidence of the new day, passed on the
jug, and spoke to Packy. "Who's going to take over as boss
animal man?"

Packy slowly shook his head. "Skinner Suggs, the boss
hostler, don't know nothin' about bulls, an' I don't know
nothin' about nags. 'Sides, I don't guess we got much need
for a boss animal man now." The boss elephant man pushed
his fingers through his thinning gray hair. "Goddamn Pony,
always been with the show. Took me on when the show only
had five bulls."

Goofy Joe passed on the jug. "Packy, you movin' your gang
south to help Skinner get down the cliff?"

Packy lowered the jug from his lips and nodded. "Some,
I guess. Most'll be goin' back to Miira . . . to finish buildin'
their houses. Funny how we call the town Miira."

He shook his head and spat on the ground. "Crummy little shacks. Damned hobo jungle. Trouper's got no business ownin' a damn house anyway." He stood, stumbled around in a circle, then faced the fire with his hands held out. "Trouper's got no business—no *business*—on this here damned planet." He stabbed at his chest with his thumb. "Lookit us! Goddamned road gang!" He sat down with a thump. "Goddamned road gang."

Fisty Bill took the jug and depleted its contents. After he lowered the jug, he pointed with his thumb back toward the sleeping crews. "Seems like you and Waxy'll have to move in together."

Packy looked in the indicated direction and saw Little Will pretending to be sound asleep next to Shiner Pete, Waxy's son. Packy shook his head. "Bill, you got an imagination that'd put Mootch Movill to shame. She's only thirteen; and what's Pete? Fourteen, fifteen?"

Stretch shook his head. "Back where I come from, thirteen is a little over the hill."

"I bet Waxy'd have a little something to say about that." Fisty Bill looked up at Goofy Joe. "What's Waxy doin' now?"

"After Mange trimmed off Waxy's wing, Waxy wanted to get back to working harness. Warts got to him first."

"The route book man?"

Goofy Joe nodded. "Warts's gettin' someone from each of the cars to keep records. Who's alive, who's dead, who gets born, who owns what. Since he's doin' it for Warts, Mange has Waxy keeping records on the horses, too. Wants to keep track of the nag . . . pop . . . population 'e says."

Fisty snorted. "Talk about your one-armed paper hangers."

They continued in silence for a moment, passing a newly opened jug. Packy finished a blast, passed on the jug, and looked at Stretch. "Stretch, what's goin' to happen to them?"

"Who?"

Packy waved a hand in the general direction of Little Will and Shiner Pete. "Them. Romeo and Juliet. All the show kids."

"Damned if I know." Stretch shook his head. "I keep waiting for something—a ship in the sky, a call on the radio. The route man could keep plugging and get us out of here. Maybe. Maybe somebody or something will see Number Ten circling around out there. Most everybody's hoping something of the sort." He rubbed his chin. "But the kids're different. They'll just get on with it."

"On with what?"

"Life. Living. For the real young ones, this is home."

Fisty Bill looked down and shook his head. "Sonofabitch. Can't believe we're just goin' to roll over and die like this. I mean . . . dammit, Stretch, when you think of the things we've gone through."

"Arnheim's ghost's got us by the short hairs, for sure."

"I don't want to ever hear that damned name again!"

"Nobody does, Fisty."

Stretch thought for a moment. "Fisty, when you come right down to it, what good are most of us here? I'm the advance car boss, but there's nothing to advertise, no place to hang the banners, no rubes to read 'em. You boss the opposition brigade, but you got no opposition."

He pointed a finger. "Packy and his bullhands have something to do, but it's timbering and roadganging. Anyway, all those bulls are females. What happens when the last of those dies off? What are the bullhands then? A show without an audience just ain't no show."

Goofy Joe nodded. "Down in Tarzak we got a lot of canvasmen with no canvas. They're turnin' into a bunch of bricklayers. Damned sorry bunch of hod-carriers they make, too."

Fisty Bill reached out his hand and took the jug. After a long pull, he passed it along and looked toward the far wall of the gorge. The sound of the river seemed far away. "Sometimes I think Waco and Fireball had the right idea. Just wander off in the jungle and say the hell with it all."

Goofy Joe held up his hands. "Laydeeeezzz an' gen'men. Step right up'n see the great show stick its finger up its nose, roll over'n die." He laughed as he dropped his hands into his lap. "Boys, down in Tarzak you should see Warts. The route book man's tryin' to keep a show goin'. A *show* would you believe?" He pointed a finger at his circle of sodden listeners. "You know that right after the Tarzak cars went down— couldn't of been an hour after—that damned Pendiian'd talked everybody into holdin' a parade? A *parade*. Do you believe that?"

Packy frowned at the canvasman. "A parade?"

Goofy Joe nodded. "Damned right. We did it, too. Right there with nothin', in the middle of nowhere, in front of nobody. A flipping damned parade."

"A parade." Packy pushed himself to his feet and stood weaving before the fire. He looked past the string of Percherons

to where the bulls were standing quietly. "A parade." Packy
looked down, rubbed his eyes, and began stumbling toward his
bedroll.

"I wish we'd a done that."

Four days later it was a somber sort of parade that made its
way from the Snake Mountain Gap, across the Push River
Bridge, into the town of Miira. The bulls, horses, bullhands,
and hostlers were stained the same ochre yellow as the dust
that rose from the road. Before putting the bulls into the *kraal*
for the night, Packy Dern led the bulls to the shallows of Table
Lake, just below the trench grave they called the Big Lot, to
allow the bullhands to wash themselves and their pachyderms.

Grass and small flowers of yellow and blue covered the
graves from the original burying where Pony Red Miira had
kicked in the first clod of dirt. Now there was fresh soil in the
trench. Pony Red was holding up some of it; the rest was
supported by the eleven troupers from Number Three that had
died building the Ikona–Tarzak Road.

The bulls secured in the *kraal* and fed, Little Will and Packy
went to their house to complete it. When they arrived, the
plank walls were washed white with chalk and clay, the
thatched roof had been replaced with one of shingles, and the
dirt floor inside had been covered with wood. They both stood
in the doorway staring at the low wooden table and the stuffed
cushions that served both as chairs and beds.

"Well, how about it?"

They turned to see Waxy Adnelli, the left sleeve of his
tattered shirt tied into a knot. Packy pointed with his thumb
toward the interior of the one-roomed structure. "What the hell
happened?"

Waxy grinned and swept his right arm about indicating the
many finished white houses of Miira. "A big crew of canvasmen and razorbacks were sent here from Tarzak to get lumber.
I worked a little deal."

Little Will looked back inside. "It's beautiful." She pulled
on Packy's arm. "Isn't it, Packy? Just look."

Packy looked back inside. First his frown relaxed into an
expression of resignation, then his shoulders slumped. "It's
pretty. Pretty as hell. A regular damned mansion." He tossed
his bullhook inside, turned, and walked toward the lake.

Little Will looked at Waxy. "What's the matter?"

Waxy scratched his chin, shrugged, spat on the ground,

then looked at Packy's receding back. "Stupid, stupid me. I guess I never thought it out too clear." He looked back at the house. "As long as we were holed up in shacks and the caves, we were just making do until help arrived."

He pointed at the house. "This just told Packy that no help is coming; we're dug in here for the long haul." Waxy stared at the house until his eyes began to glisten. "Yeah. I guess that's what it means." He turned and walked the small path that wound among Miira's new houses.

Little Will ran from the door and headed toward the lake. By the time she had caught up with Packy, the boss elephant man was seated upon the sand, staring across the water. She knelt beside him. "Packy, it's a nice house."

Packy nodded, half-smiled, and patted her shoulder. "Sure it is, kid. Sure." He looked at his hands, cut and scarred from the endless days of work cutting through the Snake Mountain Gap. He clasped his hands, let out a brief laugh, and nodded again. "I guess we were doing the same thing building a damned road. I just never thought about it." He removed his glasses and rubbed his eyes. "Damn, but I miss the show. Damn, but I miss it."

"We all do. But it isn't dead yet, Packy."

The boss elephant man held his hands out toward the waters of Table Lake. "John J. O'Hara himself could walk across that water and tell me that, and you know what I'd tell him? I'd say, that's one helluva water-walking act you got there, Mr. John, but where's your goddamned audience?"

He stood and pointed toward the water. "Where's your starship but a whiff of ashes around some lump of nowhere? Where's your center ring but tossed out into freezing damned space along with the white tops and dead bulls? Where's your clowns? You know where they are? They're in damned Tarzak, clearing roads, digging up roots, building damned houses out of damned mud!"

Little Will stood next to Packy and took his hand as he lowered it. "Don't talk like that about Mr. John. He was a good man."

Packy nodded. "Too damned good." He looked down at her. "How do you fight a ghost? I'm fit near to split I'm so damned mad. But how do you fight a damned ghost?"

She turned back toward the house. "Let's go home."

"Home." He nodded and began walking. "Home."

NINE

For three days Packy sat in the house, staring through a window toward Table Lake. During that time Little Will and Shiner Pete would walk the forests, and climb the hills, exploring.

They were high upon one of the Snake Mountain's foothills when Shiner Pete pointed toward the west. *"Look."*

Little Will looked past the lake and the jungle beyond to see white-capped peaks in the distance. *"Pete, they look just like the white tops."* She looked at him. *"We're still a show, aren't we, Pete?"*

He sat down on the grass and wrapped his arms around his knees. *"I don't know."*

She sat beside him. *"You said the show couldn't be killed."*

"Maybe I was wrong." He shook his head. *"Waxy's down. He's so down. Everybody is."*

"Pete, just who was Karl Arnheim?"

"All I know is he got us in the fix we're in. Every time I ask Waxy about Arnheim, he don't want to talk about him."

"Neither does Packy."

They sat in silence for a long time, looking at the white-topped mountains. Little Will lowered her glance and stared at the jungle between the mountains and the lake. *"Pete, what do you think happened to Waco and Fireball?"*

"Dead most likely." He pushed himself to his feet and held out his hand. *"Come on. Let's go back. This is getting to be as much fun as staking babies out on anthills."*

"Number Ten is back down."

Moments after word of Number Ten's return had spread throughout Miira, Little Will, Packy and the others from Number Three gathered in the square marking the center of town. The sun was hot and the air quiet as Waxy Adnelli stood before a box and shook a handful of papers in the air. "I got this stuff from Warts down in Tarzak." He put the papers upon the box and began reading.

"Across that ocean next to Tarzak is another continent. Number Two went down there. Number Two's radio was working . . ."

And the inhabitants of Miira learned that car Number Two was located across the sea upon a continent the troupers in Number Two were calling Midway. One hundred and nine troupers went to the big lot when Number Two hit. Among them, Bone Breaker Bob Naseby, the show's surgeon, was fatally injured when Two plowed up some real estate upon touching down. This left the total medical knowledge on Momus in the hands of Butterfingers McCorkle, Bone Breaker's flunky, and Mange Ranger. Leadfoot had given Number Two instructions on how to get to Tarzak. Boat building was already in progress.

And the inhabitants of Miira asked about friends, loved ones, family, enemies that had gone down with Number Two.

Fish Face Gillis, kid show director, dead.

Na-Na, the two-headed lady, dead.

Pod, the three-legged man, lost a leg.

Dog Face Dick, the wolfman, alive.

Big Sue, the giantess, alive.

Teena and Weena, midgets, both alive.

Amazing Ozamund, magician, alive.

Madam Zelda, fortune teller, alive.

Slippery Sash, escape artist, dead.

Electric Lips, barker, dead.

Motor Mouth, barker, alive.

Mootch Movill, shooting gallery concessionaire, alive . . .

After he had read out the list of living and dead, Waxy continued with Wart's report.

Number Ten said that there appeared to be a possible route through the Upland Mountains north of Kuumic, and through the swamp and jungle from Kuumic to Miira. The grades appeared to be gentle, with no swamps to drain, and only one major river crossing.

An expedition from Kuumic had made it across the desert to Tarzak, provisioning themselves with cobit root along the way. They protected themselves from the desert sun by using loose hooded robes made from their clothing. The expedition reported that there were large numbers of fissures along the route (confirmed by Number Ten) that gave off a hot, constant flame. It was supposed that the fires were fed by some enormous natural gas reservoir. The expedition used these fires to cook their cobit and to keep warm during the desert nights.

Farther around the planet were various and sundry islands of assorted sizes, and then a huge, jungle-covered continent with high mountains and wide plateaus. Number Ten then crossed a wide sea, then returned to this continent. Since it was between Midway and the western continent, the mass of land where nine of the *Baraboo's* ten cars had put down was called the Central Continent. Midway is midway, while the continent west of the Central Continent was called the Western Continent.

After some commentary regarding the originality of the continents' names, Waxy continued.

The sea west of Central was called the Western Sea, while the body of water between the Central and Midway continents was called the Sea of Baraboo. Before landing back in Tarzak, Number Ten noted what appeared to be an enormous geological rift that split the northern third of the Central Continent. The high peaked cliff visible across Tarzak's harbor was the southern end of this rift. Leadfoot Sina, chief pilot of Number Ten, reported that this might mean shaky times in Tarzak town.

The measurements taken by Number Ten showed that there was no measurable winter on Momus, the Moman year was eight-tenths of an Earth year long, divided into three hundred and four days of roughly twenty-three hours each. Warts had divided the three hundred and four days of the Moman year into ten months of five weeks of six days each.

The year began with the month of May, followed by: Rain, Mud, Wind, Thunder, Hail, Flood, Quake, Layup, and Winter. The days were called: Workday, Bluesday, Herdsday, Quadsday, Payday, and Funday.

To fill in the remaining four days, Warts had created an eleventh month, The Season, consisting of the days of Put Up, The Stand, The Show, and Teardown. Midnight of Teardown, the fourth day of The Season, would be the anniversary of The Crash.

Waxy lowered the paper from which he had been reading. "This four-day month called The Season. Warts's put out the call for everyone to show at Tarzak for parade."

There was a grumble among the inhabitants of Miira. Packy Dern walked forward into the square and shouted: "The bull-hands'll be there—with bells on!" He looked around at the now silent crowd, then he turned to Waxy. "How long do we got before The Season? What day is it?"

Waxy studied another sheet of paper. "Let's see, this is the two hundred and sixty-eighth day since the crash, which makes... ummm, this the month of Winter. Bluesday, the eighth of Winter. That means there're twenty-two days before The Season."

Packy looked around at the faces. "My road gang. Get it together. We're moving' out in two hours to join the boss hostler's gang to finish gettin' down Blowdown Cliff. From there we go on to Tarzak to make parade."

THE CALENDAR OF MOMUS

Months:	1 May	6 Hail	11 The Season
	2 Rain	7 Flood	1 Put Up
	3 Mud	8 Quake	2 The Stand
	4 Wind	9 Layup	3 The Show
	5 Thunder	10 Winter	4 Teardown

Days:	Workday	Bluesday	Herdsday	Quadsday	Payday	Funday
	1	2	3	4	5	6
	7	8	9	10	11	12
	13	14	15	16	17	18
	19	20	21	22	23	24
	25	26	27	28	29	30

TEN

The Ikona–Tarzak Road was finished and it was Put Up, the first day of The Season. Little Will sat astride Reg's neck, leading the bulls of Miira down the road toward Tarzak. The bulls each pulled wagons piled high with lumber, while the horse-drawn wagons filled with people from Miira and the Emerald Valley had raced on ahead. In exchange for the lumber, the bulls would bring back core blades, gears, metal, and salt-packed fish. The people from Number Two would not be there; they were still building their boats. But Kuumic would be represented by a delegation that had crossed the desert.

As Reg reached the crossroad going off to Sina, the desert, and Tarzak, Little Will tapped Reg's left shoulder with her bullhook, and headed toward Tarzak. She closed her eyes and tried to remember the parades she had ridden in with the show. She had been in costume, the bulls had been decked out in spangles, and the windjammers filled the air with lusty marches. But the costumes, spangles and instruments had been tossed out to lighten the *Baraboo* as it tried to make orbit around Momus.

It hadn't mattered what planet they had played, beings of every sort and description would line the ways and cheer the parade after their own fashion. As Little Will opened her eyes to see Reg crossing the last metal bridge into the town of Tarzak, there were no crowded, cheering ways. The white-washed mud huts of Tarzak were silent as the inhabitants continued with the day's occupation. They had all seen bulls before, and there was work to do.

Packy Dern rode on a horse toward her from the direction of Tarzak. He pulled up beside her. "Little Will, lead them through the town to the clearing on the other side. We have a *kraal* put up there for the bulls."

She nodded and Packy made a clucking sound and rode on ahead. Little Will sighed and patted Reg behind the bull's right ear. *"Just a little more, Reg. Not much of a parade, is it?"*

Far into the jungle from Miira, Waco Whacko emerged into a large clearing carrying the fruit he had gathered. He walked through the tall grass to the bark shack he had built, stooped inside, and deposited the fruit on a stone slab. Stepping outside, he examined the clear sky, then looked down and walked up the rise in the center of the clearing. As he approached a moss-covered mound, they began:

"Waco. Waco, Talk to us, Waco."

"It's not our fault, Waco. Please talk to us."

Waco studied the moss covering, tested its moisture with his fingers, then stood. "I promised your parents I would care for you. I did not promise them to entertain you, or love you." He turned away. "If you want conversation, talk to each other." He walked away from the mound.

"Waco! Waco! Don't leave us, Waco!"

When he was out of range of the Ssendissians' thoughts, he turned back and looked at the mound. One night twenty days before, Waco had been dreaming. He was walking through jade forests hung with jeweled leaves and fruit, the forest carpet beneath his bare feet made of satin. He had awakened to find himself up to his knees in quicksand.

The Ssendissians eggs then laughed at the joke they had played upon him. After four hours, Waco had pulled his exhausted body from the deathly trap and collapsed among the rot of the jungle floor. The next morning he had moved the eggs into the center of the clearing and had placed his sleeping quarters out of the infant Ssendissians' range.

He studied the mound, searching his soul for some small

remaining spark of affection. The thing he searched, he concluded, was dead.

There was a loud splash, and Waco crouched and turned his head in the direction of the small lake that bordered one edge of the clearing. His eyes squinted, but the brightness of the sun and the shade of the trees surrounding the lake obscured his vision. He began moving toward the lake.

Several times he had felt that he was being watched, and once he had caught the flash of a huge creature as it bolted out of sight. When he had arrived at the point where the creature had stood watching him, Waco smelled a curious odor and observed a wide expanse of flattened vegetation. In its flight, the creature had made a swath through the jungle almost fifteen feet wide. Trees six inches thick had been pushed aside to right and left as though they had possessed no roots.

Waco crouched lower in the grass as he approached the trees at the edge of the lake. He could hear nothing save the buzzing of an occasional water wasp in the hot, still air. He moved quietly through the trees and squatted behind a berrybush. The water rippled from his right. He looked in that direction and saw a woman sitting naked in the water, near the rocks that lined the lake's shore.

She cupped her hands, lowered them into the water, then brought them up to rinse her face. She bent forward and dipped her long black hair into the water. As she sat up, she raised her arms and twisted the excess water from her hair. Waco studied her tiny mouth, pug nose, and almond eyes. He stood up, walked to the edge of the lake, and called out. "Well, Hanah Sanagi, look at you."

Fireball Hanah Sanagi started for an instant, then lowered her arms as she saw him. "Waco. Everybody said you were dead." She lowered her arms into the water again and brought them up to splash water on her breasts. She looked again at Waco. "Getting an eyeful?"

Waco turned away. "I apologize. I didn't expect to find anyone out here."

Hanah stood. "I didn't expect to find you either. You can look, Waco. From what I hear, I don't have anything to worry about."

Waco frowned as he looked back at her. "What is that supposed to mean?"

Hanah walked from the water, wiped the water from her body with swift strokes of her hands, then picked up her clothes

from beneath a tree. She returned to the water, squatted upon
a rock, and began rinsing and wringing out her clothes. Waco
walked around the shore until he stood beneath the trees behind
her. "I asked what you meant by that?"

"You're a garry, aren't you? That's the word I heard. All
those years living with Buns and Bullhook."

Waco flushed and turned away. "Don't believe everything
you hear."

"Are you?"

Waco lowered himself to the ground and leaned against a
tree. "Am I what?"

"A garry." She finished wringing out her clothes, then
turned and walked to a large, smooth rock that was bathed in
the hot light of the sun. She spread her clothes to dry.

Waco shook his head, picked up a stick, and flexed it until
it snapped. "It's not anyone's business." He looked at her
again, and she was stretched out on the rock beside her drying
clothing. Waco tossed the pieces of stick aside. "What are you
doing here?"

Hanah smiled as she drew her hands down from her breasts
along the length of her body. "That's none of *your* business."
She stretched in the sun, fanned out her hair, and clasped her
hands behind her head. "How are the eggs, Waco? Are they
still alive?"

"Yes. They're still alive." He rubbed his eyes, then looked
back at Hanah.

She turned her head, glanced at Waco, then closed her eyes
and faced the sun. "I left when they began chewing up Number
Three to make tools. They're building a road to connect the
cars. I wandered a lot. I guess I felt like pulling the plug a
time or two." She shrugged. "But I didn't." She looked back
at Waco. "Say, have you seen one of those lizards that live in
this swamp yet?"

Waco shook his head. "No. I came close a couple of times.
The tracks they make seem to indicate that they are fairly
large."

Hanah laughed. "I'll say they're large. I got a good look
at one while it was playing patty-cake in a big mud puddle.
It made a bull look like a puppy dog." She shrugged. "Once
it saw me, though, it took off like its tail was on fire."

They were both quiet for a long time. Waco studied the
naked woman. "Hanah?"

"Yes, Waco?"

"How do you feel now, about Number Three?"

She opened her eyes and looked at the clear sky. Then she sat up and began turning her clothes over. "I've worked it out of me. I don't know how long it's been that I've been wandering around the jungle, but at some time or other, I discovered that I'd gone for a couple of days without thinking about the car." She turned over on her stomach and spread out. "I can take it, I guess. I've just been exploring the jungle since. It's an interesting place. I don't know that I really want to be back with the old crowd yet. Or ever." She lifted her head. "Waco?"

"What?"

"Are you a garry or not?"

The snake charmer smiled, looked down at the ground, and shrugged. "I don't know." His face grew serious. "Everything and everyone disappoints me. I didn't want to risk anything."

"You're a virgin? Both ways?"

"All ways." Waco picked up another stick and fiddled with it as he looked up at the sky. He looked down at the ground and shook his head. "There are a lot of unhappy people in the universe, Hanah. I'm not unique."

Hanah Sanagi studied the snake charmer. "Waco, how long will it take for those eggs to hatch?"

He sighed, then shrugged. "On Ssendiss it takes about two hundred and eighty Earth years." He held up a hand toward the sky. "With the different climate, gravity, soil nutrients, I don't know. I don't even know if they'll live to be hatched."

Hanah lowered her head to her arms. "That's a lot of years."

"A lot of years."

"Waco, when my clothes are dry, show me where your digs are."

The snake charmer jumped to his feet. "Why?"

Hanah wiggled on the warm face of the rock. "Oh, I don't know. If nothing else, you could use a cook. If you were any skinnier you wouldn't even cast a shadow. Besides, two hundred and eighty years is a long time."

The former snake charmer settled back against the tree and studied the former pilot.

ELEVEN

After all had assembled in the clearing next to Tarzak to begin The Season, they sat surrounding a large log fire. First they ate cobit and freakfish, prepared by the cookhouse gang, then they worked on jugs of sapwine. As the sun moved toward the horizon, Blacky Squab, the lithographer, and his printer's devil, Meph, handed out the printed maps of Momus.

"Now, don't you bend that paper too much; it'll break."

"*Holy*.... Blacky, you smell like year-old sardines!"

"That's the ink. Careful you don't smear it. It's not quite dry yet."

"How long's it going to take to dry?"

"Don't know. I haven't had any dry yet."

"Jeez, Blacky, stand downwind!"

"What's this paper made out of?"

"Cobit milk, clay, and a stringy plant that grows in the wetland down in the delta—there, I told you not to bend it. Here's another."

"Phew!"

"Blacky, what's these little squiggles? Damn paper is lumpy."

"Those're the roads. Put your glasses on. *You*—don't bend that!"

"My glasses got busted in the Snake Mountain Gap."

"You just never learned to read. Here, don't bend the paper, and don't smear the ink . . ."

The longer they studied the maps, the quieter they became. The marks of their year's work were small in comparison with the size of the planet. They, in turn, felt small; helpless. The sapwine began to flow at an increased rate. When the sun fell below the horizon, the sky still tinted with bluish-red, the fire in the center of the clearing was replenished with fresh wood. They sat and watched the fire. Shiner Pete Adnelli sat next to Little Will. They stared into the fire and held hands.

Across the fire from them, Stretch Dirak, the advance manager, weaved to his feet and walked into the clearing, a sapwine jug dangling in his hand. He looked around the circle of faces. "Well, what in the hell are we going to do? What's next?"

Packy Dern looked up from the fire and shouted across the clearing. "The Miira–Kuumic Road."

"Bah!" Stretch shook his head. "I don't want to hear about any more damned roads! What're we going to do about getting off this mudball?" He searched the circle of faces. "Leadfoot, where are you?"

Leadfoot waved a hand. "Over here. And we're not going to do a damned thing about getting off the skin. We're stuck."

"Stuck?" Stretch walked around the fire until he stood before Leadfoot. "What about Number Ten?"

Leadfoot shrugged. "What about it?"

"Can't you rig something?"

Leadfoot shook his head, then laughed. "I'm a pilot, Stretch. Just for the hell of it, let's say that we can make up the fuel that bird eats, which we can't. No one here knows how. But let's say we can. Then what? We can get up into orbit. Sight-seeing tours, and that's it. Maybe we can get a couple of million miles away before the air runs out. If only a couple of us goes, maybe more."

"What about an air recycler?"

Leadfoot shook his head, then looked up at Stretch. He shook his head again, then stood and walked out into the clearing. "Let's say there's no air problem—and no water problem—and no food problem. At Number Ten's top speed, it would take thousands—*thousands*—of years just to make it to a trade route." He shook his head, then looked around at the circle of faces.

"While I'm at it I might as well ex the idea of a light drive." He held out his hands. "Does anyone here know how to build one?" He looked around at the silent faces. "Anyone?" Leadfoot thrust his hands into his pockets and faced the fire. "I know this much about light drives. Just to build it, providing someone knew how, takes a huge industrial base just to manufacture the components. It would take generations just to put together that industrial base."

He stared at the fire a moment longer. "Besides, the only drive I know anything about is too big for Number Ten. See . . . we'd have to build a ship, as well." He looked at the advance manager. "Hell, Stretch, we don't even have the know-how or the parts to put together a deep space radio." Leadfoot went back to his place and sat down.

Stretch rubbed the back of his neck, then threw his empty jug into the fire. "Damn!" He turned away from the fire, went back to his place and sat down.

Again silence, save the crackle of the fire, then a slender figure across the fire from Stretch stood up. "Most of you don't know me. I'm Rhoda Lerner, in wardrobe. I joined the show in Ahngar just before . . . this." She frowned and placed her hands on her hips. "Well, I just want to know something. What happened? I've been with this down at the corners, hard luck gang for most a year now, and nobody talks about it. What happened? Why?" She looked around the fire until Warts Tho stood up and moved into the clearing.

The Pendiian rubbed his bumpy chin. "There's a lot of you that joined last season. Karl Arnheim sabotaged the *City of Baraboo* and marooned us here. Arnheim and John J. O'Hara had a long feud going. Arnheim's company built the ship for the Governor, but he never intended to deliver. Instead he was planning on selling the thing as a warship to someone else for about double what O'Hara contracted to pay him. In any event, O'Hara snatched the ship before Arnheim could complete the deal with the other party. O'Hara paid for the ship, but Arnheim lost his shirt all the same. Ever since, Arnheim's been after the show." Warts held out his hands. "Except Arnheim's dead now."

Mange Ranger, the veterinarian, stood up. "Warts, don't forget; Arnheim was crazier than a sock full of bedbugs." Mange looked around. "Bone Breaker told me that on the ship when he examined Arnheim's body." Mange sat down.

Warts shrugged. "That's about it." He returned to his place

and sat down. Rhoda the wardrobe lady, hands still on hips, looked around at the silent faces, then sat down. Boss canvasman Duckfoot Tarzak sat shaking his head. Little Will leaned over and shook the huge man's arm.

"Duckfoot?"

The boss canvasman continued shaking his head. "Dammit. Dammit, Little Will. If we don't do something soon, we are whipped." He looked up at the troupers surrounding the fire and pointed his finger at them. "Look at them. This is supposed to be a celebration—a holiday." He lowered his arm. "Just look at them."

Little Will studied the faces. All of them were lost in thought. All of them read: whipped, done, defeated. In the cart.

A horrible aroma assaulted her nostrils and an ink-covered hand gave her one of the evil-smelling maps of Momus. The aroma moved on and she studied the lines and smears that represented the planet upon which she was sitting.

As she studied the map, the defeated faces around her fell into a collage of other impressions: the geological fault that had done away with a week's work in the Snake Mountain Gap, Goofy Joe at the fire talking about fighting ghosts, Packy crushed at seeing his temporary shelter turned into a permanent home, Shiner Pete saying that you can kill troupers and you can kill animals, but you can never kill the show.

On the map was represented the huge geological rift that extended from the harbor at Tarzak straight north off the end of the Central Continent. The formation had no name. All of it came together in her head: the place, the situation, the mood, what the name should be. It was also clear to her who should say the name. She closed her eyes and searched the crowd with her mind. When she found the one she was looking for, she planted the name.

"Ah-*hah!*"

Everyone looked toward the source of the exclamation. Cholly Jacoby, the tramp clown, sprang to his feet and walked quickly into the clearing. He stood next to the fire, held up his map in order that he could read by its light, then he lowered the map to his side. He looked around. "Blacky?"

The lithographer stood and walked over. "What?"

Cholly stabbed at the map with his finger. "What's that?"

Blacky shrugged. "I don't know. It's sort of a mountain. Leadfoot drew it that way."

Cholly nodded. "I see. I see." As Blacky returned to his place, everyone faced their maps toward the fire to try and see what had captured the clown's interest. Cholly turned toward Leadfoot. "Leadfoot, what is this thing?"

Leadfoot got up and walked over to the clown. He looked to see where Cholly's finger was pointing. "Oh. That's a long geological rift in the planet's crust. It begins a little north of Tarzak here"—he pointed—"and goes straight north right off the end of the continent as far as I could see from low orbit. See, it's a big fold in the crust. Maybe plates in the planet's crust grinding together. It probably means frequent quakes near the fault zone."

Cholly looked at Leadfoot. "How come it's not named?"

Leadfoot looked at Cholly, eyebrows upraised. "What was I going to call it?"

Cholly snorted. "It's obvious." He looked around at the faces. "Arnheim's Fault."

For ten full seconds the troupers stared at the clown; then the laughing began. Between their tears they borrowed the few pencils that remained, or used pieces of charcoal, and marked the name on their maps. True, it was Arnheim's Fault. Cholly bowed, doffed the derby that he no longer wore, then retired to the circle.

That night they ate, drank and sang the show songs. Dr. Weems borrowed a hostler and four horses, went to Number One, and came back with the calliope. The boiler was fired up, and then the shrieks of the steam music joined the laughter, the combination forever putting to rest the ghost of Karl Arnheim.

The next three days saw clowns, jugglers, riders and others perform their acts. Little Will proudly stood beside Reg as the bulls paraded tail-and-trunk around the crude ring of cut logs on The Show. On Teardown, the fourth day of The Season, the troupers headed back toward their towns to continue all the mundane tasks of day-to-day survival. No one could ever be accused of saying that they looked like one, but they were once again a show.

TWELVE

Upon returning to Miira most of the road gang repaired harness, tools, and wagons. The remainder constructed a piling, beam, and plank bridge across the Fake Foot River, opening the southern route around Table Lake, the first step in constructing the Miira—Kuumic Road. Daybreak of the morning following the completion of the bridge saw the bull-hands lead their charges from the *kraal* to the bridge against a hushed background of harness jingles and the low grumble a planet seems to make when more than one elephant at a time walks.

The bulls were clucked to a halt, the soil of Momus stopped shaking, and the grumble was replaced by the shouts, curses, profanities, blasphemies, obscenities, and other affectionate expressions of the hostlers bringing into line their wagons and timber-skidding teams. As morning's progress filled in the night's grays with color, Cookie Jo Wayne pulled up her cook-house wagon at the end of the column.

Little Will's thoughts skipped among her memories of the many mornings standing in line with the bulls. There were the chilly mornings in the Snake Mountain Gap, standing next to Reg. But there were the many mornings sitting on Bullhook

Willy's shoulders next to Ming. The shadows of the bulls had
stood against strange skies of orange, red, purple, and blue.
At times the air would be so dry her tongue would stick to the
top of her mouth. Elsewhere, moving onto the lot of another
strange city on another strange planet, the air might be so humid
that everyone's clothes were drenched before the sun peeked
over the horizon. On one planet, every morning was greeted
by flurries of fat snowflakes that would melt as soon as they
touched the ground.

She looked at her gold-tipped bullhook and remembered her
father putting Ming through her paces. Both bulls and bullhands
were killed, or just grew old and disappeared. But the more
the show changed, the more it became to her a fixed place in
a constantly changing universe. She turned, looked down the
line of bulls, and watched Ming until the waving of a hand
caught her attention. Shiner Pete was climbing into the harness
wagon.

"All ready to go, Little Will?"

She waved back. *"All ready."* She turned to Reg and petted
the bull's shoulder. *"Are you all ready, girl?"* Reg snorted and
nodded her head.

"Little Will?" She looked forward and saw Packy motioning
with his hand for her to come on. She walked up and stood
next to the boss elephant man as he held out his map, and
pointed at the lines and scribbles that had been entered upon
it by the trailblazing gang. "What the hell does that say?"

She glanced at it, then looked up at Packy. "It says, 'Soft
area. Follow the north trail.'"

Packy slowly shook his head as he looked again at the map.
"Well, I guess it's my glasses instead of Short Mort's writin'."
He looked back at Little Will. "You think you can read this
map, follow the blazes, and push Reg at the same time?"

"I think so."

Packy rubbed his chin, then pointed toward the bridge.
"Then when we get across the bridge, move Reg to the front
end. I don't want us rollin' into a quicksand bath because my
glasses don't work so good."

Little Will took the map. "What did Mange say about your
eyes?"

"He's a damned vet." Packy dismissed the subject with a
wave of his hand, then raised an eyebrow and glared at Little
Will. "And don't you go peekin' inside my head—or anyone
else's—without permission. Hear?"

They both turned and looked as Waxy Adnelli came from
the door of his house and walked up to Packy. Waxy looked
past the bridge toward the southern edge of the lake, then
looked back at Packy. "You about ready?"

"About."

Little Will observed Waxy's apparently permanent frown.
"Good morning, Waxy."

Waxy shook his head. "I'll let you know."

"Is something wrong?"

Packy studied the town of Miira's record keeper. "Waxy,
you do look sort of in the middle of something sticky."

Waxy snorted, rubbed his chin, and pointed his hand toward
the south. "Turtlehead came up from Tarzak last night. You
know what Warts has me doin' now? I'm supposed to interview
everybody and record their remembrances of the show."

"What's wrong with that?"

"With the old wheeze population we got, do you have any
idea how long that's goin' to take? And Warts wants copies
before we go down to Tarzak for The Season next. What am
I supposed to record on? Blacky Squab hasn't sent any more
paper up here in more'n a month. I'm already keepin' notes
on the damn walls."

Packy grinned and shook his head. "Sounds like you found
your life's work."

Little Will placed a hand on Waxy's shoulder. "Look upon
it as a challenge."

Waxy shrugged off her hand. "This is too early in the day
for cracks from the back of the blues." He looked at Packy.
"I don't *have* to do this stuff. It's not like I was bein' paid."

Little Will pointed a finger at Waxy. "You are too being
paid. Stew Travers gave you a whole sack of cobit roots for
marrying him to Diamonds Mary." She turned to Packy. "What
are you going to pay to have Waxy marry you to Cookie Jo?"

Packy snorted. "I already got me an elephant, short stuff.
What do I need a wife for?"

Little Will frowned and grinned at the same time. "You
don't *know?*"

Waxy waved his arm about. "Enough, you two! I got serious
problems." He lowered his voice and moved more closely to
Packy. "That's the thing." He pointed his thumb at this chest.
"Me marryin' people. My Great Boolabong, Packy! Poge Loder
came to me after I married Stew and Diamonds and told me
I'd burn in hellfire, brimstone, and such for doin' that."

"You worryin' about that, Waxy?"

"No. Not that." Waxy sighed. "It's just that some others want to get married, too. That'll have Poge screamin' damnation in the square twenty-three hours a day." He looked at Little Will, then up at Packy. "And what if he's right? Who am I to be marryin' people?"

Little Will smiled, a glint of mischief in her eyes. "Waxy, who better than the boss harness man to tie the knot?"

Waxy's glowering face studied Little Will for a moment. He then spake: "If you know what's good for you, sprout, don't risk readin' my mind right about now." He looked at Packy. "Look, the reason I'm here is to find out if you can find something for Dot the Pot to do on the road gang."

"There's nothin' for her to do now that Queenie's dead. Why do you want her out of town?"

"Why?" Waxy's voice lowered. "She's after my *bones,* that's why!"

Packy held out his hands. "There's nothin' I can do, 'cept give the bride away."

Waxy turned abruptly and marched back to his house. "Goddamn bullhands been shovelin' plop so long their heads're packed solid with it!"

A call came from the column, and Packy answered it by waving his bullhook above his head. He lowered the bullhook and faced Little Will. "Get on back to your rubber mule, bullhand. We got a mess of trees to push over and clear before making camp." She began walking toward Reg when Packy called out. "Hey!" She turned and looked back at the boss elephant man. "And you put that nonsense about Cookie Jo out on the lot. Don't want to be givin' her any dumb ideas."

Packy clucked at Robber and the column began to move, lifting the dust into the still morning air as it followed the boss elephant man across the Fake Foot River Bridge.

Deep in the Great Muck Swamp, Waco Whacko awakened from a troubled dream. He lifted himself up on one elbow and studied the interior of his hut. Nothing seemed unusual except for the many improvements that Fireball had made. He looked at the woven curtain he had made to separate their sleeping quarters.

"Fireball?" he whispered. Getting no reply, Waco lowered himself back down upon his sleeping mat and closed his eyes. He tried to drift into sleep, but strange, threatening thoughts interfered. He and Fireball lived almost as brother and sister. Her company, once thought by Waco to be an intrusion on his isolation, turned out to be not only pleasant and entertaining, but had become a vital part of his existence.

In his head he conjured up a vision of the shuttle pilot. Hanah Sanagi. Long black hair against the creaminess of her skin; her face always something of joy, sensualness, or serenity—

Waco suddenly sat up. "Yes, Waco, you stupid bastard," he said quietly to himself. "You've done it again." Love. Goddamned love.

Although it seemed like yesterday, it must have been months ago that Hanah Sanagi and he sat outside, facing each other across the night's cooking fire. And Hanah was talking. Waco had noticed that he wasn't listening to her words; he was watching the movement of her lips, the black flash of her long-lashed eyes, the subtle motion of the muscles beneath the skin of her long neck. And he had stopped—had frozen everything that he could or ever would feel. He had left the fire and had walked the darkness until he stood next to the mound of eggs.

"Are you leaving us, Waco? Will you leave with the female?"

He looked up at the stars. "No. I won't leave you."

"We can feel your feelings, Waco. There is a war within you. Who will care for us when you leave?"

Waco lowered his glance, rubbed his eyes, and shook his head. "I won't leave you. I promised your parents."

"You think you do not feel, Waco. But we can see past the walls you have built in your mind. You feel, Waco. You love the female."

"Silence!" Waco breathed hard for a moment, then closed his eyes. "It doesn't matter. It will never matter. I made my promise."

He turned and looked down the hill toward the wash of yellow light made by the cooking fire. Beyond that place of light was the absolute blackness of the jungle and the cloud-covered night sky. Almost in the center of that light, Hanah knelt as she made tea from the strange-tasting leaves she had discovered. That light, that woman; the center of Waco's universe. He lowered a shield of icy indifference over his realization. There would be—could be—no love.

To love is to risk too much.

He returned to the fire, had his cobit bread and tea, and

listened with detachment as Hanah talked about trying to capture and train one of the swamp monsters. He had joined the conversation, his internal war placed far behind him.

He had thought it was far behind him. As he sat upon his sleeping pallet cursing himself, his feelings, and Hanah Sanagi, he knew that he had once again opened himself up to the sickness. He pulled on his clothes and spoke in the direction of the grass curtain. "Hanah? Hanah? We have to talk."

He stood, pulled on his shirt, and looked around the edge of the curtain. "Hanah?" She was not upon her sleeping mat. He turned, walked through the hut's entrance, and stood in the early morning light searching the treeline. He heard a low moan, and when he faced the direction of the sound, he saw Hanah's half-dressed body collapsed upon the mound of eggs.

"Hanah!" The scream came from his gut. He ran up the hill, pulled her body from the mound, and cradled her head as he knelt upon the grass. "Dammit, Hanah. I *told* you to stay away from them. I *told* you!"

Her eyes fluttered open and her mouth worked at soundless words. Waco faced the mound. "Stop it! Stop whatever you're doing! Stop it, or I'll smash every damned one of you!"

Hanah seemed almost to turn to liquid in his arms as a timid whimper fought itself from her mouth. "I didn't . . . Waco, I didn't. In my sleep. They came to me . . . in my sleep." Her whimper evolved into racking sobs as she lifted her arms and wrapped them around Waco's waist, her face buried in his chest.

He placed his cheek against the top of her head. "Why? Dammit, why?"

And the eggs spoke to him. *"A precaution, Waco."*

"Against what?"

"You love her. We need you, but you love her. She is dangerous to us."

"She is no threat to you! I promised your parents!"

"Promises can be broken, Waco. She must die."

"Die?" Waco placed his right arm beneath Hanah's knees and stood lifting her. "I'm moving her out of your range. She does not die!"

"She dies. We must protect ourselves. We will kill her mind before you can take her away from us."

Waco moistened his lips. "Don't do this. Don't do this to me."

"We must protect ourselves, Waco."

Waco lowered his head until his cheek was against Hanah's. "Don't you understand that you are going to need someone else to take care of you after I'm dead? It will take almost three hundred years before you may leave your shells. I will only be alive, perhaps, another fifteen or twenty years, if that."

The eggs were silent.

Waco lifted his head. "There will have to be someone to take care of you after I die. For that, I must have a child. To do that, I need this woman. I need . . . Hanah. Kill her and you kill yourselves." He turned away from the mound. "May I take her away, now? Speak to me!"

The thought came, timid and repentant. *"If we let you have her, Waco, do you promise not to punish us?*

"I promise."

Waco walked from the mound carrying the now unconscious woman. He whispered into her unhearing ear, "Damn me. Damn me, but I love you."

Many nights later, in the road gang's camp deep in the Great Muck Swamp, Little Will drew her lips away from Pete's, her glance cast down. *"My face, Pete, it feels so hot."*

"Mine, too."

She looked around at the dark of the camp. *"What if someone saw us?"*

"What if they did?" He nestled her head in the crook of his arm. *"Come on, Little Will. You're stiff as a board. Packy's going to be getting us up at the crack. He wants five miles of road cleared before tomorrow night. Go to sleep."*

"I can't." She sniffed.

"Now what's wrong?"

She buried her face in his chest. *"I don't know. I'm so confused."*

He wrapped his arms around her. *"Now, look, you. You love me and I love you. That's how it's always going to be. There's nothing confusing about that."*

She looked up into his face. He wiped the tears from her cheeks. *"Pete . . ."*

"Quit crying, Little Will. We haven't done anything."

"Pete?"

He kissed the tip of her nose. *"What?"*

Her hand stole beneath his shirt and caressed his chest. *"Pete, I love you."*

Pete swallowed, and quickly glanced around. The rest of

the road camp was dead asleep. *"Er . . ."* He swallowed again. His face was burning up, and in other districts strange and wonderful things were happening. *"I, uh . . ."*

"Pete?" Her hand began unbuttoning his shirt.

"Wha . . . what?"

"Say you love me, Pete. Say you love me more than anything else in the world." She opened his shirt and kissed his chest.

Pete wrapped his arms around her, held her tight, then released one hand to lift her chin toward his face. *"I feel so crazy right now. I love you, Little Will. I love you more than anything else in the Universe."*

He swallowed, then touched his lips to hers.

THIRTEEN

Twenty miles of new road through the swamp, and the lead gang of bulls had made it to the gentle foothills of the Upland Mountains. There was a natural pass through the mountains, then a gentle slope down into the Great Desert all of the way to where Number Seven had gone down. Once there, the Miira–Kuumic Road would be done.

Packy Dern sat in front of the campfire. He looked at Pete Adnelli, then turned and looked at Little Will. Again he looked at Pete, then back at Little Will. He shrugged and looked down. "I don't know. On Earth, I'd know. Here things are different." He looked at Pete. "I'm pretty darned sure what Waxy's going to say, though."

Pete squeezed Little Will's hand. "It doesn't matter." He leaned over and kissed her cheek. "I'm thinking about going back to Miira with the supply wagon and asking Waxy."

Packy scratched his head. "I don't know, kids. You two are awful young." He shrugged. "But the two of you are beautiful, and," he pushed himself to his feet, "I'm just an old man."

Pete looked up at the boss elephant man. "Packy. Where're you going?"

Packy looked around at the road gang eating their evening

meals, glanced at the cookhouse wagon, then looked back at Pete and Little Will. "I think I'll go see if I can find myself an old woman."

In their new hut, farther from the egg mound, Hanah and Waco sat together in the dark, watching the light from the cooking fire outside. His arm was around her shoulders, and she leaned her full weight against him. Waco turned his head and looked down into Hanah's face. Her eyes were transfixed by the light of the fire.

"Hanah, what are you thinking?"

The frozen expression on her face slowly melted as her eyes closed. "I was trying to remember the checkout sequence for launching the car. I knew that better than my own name." She was silent for a long time. "It's all scrambled up, now—great gaping blanks." Her head shook slowly. "I don't know. Those eggs. They've taken so much from me." She looked up into Waco's face. "Waco. I can't even remember my mother's face."

He placed his hand against her head and pressed her face against his chest. "Ssendissians have great powers, Hanah. The adults take them for granted and they know when and how to use them. Those eggs are just babies."

Hanah sighed. "What they did . . . what they said." She shook her head. "About the last word I'd use to describe them is 'babies'."

Waco looked at the fire while he searched for the proper words. "Ssendissians pass on their memories to their children. Each one of those eggs possesses the memories, knowledge, and mental skills that would take a human thousands of years to acquire." He paused and looked down at her. "But they are still babies. They aren't mature in how to use their powers. What would a human baby be like if it could destroy minds at whim?"

Hanah shuddered. "It frightens me." She pointed toward where the old hut once stood. "How do we know we're out of range here?"

"We don't. I didn't think the range expanded as they grew older, but it does. I'm certain that they wouldn't be particularly honest on the subject. Again, they are just babies."

Hanah looked above the fire toward the darkness which contained the mound of eggs. "It must be lonely for them."

Waco looked toward the darkness. "I never thought of it.

It probably is. Ssendissian parents are constantly in contact
with their children before they hatch. They instruct, teach . . ."

Hanah looked up at Waco. "And they love. They love and
they teach their children love. Don't they?"

"Yes."

She pointed toward the darkness. "If they have their parents'
memories, they know what their parents experienced as babies.
They know what being loved means." She lowered her hand
as she looked up at him. "You haven't given them that."

He shook his head and remained silent.

"I can't blame a baby for crying and striking out when it
is mistreated. And by denying them your love, you have mistreated them."

Waco closed his eyes. "Loving is not always an easy thing
to do."

She lifted a hand and placed it against his cheek. "You said
you loved me."

"Yes. But I did not say it was easy."

She pulled his head down until their lips touched. When she
released him, she again faced the fire. "It will become easier
for you to love the longer you are loved."

Waco joined her in looking at the fire. His soul shuddered
at the thought of trading in comfortable desolation for the un-
certainties of loving and being loved. He looked up toward the
mound and whispered. "Have you been listening?"

The answer came into his mind. *"Yes."*

"Then your powers extend to here?"

"And beyond."

Waco nodded. "I have been wrong. From now on I shall
love you as if I was parent to you all. And so will this woman,
if she chooses. But you must let her choose."

There was silence from the mound, but Waco felt Hanah's
hand squeeze his arm. He looked down, and Hanah Sanagi was
smiling.

The grade down the foothills from the Upland Mountain
Pass was gentle, the work consisting chiefly of moving boulders
and clearing the thorned desert scrub. It was hot work, and
dusty. At night the special cold of the desert had the bullhands
near their fires.

It was Payday, the eleventh of Quake, and the talk around
the fires began with excited anticipations about seeing old
friends who had gone down with boss property man Grabbit

Kuumic in Number Seven. Eventually the talk turned to how the town of Miira would represent itself in the parade come The Season in Tarzak two months hence.

Little Will heard none of the talk, and when the desert chill finally drove her companions beneath their angelhair blankets, she remained sitting up alone, staring into the fire. Eleven days ago, Shiner Pete had taken the supply wagon into Miira to ask his father about marrying her. Each night at the fire since, her doubts about Waxy's approval grew.

Her body shuddered with a chill, and she added more wood to the fire. The supply wagon had returned that morning, and Pete hadn't been with it. The hostler who drove the wagon, Bye Jim, would only say that things seemed "durned tense" in Miira town. When asked to elaborate, Bye Jim scowled, thought for a moment, then shook his head. "Jes' tense. *Durned* tense!" He then began searching for help in loading the wagon.

Little Will looked around at the camp and saw the dark shapes that were her sleeping comrades. Many of them had paired up, sleeping together. Because there were no bushes or trees behind which to seek privacy, the desert form of love consisted mainly of hot breathing and furtive gropes beneath blankets. She turned and looked over her left shoulder.

Next to one of the blanket-covered mounds, Packy's bullhook was planted in the sand. Hanging from the handle was Cookie Jo's plaid cap. Little Will turned back to the fire, wishing that her thoughts could carry all of the way back to Miira and Shiner Pete.

At that moment she heard the Perches tied up along the nag line getting restless. She stood and walked around the sleeping forms, wondering if some strange animal was bothering the horses. While they were working their way through the Great Muck, several members of the road gang caught glimpses of some the planet's animated wierdness—huge dragons, laughing lizards. The sizes involved increased with each telling around the fire.

She approached the string of huge horses and saw Shiner Pete walking toward her, his hands thrust into his pockets, his blanket roll hanging limply in the crook of his left arm.

"Pete!"

He jumped as her call slammed his consciousness. *"Uh . . . hi, Little Will."*

She hugged him, kissed him, and upon getting less than enthusiastic response, she looked up into his troubled face.

"Pete, what's wrong? Aren't you glad to see me?"

He lifted a hand and touched her cheek. *"Sure. Sure I am."* He kissed her again. *"It's just that things didn't work out so good."* He shivered against the cold, bent over, and picked up his blanket roll. *"Let's get under some covers. I just realized that I'm freezing."*

Later, as they snuggled together beneath their blankets, Little Will buried herself in the crook of Pete's shoulder. *"Now, Pete. What is it? What did Waxy say?"*

"I never asked him." He was quiet as Little Will's body stiffened. *"I meant to, but you don't know how things are in Miira. It seems like everybody's mad at Waxy and Waxy's mad at everybody. Poge Loder and some others've got the whole town upset about Waxy marrying Stew and Diamonds. It got so bad that Stew and Diamonds moved out of town and went north to live in Dirak."*

This, it seems, was only the beginning. Waxy had been so angry about Stew and Diamonds being driven out of town that he had "officially" annulled Poge Loder's marriage to Baggage Horse Betty, effectively making bastards out of Poge's three children. In retaliation, Poge publicly accused Dot the Pot of adulterating with Waxy. When Dot learned of this, she broke Poge's nose. When Waxy learned of this, he "officially" annalled the wedding of Poge Loder's parents, making Poge a bastard in name as well as in disposition.

Now, Poge never recognized any of Waxy's "official dissolutions," but his wife, Baggage Horse Betty, did, for reasons of her own, no doubt. And now that she was free and clear of Poge & Sons, she moved out and was beginning to let wheelwright Sunburst Sid call upon her. In Sunburst's house.

To make a complicated story less so, Waxy performed two weddings in absentia: Baggage Horse Betty to Sunburst Sid (purely an act of altruism to keep them from sin), and Poge Loder to his own mother (ending Poge's bastardism, but rendering his status something more colorful). Poge then set up his own marriage concession, arguing that if Waxy could, so could anyone. He then proceeded to marry, in absentia, Dot the Pot to Daisy, a retired Percheron; and then he married Waxy to Waxy, telling Waxy in public and in person the full meaning of this enigmatic relationship.

All in all, the time was not ripe for a fifteen-year-old son to ask his father if he could marry a fourteen-year-old girl. Shiner Pete decided at that point to take a horse and head back to the road gang before things started getting ridiculous.

Little Will, now possessing a better understanding of the phrase "durned tense," squeezed Pete's hand and asked: *"What are we going to do?"*

Pete looked up at the stars and was silent for a long time. *"Little Will?"*

"Yes, Pete?"

"Can you place a thought in someone else's mind?"

She frowned as she thought back to The Season the first. She had placed the name "Arnheim's Fault" into Cholly Jacoby's mind. She moistened her lips and looked up into Pete's face. *"I think so. I've done it before."*

"I've played with it some, and I think I can, too." Pete closed his eyes and nodded. *"I have a plan. If it works, we'll wind up married."*

"What if it doesn't work?"

Pete sighed. *"The way things are going in Miira right now, I'll probably wind up married to Packy and you'll be the proud mother of the whole blamed herd of bulls."*

Waco pushed himself off from the bottom of the lake. As his head broke the surface, he inhaled deeply of the rain-washed air.

"Waco!"

He paddled around to see Hanah Sanagi standing on the shore. "What?"

"Just a minute." She removed her clothing, dived into the water, and swam toward him with clean, swift strokes. She came to a stop next to him. "I checked out the racket."

Waco paddled in place, slightly uncomfortable. "What was it?"

"There's a road through the jungle a little north of us. The gang that built it is heading back toward Number Three."

"How close is the road?"

"Along the top of that crest, out of the swamp. Four or five miles."

"That's still pretty close." Waco looked down at the ripples in the water. "Maybe I'd better move the eggs deeper into the jungle. They're dangerous." He began swimming toward the shore."

"Wait, Waco."

He turned and faced her. "What is it?"

"You don't have to move them right this minute, do you?"

"It's not that. I'm . . . just not . . . you know."

She swam next to him and touched his cheek. "No, don't pull away. Waco?"

"What?"

"Waco, just close your eyes."

"What for?"

"Don't ask so many damned questions. Close your eyes."

He closed his eyes. "Now what?"

Hanah smiled. "Now, take a deep breath." As Waco complied, she wrapped her arms and legs around him and kissed him as the water closed over their heads.

FOURTEEN

When the road gang returned to Miira after completing the road to Kuumic, it was hard to ignore the signs. Upon Waxy's house was a sign that read: "The Pope." Farther up the street, hanging from the edge of Poge Loder's roof, was a sign that read: "The *real* Pope. ½ price!" Farther up the street, painted in Waxy's unmistakable style, a sign leaned against Sunburst Sid's house, which read: "In here sleeps the cheap pope's ex-wife." Against the *kraal* fence was a sign that read: "Waxy's harem. Anything on all fours apply within."

True, the signs were troubled.

After securing the bulls, Little Will and Shiner Pete sat upon the logs of the *kraal* fence looking down at the town. Packy and the other bullhands had descended the grassy slope and were walking Miira's dusty street to get to their houses. Little Will swallowed against the hard lump in her throat and turned to Pete. "Where do we begin?"

Shiner Pete shielded his eyes against the sun and examined the town. "This is like harness that's been all tossed around and scrambled in a trunk. It just looks like a bunch of hooks and knots; but you can fix it. What you have to do is, one by one, untie each knot, unhook each hook." He pointed his finger at Sunburst Sid's house. "There's where we start."

Dot the Pot Drake sat on a long stone bench in the shade of her house's porch near the *kraal*. Cookie Jo Wayne having secured the cookhouse wagon and horses, joined Dot on the bench. After an initial exchange of greetings and news, Cookie Jo pushed her silver-blond hair from her eyes and nodded toward the town. "How are you and Waxy getting on."

"About like dogs'n'cats. You and Packy?"

Cookie Jo sighed and shook her head. "I don't know."

They absent-mindedly watched the heat of Miira's street make the air above it dance. There were the sounds of angry voices coming from Sunburst Sid's place, and Dot raised her eyebrows when she saw Baggage Horse Betty march from Sunburst's door. "Now, will you look at that."

Cookie Jo watched as Sunburst stood in his doorway, calling out to Betty. Betty turned to reply and saw Waxy's "In here sleeps the cheap pope's ex-wife" sign. Picking up the sign, Betty turned abruptly and walked with rapid strides toward Poge Loder's place. Cookie Jo looked at Dot. "What do you suppose is happening?"

Dot the Pot shook her head and watched as Betty leaned the sign next to Poge's door, picked up a rock, and scratched the "ex-" out of the sign's wording. When she was finished, she examined the results of her efforts, then took a deep breath and disappeared into the darkness of Poge's doorway. After a few moments, Poge appeared in the doorway, went to where his "The *real* pope! ½ price!" sign was hanging and took it down. He turned, read the sign leaning next to his door, picked up the sign, and carried both of the signs indoors. A moment later, Poge ran from the doorway toward Dot's house. As he approached, Dot nodded. "How you doin', Poge?"

The man nodded, ran past the house to the *kraal* fence, picked up the "Waxy's harem" sign there, then turned and ran back to his own house. Seconds after he had entered it, Poge's door curtain covered the entrance to his house.

Dot leaned back against the front wall of her house. "Now if I was Mootch Movill, I'd say there might be a story in that."

Cookie Jo leaned forward, and a few moments later, Waxy walked from the door of his house. His eyes were confusion capped by a frown. He stood in the sun for a moment, scratched his head, and looked back at his house. Lowering his hand, he rushed to his "The Pope" sign, pulled it from the wall, and threw it inside the house as though the sign embarrassed him. The deed done, Waxy sat down upon a split-stump chair next to his door and stared in the direction of Poge Loder's place.

After a few more moments, Cookie Jo and Dot watched Poge Loder emerge from his doorway at the same time that Waxy got to his feet. Slowly, as though their feet were dragging through winter syrup, the two men approached each other, meeting in the center of the street. The two women could see that the two men were talking, and that it was talk instead of screaming was an event.

Cookie Jo shook her head. "I don't get it. I thought you said those two had been going at it like Arnheim and the Governor."

Dot nodded, observed the two men shake hands, then rubbed her eyes as the two men turned and walked back to their homes. When she opened her eyes she studied the deserted street, heard laughter nearby, and turned her gaze toward the *kraal* fence. She pointed at Little Will and Shiner Pete. "Now aren't those two just falling all over themselves just a bit?"

Cookie Jo studied the pair and looked back at Dot. "You don't suppose they were working a little of their think-and-do?"

"That's exactly what I suppose. Naughty, naughty."

Cookie Jo lifted her head, studied Packy Dern's house for a moment, then turned to Dot. "I don't imagine that they take requests."

"Hmm." Dot rubbed her chin, looked at Waxy's house, and nodded. "I bet they do." She grinned and looked at Cookie Jo. "If they don't someone who shall remain nameless might just rat on them to Waxy."

The two women stood and headed for the *kraal* fence.

Waxy sat on his cushion before his low plank table trying to write yesterday's entry in the Miira book. He chewed upon his reed pen for a moment, then tossed the thing down. "I don't understand it." He held his arm out toward the walls of the room. "I do not understand it! I hate that sonofabitch!"

His fist slammed down upon the table. "And there I was, pleasant as you please, standing in the middle of the damned street, in broad daylight, shaking hands—" He shook his head. "Maybe I'm sick."

He looked down at the papers, then swept them from the

table with a single stroke of his arm. "Boring! That's what you
are! D-e-d deadly dull, goddamned paperwork!"

He leaned his back against the wall and looked at Miira's
street through his open doorway. "Got half a mind to put my
damned sign back up."

A great calm washed over him. He leaned the back of his
head against the wall and closed his eyes. The faint sounds of
the windjammers pounding out ragtime in the main top began
thumping at the insides of his eardrums as the full complement
of seventy-five bulls went tail-and-trunk around the hippodrome
inside his eyelids. The image singled down to one bull. It was
Queenie all decked out in silver sequins for the spectacular.
Next to Queenie's left front stood the bullhand, Dorothy Drake,
in dark blue sequins, her glossy black hair pinned up from her
neck and capped by a long blue plume.

Waxy smiled as he let the vision and the sounds play in his
mind. Dorothy turned, kootched along with her pachyderm,
displaying her long, shapely legs. Her legs. They were clad
in French knit hose—the kind with seams down the back.

"Yum."

She whirled about, and soon Waxy could see nothing but
the sequined bullhand in the spotlight. The top of her costume
seemed to strain against her ample bosom.

"Damn, but how did she ever get a handle like Dot the Pot?"

She smiled, the scarlet of her lips against the white of her
teeth, the rich satin cream of her skin, the sparkling black of
her eyes . . .

. . . the image wavered, her eyes changed to the color of
blue, then back to black, then one was blue and the other black,
then both were blue and stayed that way.

He heard a tiny voice. *"I told you they were blue."*

"I thought they were black," answered another tiny voice.
"Well, you should've checked."

Waxy studied the image, comforted by Dorthy's smile and
the continuity of her eye pigmentation.

"Well, I'm glad that's settled." Beautiful blue eyes. And,
Great Boolabong, those legs! Those long, lovely, luscious—

Waxy opened his eyes. "I've never even seen the damned
show!" He frowned. "I've always been repairing and polishing
harness! I've never seen Dot in anything but bullcrap-covered
overalls!"

He scratched his head and tried to remember the time. There
must have been a time when Dot was in costume. He closed

his eyes, and there was Dorothy Drake inside his house. The *smells!* She was cooking. The cobit bread cut like fine, aged beef filet. Waxy chewed, and by damn it *was* beef! Dorothy, darling, Dorothy. *Where ever did you get beef on Momus?*

Anything for you, Waxy love.

Waxy stood, walked around his table, and stumbled out into the street. Corn on the cob, lobster, scrapple, potpie, turkey, cranberry sauce, watermelon, *spaghetti!*

Lovely, lovely Dorothy, where in the hell did you get spaghetti? With antipasto? Chianti? Mama mia! 'At's-a some spicy meatball!

Anything for you, Waxy—

Waxy opened his eyes, realizing that he had just run into someone. He looked at the person's face, and it was Packy Dern.

"Uh, hi Packy."

Packy looked about the dusty street, then frowned at Waxy. "Hi, Waxy. Uh, where're you goin'?"

"Damned if I know."

Packy nodded once. "See you there." The boss elephant man continued his stumble down the street.

—and the lovely Dorothy Drake again filled Waxy's vision. His feet walked upon clouds of whipped cream, the vision just out of reach. Those legs, that body, that smile, *spaghetti!*

Waxy, I can help you with the paperwork.

"Dorothy," he called. "Dorothy!"

"What is it, Waxy?"

He opened his eyes and found himself next to the *kraal*, standing in front of Dot the Pot's porch. She was garbed in tattered overalls, her hair was snaggled, and Waxy suddenly remembered the lady busting Poge Loder's nose. Still, before him flashed images of the bullhand, her bosom straining against her blue-sequined costume, French knit stockings, the smell—the *smell* goddammit—of spaghetti!

Waxy closed his eyes, rubbed them, then looked away from the glorious vision just to clear his mind. He saw a boy and a girl sitting upon the *kraal* fence. They both screamed in surprise and fell over backwards when they realized that they were looking at themselves.

Little Will and Shiner Pete held hands as they stood before Waxy's table, Cookie Jo and Dot the Pot standing behind them. Waxy sat upon his cushion while Packy stood next to him, his face a study in perpendicular outrage. Waxy tapped his reed pen upon the table and looked, first at Little Will, then at Shiner Pete.

"Why?"

Shiner Pete looked Waxy square in the eye. "Little Will and I want to get married."

Waxy dropped the pen. "Hoo! Would that turn Poge's crank." He studied the pair, then held out his hand. "But why all this other stuff?"

Pete shuffled his feet around some, then spoke. "You didn't seem too keen on marriage the last time I was in town. We thought if we could square away your troubles with Poge—"

"What's that got to do with me and Dot?" Waxy pointed at the boss elephant man. "And Packy and Cookie Jo?"

Dot the Pot stepped forward and placed her hand upon Little Will's shoulder. "I asked them to do Cookie Jo and me a favor. If it's anybody's fault, it's mine."

Cookie Jo glanced at Packy, then at Waxy. "And mine." She looked at Packy, but the boss elephant man turned his glance toward Waxy. "Look, old son, can't we just put this thing to rest?"

Waxy leaned back against the wall, his eyebrows attempting to mate with his hairline. "I don't know." He looked at the boss elephant man. "What about you?"

Packy's face reddened as his voice lowered. "Well, I was going to ask Cookie once we got back anyways—" Cookie Jo issued a small scream and almost flattened Packy against the wall.

"You never said. Packy, you never said."

His composure almost restored, Packy looked into Cookie Jo's eyes. "Cookie, some things go without saying." He shrugged. "'Sides, I didn't know if you'd go for it."

Waxy looked at Shiner Pete and pointed at Cookie Jo. "What did you do? Did you have her slinging hash in the altogether?"

Pete's face flushed and he remained silent. Waxy scratched his chin, then looked up at Dot the Pot. "Well?"

"Well, what?"

"You going to make me say it?"

Dot grinned. "You can bet your brass buttons on that, Waxy."

"That spaghetti was hitting below the belt."

Dot withdrew her hand from Little Will's shoulder and leaned over Waxy's table. "You want spaghetti? I'll figure out how to make it."

Waxy looked down and hunched his shoulders up and down. "What're you going to do with a one-armed man?"

"It's not your arm I'm interested in." Dot moved around the table and knelt next to Waxy. "You are such a jerk."

Waxy looked up at Shiner Pete and Little Will. "I guess that leaves you two." Waxy waved his arm about. "Does Poge know about any of this?"

Both Pete and Little Will shook their heads.

Waxy pursed his lips for a moment, and then nodded. "Good. Never tell him. *Never*. Neither him nor Baggage Horse Betty." Waxy grinned. "There's a time and a place for everything. Now, as to you two—"

Weeks later, far to the south in Tarzak, Warts, the Pendiian route book man, was conferring with his assistant, Agdok Shtimaak, one of the turtle-shelled inhabitants of the planet Wallabee. Turtlehead held out a paper with a two-fingered hand. "Then there is this copy of the entry for the town of Miira."

Warts sighed, took the sheet of paper, and read it:

Workday, the 1st of Layup, Second year since the Crash
Waxy Adnelli on the Miira Books
        Today the road gang returned. No one died, and the Miira–. Kuumic Road is finished. Everybody is getting ready for The Season the second in Tarzak
Marriages annulled:
        Baggage Horse Betty Loder to Sunburst Sid Bates;
        Dot the Pot Drake to Daisy the Percheron;
        Poge Loder to his mother, Agnes Loder;
        Waxy Adnelli to Waxy Adnelli;
        Poge Loder to the Miira town cesspool;
        Waxy Adnelli to various and sundry plants and animals in the immediate vicinity of the town.
Married today:
        Poge Loder to his wife, Baggage Horse Betty, to be made retroactive enough to take care of the three Loder boys;
        Mortimer Loder and Agnes Loder, to be made retroactive enough to legitimize Poge in the eyes of the religion to which he is afflicted;
        Boss elephant man Packy Dern to Cookie Jo Wayne;
        Waxy Adnelli to Dot the Pot Drake;
        Shiner Pete Adnelli to Little Will Kole.
And may the Great Boolabong look over us, each and every one.
Warts handed the paper back to his assistant. "Turtlehead,"

he said, "our primary purpose is to preserve John J. O'Hara's vision of the show. We must devote our every effort at making a success out of The Season the second." He waved a lumpy hand at the paper. "I think that human mating and religious rituals are something better left to specialists."

Turtlehead glanced at the paper, then looked back at Warts. "Do you still want me to move to Miira and help Waxy?"

Warts nodded. "Waxy has complained about the workload." Warts tapped a lumpy finger against the paper. "Still, I wonder why Poge wedded the town cesspool? Is it symbolic?"

"It would seem to be, since such an arrangement hardly seems productive." Turtlehead placed the paper into the Miira Book, then looked back at Warts. "Perhaps it was arranged. It was the custom upon my planet."

Warts scratched his lumps and nodded. "Perhaps. After The Season, I might ask Waxy to explain a few of these things. Meanwhile, there is The Seaaon for which to prepare." Warts noticed a curious expression upon Turtlehead's face, that of it which could be seen beneath his shell. "Is something bothering you?"

Turtlehead angrily tapped one finger against the cover of the Miira Book. "It seems rather callous for Waxy to wed all of those plants and animals, and then to dump them for one female human."

Warts nodded. "As I said, perhaps the subject is better left to specialists."

FIFTEEN

As the bulls crossed the delta bridges on the way to Tarzak for The Season the second, Little Will noticed changes. From her rolling perch upon Reg's neck, the sun reflecting from the many whitewashed adobe houses lining the streets made her squint her eyes. Across the delta, the houses of the fishing village started by Leadfoot Sina dotted the dark yellow dunes above the blueness of the sea. A single pier extended from the beach over the water. Tied to the pier were two large fishing boats with fixed masts and several smaller craft.

The street-side walls of some of the houses in Tarzak sported decorations in celebration of The Season. There were multicolored bunches of flowers, garlands woven from scarlet-colored delta blood-tails, and painted designs and show scenes. Here and there was a sign identifying the house's inhabitant as a metal-worker, mason, carpenter, well-digger, or any of several other occupations. Upon the wall of Cholly Jacoby's house was painted: "Clowning—Cheap Laffs." Goofy Joe's house sported a slogan: "All the news that it pays to tell." Upon the wall of boss canvasman Duckfoot Tarzak's house was the simple message: "Complaints—and they better be good."

The people were different as well. Many wore long, hooded

robes to protect themselves from the sun after the fashion of those in the desert town of Kuumic. There were many new Momans, perched upon shoulders or carried in arms and back-slings. The big change Little Will noticed, however, was in the faces of those who watched the bulls move through the town. This time the people watched. The indifference of The Season the last was gone. The faces were smiling, but Little Will could see lips silently mouthing numbers. They were counting the bulls that had made it to the celebration.

Little Will closed her eyes. They would find three bulls missing from the parade. Queenie and Cambo were dead, and Duchess was in the *kraal* back in Miira. Duchess was too weak to make the trip. Next season there would be fewer bulls; and then as each season came, the people of Tarzak would find themselves counting even fewer bulls. The image came into Little Will's head. The bulls were the tie to the past—to the show. To many, while the pachyderms still made parade for The Season, that mason was still a canvasman, that cobit-root gatherer was still a juggler, and that painter was still a propman. Bullhands were still bullhands, which meant the show still lived. The number of bulls making the annual parade was beginning to become a way of reckoning time—the time remaining on the show's ticket.

On the way to the *kraal*, the parade passed by where the celebration was held the year before. This year planks from Miira and Porse formed a circle of stands around a sawdust covered ring. At one side of the ring, Doc Weems was polishing the calliope, while jugglers, riders, tumblers, and equilibrists practiced their acts.

Things—puzzle-pieces—came together in Little Will's head. The image was unclear, but it was a wash of despair, loneliness, death. She shook it from her mind.

On the evening of Put Up, the first boat from Midway made landfall at Tarzak. Most of those attending The Season were there to greet those who had gone down with Number Two. Unaware of the vessel's approach, Little Will was with Shiner Pete, Waxy and Dot the Pot in Warts's house as Warts went over the past year's records from the town of Miira.

The lumpy Pendiian looked up from the papers he was reading and looked at Waxy. "Who are the Texas Rangers?"

Waxy rubbed his chin. "Well, as I remember Bullhook Willy telling it, the Texas Rangers was a program in the old United

States that gave employment to the mentally handicapped."

Warts nodded. "I see. And this organization was employed by Al G. Barnes to execute the outlaw elephant, Black Diamond?"

"That's about the size of it."

"As the bullhands view it, then, these outpatients did a poor job of the execution."

Dot the Pot tapped her finger upon the papers Warts was reading. "Those coppers pumped over two-hundred rounds into Black Diamond. I hear there was some question as to whether Diamond died from gunshot wounds or starvation."

Warts held up his hand. "Coppers?" He turned to Waxy. "I thought you said that the Texas Rangers was a work program for the mentally handicapped."

"I did. Where do you think coppers come from?"

Warts stood, his bumps gathered into a stormy glower. "Upon my planet, Waxy, I was a translator in the Bureau of Regret—our department of police!"

Waxy glowered back. "Well, Warts, nobody ever said you was perfect! In fact—"

"Pardon me, fellow *artistes*." A familiar face entered Warts's house. The kisser in question was attached to Mootch Movill, shooting gallery concessionaire.

"Mootch!" Little Will rushed and embraced the shaggy man. "The boat from Number Two is in!"

Mootch placed his hands upon her shoulders and held her out at arm's length. "I have quite accepted this effect I have on young lovelies, my dear." He lowered his head and squinted his eyes. "But who *are* you?"

Her eyebrows went up as her mouth opened. "Little Will."

Mootch's eyebrows reached for some altitude. "Bullhook Willy's girl?" She smiled and nodded. Mootch shook his head. "Time passes. My apologies, my dear, but when last I saw you, you were but a sprout. You have reached num-numdom." He patted her shoulder. "You're a balm to the retinas, my girl. How's the boss elephant man?"

Little Will's smile vanished. "Packy Dern's boss elephant man, now. Bullhook Willy's dead."

Mootch shook his head. "My apologies. We don't get much in the way of news over to Midway."

Little Will held her hand out toward Pete. "You remember Shiner Pete? We're married."

"Hoo." Mootch shook his head. "Tempus is fugitin' all over

the place." He nodded at Pete. "My assesserbations, my boy."
As he gathered Little Will in his arms and hugged her, he
looked up at Dot the Pot. "You're looking in the peak, Dot
darlin'."

Dot put her arm around Waxy's waist. "Waxy and I are
married."

Mootch released Little Will, reached out and shook hands
with Waxy. "My fellicitudes, Wax." He nodded toward Waxy's
missing arm. "You're looking slightly lopsided these days."

"The price of a landslide, Mootch. I keep the Miira books,
now."

Mootch released Waxy's hand and turned to Warts. "Which
reminds me." He nodded at Warts. "As always, my bumpy
little buddy, you look like hell."

Warts nodded back. "Likewise, I'm sure."

"I seek some information." Mootch draped the hulk of his
arm over the Pendiian's shoulders. "Tell me, light of my life,
is Carrot Nose alive?"

Warts shook his head. "He died when Number Nine went
down. I'm very sorry."

Mootch sniffed and shook his head. "Regrettable. A great
tragedy." He raised one bushy white eyebrow. "And Cheesy
Kraft? Is he well?"

"No. He drowned."

"I see. I see. A pity." Mootch frowned. "And Razor Red
Stampo? How is he?"

"He was killed roadganging in the Snake Mountain Gap.
I'm awfully sorry."

Mootch Movill rubbed his chin as he looked at the roof of
Warts's house. "Ah, Fate." He looked back at Warts as he
reached into his pocket. "Many thanks, my lumpy little friend.
You have done me a great service." Mootch dropped several
copper BB's into Warts's outstretched hand.

Warts added them to the other BB's in his trouser pocket.
Everyone in the show had a few of Mootch's BB's rattling
around. They were represented as shares in the *Caddywampus,*
a fictitious business enterprise of Mootch's primarily designed
as an excuse to borrow money to support his ineptitude at
poker. Warts looked up at Mootch.

"I just told you that your best friends are dead. How did I
do you a service?"

Mootch pulled Warts to the door and pointed a hand toward
the vastness of the outdoors. "Look at all that, my boy. An

entire globe with thousands of parched souls thirsting for the first good story they've heard in a fly's age." He lowered his voice and spoke in elaborate confidentiality to the route book man. "Remind me sometime, Warts, to fill you in about the stupendous, man-eating sea reptiles our ship encountered on its journey across the Sea of Baraboo."

Warts went saucer-eyed. "Sea monsters?" He turned and reached for pen and paper. "I must record—"

Mootch slapped Warts's back. "Ah, my boy, you bring joy to an old man's heart!" He grabbed the lapels of his shredded coat. "And I am the only competent liar left on Momus."

He waved a hand at Dot, Waxy, and Little Will. "Farewell one; farewell all." Mootch Movill turned, clasped his hands behind his back, began whistling, and walked into Tarzak's busy street, off to do the good work.

SIXTEEN

Later that evening, after the bulls were paraded tail-and-trunk around the ring, Little Will sat in the blues between Packy and Shiner Pete, surrounded by the other bullhands and residents of the town of Miira. Fish oil torches lined the edge of the ring and the outside edge of the stands while in the center of the ring a large fire of logs was started. When the log fire was burning brightly, Spats Skorzini entered the ring carrying a long, wooden staff.

"Laydeeez and gentlemen! The Ring of Tarzak welcomes one and all for The Season!" The stands rocked with applause. When the noise died down, the man in the ring lowered the stick. "I am your master of the Great Ring of Tarzak, Spats Skorzini."

More applause, acknowledging both the death of Ringmaster Sam and the acceptance of Ringmaster Spats. Spats bowed, then pointed at Warts Tho. "For our first attraction tonight, Warts Tho and the record keepers of Momus!"

To loud applause, Warts came down from the blues followed by Waxy Adnelli from Miira, Arcadia Joe Wimple from Kuumic, Spook Tieras from the town of the same name, Bunion Paul Foote from Porse, Angela Dear Burack from Dirak, Honey

Buns Wagner from Ris, Hooks Javorak from Sina, and Luscious Leona Washington from Ikona. Warts read to the audience from a prepared list.

"I have compiled the figures for Momus supplied to me by the other record keepers. This past year, there have been ninety-one marriages, two hundred and three deaths, and two hundred and fifty-one live births. The population on the Central Continent now stands at one thousand, nine hundred and four." He lowered the paper for an instant. "With all these marriages, I expect we'll break two thousand by The Season the next."

Little Will heard Poge Loder's voice calling out from the back of the blues. "What about this marryin' thing, anyway?"

Warts lowered his papers. "What about it?"

Little Will turned around and looked up to see Poge standing, frowning, and scratching his head. "Well," he began, "it don't seem proper somehow for you bookkeepers to be marryin' folks. It's not like you was judges, or even a chaplain like Little Joe."

Warts held out his hands. "Marriage is a human ritual. It makes no difference to me who officiates, or even if the ritual is performed at all. However, those who do want a ritual seem to want a record made of the event; and the record keepers keep the records."

Waxy pointed up at Poge. "Are you going to start up again?"

Poge's shoulders moved up, then down. "Waxy, I'm not tryin' to start up any trouble. It just seems you bookkeepers ought to be called something with a little more class."

"Like what?"

Poge thought for a moment. "Maybe justice of the peace?"

Little Will heard a bellow coming from the opposite side of the blues. "Like hell!"

She turned and saw boss canvasman Duckfoot Tarzak get to his feet. "A name like that's liable to put ideas in people's heads. We don't want any jaypees on this planet." He pointed around at the stands. "Don't you remember the number of crooked jaypees the show had to pay off? You call those bookkeepers jaypees and the next thing you know, they'll be issuing permits, making laws, and hiring coppers to push everybody around." Duckfoot Tarzak resumed his seat.

Whitey Etren, mime from Tarzak, stood and addressed the ring. "I don't think we ought to be hasty in dismissing the idea of law and government. What are we supposed to do about the criminal?"

Duckfoot stood and faced Whitey. "Put his trunk on the lot."

"Exile?"

Duckfoot held out his hands, then lowered them. "Call it anything you want. You got a sticky-fingered fellow, we do what we always do. Either he comes up with the goods, you take it out of his hide, or his trunk is on the lot until he coughs up."

A voice called from the Ikona section of the blues. "What about murder?"

Duckfoot shook his head and scowled at the speaker. "Who is that? Bungo?"

"Yeah."

"Where've you been for the last twenty years, Bungo? Out on the lot. Out on the lot until the bum coughs up the goods. Now you ex somebody, the goods you gotta cough up is somebody's life, isn't it?"

The one called Bungo scratched his chin. "Sounds like a long time out on the lot."

"Damn right." Duckfoot faced the center of the ring. "Look, there's a whole continent west of here without a soul on it. All you rubes who want to be kings, coppers, or government paper wizards move out there. We'll hang a plague sign all around you and be done with it!" Duckfoot resumed his seat.

Waxy jabbed Warts in the ribs with his elbow. "Don't look like we're gonna be jaypees, do it?"

Warts sighed, shook his head, then looked up at Poge. "Do you have another suggestion?"

Poge held out his hands. "Maybe preacher, minister—something like that. Or maybe chaplains."

Waxy laughed. "Dammit, Poge, what in the hell're you using for brains? Me? A Bible-thumper?" Laughter filled the ring.

"Excuse me." The ring hushed at the sound of the strange, quiet voice. Turtlehead Agdok moved his shell into the ring from the Tarzak section of the blues and parked it next to Warts. Turtlehead's tiny red eyes peered out from beneath his shell up at Poge. "Upon my planet of Wallabee, the nest historians perform the record-keeping and make the nuptial agreements. They are non-theistic and possess no powers of law."

"What're they called?"

"They are called historians. The word in my language is *phreest*."

Poge nodded. "Priest. That sounds good." He sat down.

Waxy jabbed Warts in the arm. "I'll be goddamned if anybody's gonna call me a priest! I'm no—"

Warts held up his hand. "Turtlehead said the word was *freest.*"

Turtlehead shook his shell. "No. That's *phreest. P-p-p-p-h-h-r-r-reest.*"

Waxy and the other bookeepers wiped their faces. As he dried his hand upon his shirt, Waxy frowned at Turtlehead. "That's some juicy word."

Sergeant Spook Tieras, after drying his own face, nodded at Warts. "I think I prefer Poge's pronunciation."

Waxy faced the Spook. "You're from Ahngar. You don't even know what a priest is."

The willow-thin Ahngarian faced Waxy. "Would you rather be a p-p-p-p-h-h-r-r-reest?"

Waxy dried his face again. "That's not the point!"

A voice called from the blues. "Let's call 'em priests and be done with it! Let's get on with the show!"

More voices shouted agreement, quieting down after Warts held up his hands. "That's settled, then. The bookeepers will be called priests."

Waxy grabbed Warts's shoulder. "Now, just a damned second—"

Warts pulled his shoulder free and shouted at Waxy. "That is *settled!*"

Waxy snorted and spat upon the sawdust. "Well, dommi dommi, gobbi gobbi; I'm a goddamned priest."

"Excuse me," said Turtlehead, "the word is pronounced—"

The priesthood of Momus ducked.

The priests, then, in turn, recounted the happenings of their towns over the past year. The Miira–Kuumic Road was complete, Cross-eyed Mike Ikona was moving to the opposite end of the Emerald Valley to establish a fishing village on the coast of the Western Sea, since fresh fish couldn't be brought to the valley from Tarzak. The town would be called Anoki; Ikona spelled backwards.

The road gang from Miira had reported seeing huge monsters while working their way through the Great Muck Swamp, which was agreed to be the aftereffects of a bad batch of sapwine.

Kraut Messer, boss of the cookhouse gang from Tarzak, had arranged contracts for hostlers, horses, and wagons from Miira, sawdust from the mill in Porse, and special saws, tools, and fittings from Tieras. The object was to go to the frozen lakes up the White Top Mountains and bring back ice. For this he would need a road cut from where the Miira–Kuumic Road crossed the Upland Mountain Range through to the White Top Mountain Lakes. The road gang from Miira would get the contract.

Arcadia Joe Wimple reported that copper and iron had been discovered near Kuumic, and that Tiny Jim Whister, boss blacksmith, had moved to Kuumic from Tarzak in order to construct and operate a smelter. It did not appear feasible to use the natural fires from the desert for this purpose, no coal deposits had yet been found, thus charcoal would be obtained from beyond the Upland Mountains. Arcadia Joe himself would be going to establish the charcoal manufacturing facility at the point where Kraut Messer's road to the White Top Mountains joined the Miira–Kummic road. Tiny Jim had contracted for hostlers, horses, and wagons from Miira to move the charcoal to Kuumic, and to haul the finished metal goods to Tarzak and points north.

The wardrobe people in Tarzak had discovered how to make cloth from the downy fibres of the angelhair tree, and also how to dye the fabric and weave it into various colors. As part of the barter that Season, the cloth, already made into robes, would be exchanged for the goods from other towns.

On The Stand, the next night of The Season, they were in the blues and had just completed singing "The Song of *Baraboo*," music by Tarzak windjammer Flubber Mumenebe, lyrics by Tarzak clown Stubbles Joco Cruz. Warts gathered his priests before the fire. Next to them was a large wooden crate.

"My friends," said Warts, "Car Number One is all gone. Where it stood is nothing but scrub bush and grass. But as the car was being taken apart, it was discovered that the locker for the top flags was never emptied when the ship was being lightened. That is what this box contains."

He paused, then looked around at the crowd. "John J. O'Hara's dying wish was that you people—show people—would never forget who you are. The best—the very best—of all the circuses that ever existed."

A cheer from the crowd. Warts held up his hands.

"We've all been in the same clothes for two years now, and we're beginning to look a bit ragged. The young ones are growing, and it's time for new clothes. The wardrobe people, as you were told last night, have produced a large number of robes modeled after the fashion of those from Kuumic. The robe is loose, it fits any size, and it is both cool and can protect you against the sun."

Warts scratched his bumps, then folded his arms. "We must do many things to live; we only have The Season in which to be a show. In this box are the top colors. I want the division heads to come to this box and pick out the color and pattern that will forever after represent your show occupation. No matter what you must do between Seasons, your robe will remind both you and others what you really are. Who will be the first?"

The circle of troupers muttered among themselves. Packy Dern patted Little Will on her shoulder. "You go out there and find out what the bullhands'll wear."

She looked up at the boss elephant man. "Packy, you should pick it. Not me."

He smiled and shoved her toward the box. "Go on."

Little Will looked back at Packy and Shiner Pete, then walked forward and stood before the box. She looked up at Warts. "I can pick any color?"

Warts shrugged. "You're first. Pick anything you want."

Little Will bent over and searched among the flags. When she had found what she wanted, she folded the flag and walked back to Packy and handed the flag to him. Packy unfolded the flag. It was maroon and gray in vertical stripes. Little Will put her arm around Pete's waist and smiled at Packy. "The gray is for the bulls."

Packy lowered his eyebrows. "And the maroon?"

"That's because it's pretty."

Several persons rushed to the box. Cholly Jacoby walked away with a solid orange flag. The Amazing Ozamund, magician, walked away with a flag of red and black stripes. Madam Zelda, the fortune teller, came away with a flag of solid blue. Others rushed to the box and removed whatever it was that their fingers could grab. After a few moments there was no one else around the box. Waxy Adnelli jabbed Warts in the ribs. "Hey, what about us?"

Warts frowned. "Harness men?"

"No. *Priests!* We're an occupation."

Warts rubbed his bumpy chin, then shrugged. "I never thought about it. It's not like we had real show jobs."

Waxy snorted. "You telling me that the route book isn't a job? That's what we do: the route book."

"I guess." Warts shrugged again, then pointed at the box. "Waxy, see what's left."

Waxy shook his head and went to the box. He looked into it, then looked back at Warts. "You lump-headed Pendiian! There's only one flag left!" Waxy turned, bent over, then stood up holding a flag of black and white checked diamonds. "If I have to wear this, I'm going back on harness!"

Warts walked over and looked at the flag. He looked up at Waxy. "I think it is just fine." He took the flag from Waxy and held it out to the rest of the priests. The comments from the Moman priesthood ranged from "Je-sus H. Christ" to "Muthuh."

The Show began with a parade around the ring led by Packy Dern and Robber, with the rest of the bulls tail-and-trunk in tow. As the bullhands completed their circuit of the ring, they placed the bulls into the *kraal* and moved into the blues as Doc Weems honked out "The Entrance of the Gladiators" on the calliope.

Horse acts, jugglers, equilibrists, and clowns performed, but it was difficult to imagine a show without the up top crowd—flyers, wire-walkers, and iron jaw acts. But the up top acts require rigging, and they were still learning how to make rope. The Season the third promised to have a full show, complete with the upstairs crowd.

Even so, there was a bit of sparkle in The Season the second. Blue, silver, and pink sequins were on a few costumes. The sequins were made from the outside layer of freakfish carapace.

In her place in the blues, Little Will sighed and let her mind touch Shiner Pete's. *"Everyone is trying so hard. But it just isn't the show."*

Pete squeezed her hand. *"Close your eyes and listen."*

Little Will closed her eyes. The scream of the calliope filled her hearing, while the smells of people, bulls, horses, and food filled her sense of smell. She could almost taste cotton candy.

The fabric—the spirit—was still there. What reality could not provide, imagination could. Pete's thoughts touched her again. *"Remember what Waxy said. You can't kill the show."*

She kept her eyes closed, listened, and recalled the many

stands on many planets. City after city, transformed for a moment into the fantasyland of the show, the company, the circus. She felt the tears dribble down her cheeks, then felt Pete's gentle touch wiping the tears away. He spoke out loud. "You can't kill the show."

She put her arms around his neck, hugged him, and then laughed.

On the morning of Teardown, Little Will gently removed Pete's arm from around her shoulders and stood up. The sky was cloud-dotted, but the day promised to be clear and not too hot. She looked down at Pete, then turned and went to check on Reg. She made her way into the bull *kraal*, found Reg, and stroked the pachyderm's trunk. *"Is everything all right, Reg?"*

The bull snorted and nodded her head. Little Will checked to make certain that Reg and the other bulls were secure, watered, and fed. When she was finished, she climbed the *kraal* fence and headed back toward where Pete and the other bullhands slept. Half of the way there she heard angry voices. She frowned and walked around the outside of the Ring blues until she saw Duckfoot Tarzak towering over the tiny Pendiian, Warts. Duckfoot was wearing a brown and tan robe that didn't quite reach to the middle of his thighs.

Duckfoot jabbed his massive hands at his own chest. "Look at this, you lumpy moron! Am I supposed to run around half naked?"

Warts held out his hands. "We'll just have to come up with a bigger robe for you, Duckfoot. I'm sure wardrobe can come up with something. They have plenty of cloth."

Duckfoot stabbed the Pendiian in the chest. "Dammit, Warts, if people're goin' to insist on namin' this town after me, I don't want to be made to look like a fool!"

"I understand . . ."

Little Will walked up and looked at Duckfoot's knees. The boss canvasman scowled at her. "What're you lookin' at, sprout?"

Little Will looked up at Duckfoot and grinned. "Sheer dee-light." She turned and walked back to her bedroll and husband, laughing.

SEVENTEEN

On Workday, the First of May, the beginning of the third year since the crash, the column of bulls was forming for the trip back to Miira. The bullhands all wore their new gray and maroon striped robes, although most wore their trousers as well. Shiner Pete had gone ahead with the horses. Little Will and Packy were checking a slight scrape on Reg's left front leg when a delegation of eight bullhands came up behind them.

"Packy, we want a word."

Packy stood, turned around, and looked at the speaker. "What's up, Moll? Why didn't you folks leave with the horse wagons?"

The woman pointed her bullhook at the houses of Tarzak. "The bunch of us here, and our families, are staying. We aren't heading back to Miira."

Little Will stood. "What do you mean, not going back? You have to. Miira is where the bullhands live."

Moll smiled and shook her head. "Little Will, I haven't been a bullhand since Number Three went down killing Big Nance." Moll cocked her head toward the others standing behind her. "None of us has bull to push."

Packy rubbed his chin and shook his head. "Moll, there's still the White Top Mountain Road to build."

"You can build it without us. We want to stay in Tarzak. There's more people here; more things to do. Better ways of making a living than cutting dust on a chain gang."

Packy nodded. "We'll miss you." He looked around her at the others. "All of you."

"We'll get together next Season."

He looked back at Moll. "What're you going to do?"

"I think I'll try my hand at fishing. I've been looking at those boats in Sina; talked to a few people."

Little Will slowly shook her head. "Moll, won't you miss the bulls?"

"Sure. But we'll get a glimpse of one every now and then." She cocked her head back toward Mad Man Mulligan. "Mad Man is keeping Ming in Tarzak."

Little Will held her hands to her mouth. "Not Ming."

Packy's face darkened as he walked around Moll and grabbed Mad Man by the front of his robe. "Like hell you are!"

Mad Man pulled the boss elephant man's hands free from his robe. "Like hell I'm not!"

"Ming isn't yours. She belongs to the show."

"Show me the papers, Packy! There ain't no show!" Mad Man took a deep breath and exhaled as he smoothed the front of his robe. "Packy, I ain't been paid a lousy quarter-note since the crash. I been pushing bull for two years, and no pay. I figure I earned that bull. You figure different, we can have it out right here and now."

Packy looked down the column of bulls, then down at the ground, shaking his head. "Damn."

Little Will touched the boss elephant man's arm. "Packy?"

He pulled his arm away and began walking slowly toward Robber. "Mad Man's right, Little Will. Damn him, but he's right. I'm sorry."

Little Will saw Mad Man look down at the sight of her tears. He looked up again. "I know what Ming was to Bullhook, Little Will. You know I'll take care of her."

Robber began moving toward the first delta bridge. Little Will turned away from Mad Man and started walking after Packy. *"Let's go, Reg."*

Her pachyderm lumbered after her, followed by the rest of the column.

On the second night from Tarzak, the bullhands were preparing to make camp outside the timber town of Porse, when

a wagon pulled by a pair of Perches thundered down the road
from Miira. The driver pulled up the team just outside of camp,
then jumped down from the wagon as the cloud of dust that
had followed him slowly covered the horses and moved through
Porse's only street. The driver was Shiner Pete.

"Packy!"

Little Will rushed up to her husband. "Pete, what is it?"

"Where's Packy?"

She pointed toward the trees. "He's over there hobbling
Robber. What's wrong?"

He shook his head. "Not sure." He ran toward Packy.

The boss elephant man stood and brushed off his hands as
he saw Pete and Little Will running toward him. "Hold your
hosses. What's this about?"

They stopped and Pete held up his hand as he caught his
breath. "In Miira. Can't go into town. Mange says to head the
column down the Kuumic Road as soon as you hit the edge
of town. He's already headed the hostlers, horse teams, tools,
and wagons that way."

"Spill it, Shiner. What's goin' on?"

Pete shook his head. "A disease. Right now that's about all
Mange knows. Just about everybody who was left behind in
Miira when we went down for The Season's got it. Snaggletooth, The First Lady, and Walking Rug are all dead." He
looked down and closed his eyes. "I don't understand it. Waxy
and Dot the Pot are down with it, and they were with us in
Tarzak."

"What about Cookie Jo?"

"She went out with the hostlers."

Packy placed a hand on Pete's shoulder and looked back
toward where the bullhands were gathering around fires to cook
the evening meal. "What's this bug like? Nothing unusual, but
we've had a few hands griping about headaches and stomach
cramps."

Shiner Pete's shoulders slumped as he nodded. "That's it.
Dammit, but that's it. Mange said that if the bullhands show
symptoms, you should separate those who have it from those
who don't. Drop the sick ones off in Miira, then the rest of
you head out to build the White Top Mountain Road." He
pointed down the road toward Tarzak. "That means that everybody picked it up at The Season. All the towns'll have it."

Little Will placed her arm around Shiner's waist. "Can't
Mange do anything?"

Shiner Pete shook his head, then looked at Packy: "I can take the sick ones in the wagon."

Packy looked toward the campfires. "Dammit all to hell anyway." He looked back at Pete. "If Mange wants the sick separate from the healthy, I'll get one of the sickies to drive the wagon. You stay with us." He looked back at the fires. "Guess we better go and tell 'em." He began walking toward the fires.

The next evening the column turned at Miira and entered the Great Muck Swamp, the smell of Miira's burning houses still in their nostrils. In the days that followed, as they moved along the Miira–Kuumic Road, three times they met wagons filled with the sick, heading the other way.

When they reached the place where the road crossed the Upland Mountains, they found the hostlers and road gang already at work, carving their way up to the frozen lakes at the foot of White Top Mountain. That night Little Will and Shiner Pete sat at the same fire as Packy and boss hostler Skinner Suggs. Skinner had just passed a map to Packy, and as the boss elephant man studied it, Skinner talked to the fire.

"We got Kraut Messer's trail half blazed, but it's going to be a rough road to build." He reached back, picked up a rock, and handed it to Shiner Pete. "We have at least four ridges of that stuff to cut through."

Little Will looked at the rock in Shiner's hands. It was cloudy, and speared with shafts of black mineral, but the light from the fire could be seen through it. She looked at Skinner. "What is it?"

"According to Windy Fedder, it's called pegmatite. That clear stuff is quartz, and it's just like tryin' to chop through solid glass. But it's either that, or run the road half-way around the damned swamp."

Packy took the rock, examined it, then handed it back to Skinner. "Steengrease?"

"I can't see any way around it."

The punk from rotting frond trees mixed with powered charcoal and treated with the acid from the fruit of the death tree explodes after the mixture has dried into a semi-solid goo. It explodes when jarred, when ignited, when heated, or when the mood is upon it. Butterfingers McCorkle from Miira discovered it; Firehole Steen from Kuumic manufactured and used it for mining—for a brief time. Firehole's pieces were never found.

The concoction was called Steengrease.

Soon after the road was begun, the road gang was out of the jungle and into the sparse trees and grasses of the Upland foothills. Each turn and curve of the road took them higher and closer to the base of White Top Mountain. Five times wagons were sent to Miira filled with the sick. The fifth wagon returned with a few of the ones who had recovered from the still unknown disease.

By the time the nights became chill enough to require blankets for the bulls, five more bulls and bullhands had left the gang. Two bulls were steered north toward the Emerald Valley; three went south to Kuumic to help work the mines. And a coldness entered Little Will's heart as she counted the twenty-three bulls left to build the White Top Mountain Road. The image of Bullhook Willy, the full line of bulls, and the show filled her mind. The image and the coldness combined to form a resolve—a mission—to preserve what she knew and what she was.

Then bullhand Slim Kim and her bull Tori were torn apart as Steengrease exploded unexpectedly at the cut through the first ridge. And then the bulls numbered twenty-two.

The months passed, the newly stricken were replaced in part by the recovered, and the gang heard from Goofy Joe how those who had not recovered were filling Miira's Big Lot. The road gang had reached the last, and the biggest, of the pegmatite ridges.

It was too steep to go over, and there was no way around. Working on the rock with hammers and chisels left everyone with a hammer bleeding from the cuts made by numerous splinters of razor-sharp quartz. Within that same hour, Sterno Ti Myati had her left eye closed forever when a splinter punctured it.

The Steengrease was brought up. Three times before, Shiner Pete had worked with those who had worked the touchy explosive. At the fourth cut, Shiner was the sole remaining member of this select, and highly scarce, group.

For the fourth time that day, Shiner Pete worked his way up the cut with a bucket of Steengrease to fill the cracks in the cut's jagged face. Once the cracks were filled, grease-smeared strings implanted in the cracks, and Pete safely down the hill, the ends of the strings were drawn together and prepared for ignition.

Little Will stood by Reg's left front as her husband prepared to set off the charges. She was with the rest of the bullhands and elephants, far back from the hill. As Pete talked with Packy, Little Will studied the cracks in the pegmatite. She saw the slope of the hill, the amounts of Steengrease Pete had placed into the cracks. She had seen the differences in fuse lengths, and had seen Steengrease used before. She turned to the other bullhands. "All up! We have to move!"

Slobby Mike Kuboski had laughed. "I'm just a little wore. This is the first time I've had to sit on my buns all day. I don't feel much like moving."

Little Will looked at Slobby Mike, then at his bull, Dancer, then at the other bullhands. "If we don't move, the rocks from the blast will kill us." She pointed down. "A lot of the big ones are going to land right here."

There was laughter all around. They were a long way from the cut. Little Will looked at them all, then turned and moved Reg a hundred yards from the rest. The rest of the bullhands talked it up as though they were humoring a child's whims, but they followed—all but Slobby and Dancer.

Shiner Pete and Packy had looked around, surprised that the bulls had moved; but they returned to their work. Packy moved off and hid behind a tall standing rock. Pete had the fuse ends behind another rock. He prepared to slam the ends of the fuses between two rocks. Little Will moved a step forward as she saw a huge mass of rock falling upon Pete. But he hadn't even set off the charges. She bit her lip and turned to the singer-turned-harness worker, Canary Mary. "Canary, I . . . I see a mass of rock landing right where Pete is standing right now!"

The singer put her arm around Little Will's shoulders. "Don't worry, honey. Planting the charges was the dangerous part. Everyone's far enough away from the blast—"

"No!" Little Will shook her head. "You don't *understand*. I've seen this before when Stub went over the cliff in the Snake Mountain Gap. I can see things that'll happen." She pointed toward Slobby and Dancer. "A horrible thing will happen there. I don't know how I know, but I do." She pointed at Shiner Pete. "Right there will land one of the largest rocks from the blast. I know it. I just *know* it!" Canary Mary had patted Little Will's arm as Shiner Pete swung the rock down upon the fuse ends.

It was a deafening roar against the ears, clouds of gray and white powder climbing into the sky. Above the powder there were quartz shards, and many huge slabs and boulders. Many of the monsterous hunks of hill fell where the bulls had been standing—where Slobby and Dancer still stood. But Little Will was watching the lone slab that tumbled in the air, reached its peak, then began dropping toward Shiner Pete.

Pete was crouched against a rock, his face and eyes covered. The noise of the blast still reverberated from the hills. Little Will screamed at the falling rock, ran at it, and waved her hands. All saw it. The young woman ran in panic toward the cut; the rock—five tons if an ounce—changed direction and landed twenty feet from Shiner Pete. Slobby and Dancer were crushed.

That night Shiner Pete and Little Will huddled under a blanket before a fire. *"They said you moved the rock."*

Little Will nodded once. *"I think I did. Since then I've tried twice to move small things, but I can't. I don't understand it. The Ssendissians never said anything about moving things with thoughts."*

"They wouldn't. They just talk and listen with thoughts. They don't move things." He squeezed her hand. *"Maybe everybody's eyes were tricked."*

Little Will sighed, closed her eyes, and nodded. *"Maybe."* She ran the images through her head, then began crying.

Pete put his arm around her shoulders. *"You're thinking about Dancer."*

"Twenty-one, Pete. We have twenty-one bulls left with us."

EIGHTEEN

The Season the third passed almost without notice; the event being marked only by Cookie Jo being sent back to Miira with a pregnancy that was making her too ill to run the cookhouse. As Thunder of the Fourth year since the crash began, the road had reached the frozen crest where Little Will could stand on the road and look down upon the whiteness of the frozen lakes at the foot of White Top Mountain.

From that same crest she could look east, over the Great Muck Swamp far below, to where the town of Miira was lost in the distant haze. She sadly shook her head at the winding scratch in the planet's surface that the bullhands were calling "Bull Buster Road." Eleven men and women had died from accidents; another nine from illness. Over thirty had died in Miira from illness. Besides Dancer, the White Top Mountain Road had claimed the lives of two more bulls: Prima and Sailor, both from the cold. Nineteen bulls left. She looked west. And there were still the lakes to reach.

She turned and walked back to where the gang was camped in a draw that protected them somewhat from the icy winds. Mounds of blankets were gathered around wind-whipped fires as blanket-covered Packy Dern checked the bulls' blankets and feed. Before she could cross the frozen ground and join Pete's huddled form, Packy crossed over from the bulls and stopped her.

"Little Will. Tomorrow morning hook Reg up to a wagon and head back to Miira."

Her eyes opened wide. "Why? The nags do that."

"Not this time. Reg isn't taking the cold good. If you don't get your bull outta these mountains soon, she'll die." Packy cocked his head toward the campfires. "We got some sick to go in, too." He placed a hand upon her shoulder. "Pete looks like he's down with the bug. Four others." Packy turned back to the bulls. "Get some sleep. I can't spare anyone. You'll be pushing your parade by yourself"

Three days later, the air warm and lazy around her, Little Will half dozed as she sat astride Reg's neck. Reg's harness was hooked to one of the fill wagons, the wagon's bay held five very sick men and women. One of them was Shiner Pete. Reg was lumbering north up the Miira–Kuumic road toward home. At odd moments, sensing Little Will was asleep, Reg would come to a halt and begin pulling up grass from the roadside. Little Will would tap the beast's shoulder with her bullhook, and Reg would move off again. Then, again, Little Will would doze.

In her mind she saw herself a hundred steps in front of the bull, urging it on. She walked the road ahead of the bull, seeing what was around the corners. A curious dream. She stopped in the center of the road, turned back, and waited for Reg. After a while, the elephant-drawn wagon appeared from around a bend in the road. Sitting astride Reg's neck was a sleeping Little Will.

She turned away from the image and looked up at the avenue of sky between the trees. Her arms went up, and she rose above the trees. Higher and higher, until she could look back and see White Top Mountain. Higher still, until the sky above was dark. Then she looked down. The marks on the surface of Momus made by the road gang were invisible. But ahead, near Table Lake, she could see the houses of Miira. There was one afire, and the blackened remains of three others could be seen. A little beyond the houses she could see the huge swath cut through the forest when Number Three plowed to a stop. At the end of that swath there was nothing except the forest trying to heal itself.

She felt a force—five distinct powers—surrounding her. They were forces only to be felt, not seen.

Who are you? she asked.

And you? called the forces. Who are you?

Her mind whirled as she remembered the voices: Hassih, Nhissia—the Ssendissians. But they were killed in the ship long before the crash.

We are the children of Ssendiss.

And they were strong. One would push her, then the next. She felt so weak—

She looked down and tried to find the elephant-drawn wagon. As she searched, the forces swatted her down. She tumbled rapidly and the green of the Great Muck Swamp rushed up at her—

Little Will opened her eyes. Reg was again sneaking a bite at the roadside. She tapped Reg's shoulder with the bullhook and the animal moved off down the road.

Little Will felt Shiner Pete's thoughts, and she let them in. *"Is something wrong, Little Will?"*

"No. I must have had a bad dream. Go back to sleep." She felt Shiner Pete drifting off, his fever making his mind swim. Little Will looked up at that avenue of blue above the road.

At least I think it was a dream, she thought to herself. She tapped Reg on the shoulder, then settled back into a half-doze.

In another three days, the wagon was in Miira, Reg was in the *kraal,* and Little Will was in her bed next to Pete, both of them swimming in the killer fever of the disease.

Little Will and Shiner Pete flew above the clouds. *"See, Pete? I was right, wasn't I?"*

Pete swung in a loop around Little Will. *"You were right."* He leveled out and looked down. *"Look. We're over Tarzak."* He looked at the wisp of light that was his wife. *"I wonder how fast we can go."* He streaked out over the Sea of Baraboo toward the continent of Midway.

"Pete, do you think we should?" He was far ahead and did not answer. Little Will moved until she was beside Pete. Far below the mirror of the sea shined back at them, and they could see four of the fishing boats from Tarzak on the water. *"Pete, let's go faster. As fast as we can."*

The two wisps arrowed toward the East. For a moment all they could see was sky and water, then ahead on the darkening horizon was the continent of Midway. They slowed. *"Look!"* called Pete. *"It's Mbwebwe! Where Number Two went down."*

Below them were flickers of light. Pete and Little Will were still in the sky's light; but it was the beginning of one of many long nights in Mbwebwe. The flickers of light became fires, and the fires became wooden houses in flames. Men and women with torches could be seen heading toward a still dark house. Little Will cried and streaked on ahead, into the night. For awhile there was nothing but the stars above and blackness below. Little Will still cried. *"Pete."*

"What?"

"Pete, I wish we had a moon. I wish we had a moon, Pete."
In the darkness they touched, then rushed for the sun.

By the ninth night of Quake, Packy Dern was standing in the door of Mange Ranger's house. Mange and Butterfingers were slumped at Mange's paper-littered table.

"I wish I'd been here, Mange. You sure the boy's all right?"

Mange sat cross-legged on the cushion before his table, his face resting in his hands. He nodded without looking up. "He's all right, Packy. You're the father of a brand-new bouncing baby boy."

Butterfingers looked back at Packy. "The bug doesn't hit the kids. None of them born on Momus."

"What about Cookie Jo? She looks like hell."

Mange shook his head and lowered his hands. "Don't know. I just don't know." The vet rubbed his aching eyes and pointed at the table's mountain of notes. "We've tried everything. Just finished an experiment." Mange stared at the papers. "Nothing. Not a damned thing."

He swept his notes to the plank floor of the shack with a single sweep of his left arm. "Christ, I feel like a goddamned witchdoctor! Torching houses, chanting over boils..." He looked at Butterfingers. "It doesn't matter what in the hell we do. Is it a virus? A bacteria? A voodoo spell? We know it's not transferable from human to human. What is it, then? How many damned insects have we logged?"

Butterfingers shook his head. "Dunno. Must be a couple thousand by now. There must be thousands more."

Mange looked at Packy. "We have collected a billion roots,

leaves, barks, berries—hell! Dammit, we don't even have a goddamned optical microscope! Nothing! If we could just do blood tests, we might be able to find out what it is that makes the kids born on the planet immune to the damned bug."

Butterfingers lowered his head down upon his arms. "So, what do we do?" His shoulders gave a tiny heave. "Squinty Mosdov over to Arcadia is trying to figure out how to grind lenses out of that gem quartz they found there, but we're not going to see enough through that kind of equipment. An old electron microscope probably wouldn't be much help, and . . . we're long way from . . . anything like that." Butterfingers's form was still except for the shallow motion of his breathing.

Mange stood and moved away from the table. He stood next to Packy and looked through the open doorway, staring at the smoldering coals of a recently torched house. "I half feel like putting on a mask and loin cloth and doing a dance." He stepped through the doorway into the night and walked toward the large plank and shingle structure that housed the stricken whose houses were in ashes.

As they passed it, Mange pointed at the smoking ruin. "I must've told them a thousand times that torching doesn't help. Eliminated that a long time ago." He held out his hands and let them slap against his legs. "Still, every couple of nights, a torch gets tossed into an empty house."

Packy followed the vet into the infirmary. By the light of four candles, he could see the quadruple rows of plank beds extending the length of the large room.

Mange muttered out loud. "Why do a few get the bug then get better while everyone else curls up and dies? Why don't the newly born get the bug at all?" He walked past a few beds until he stood looking down at Shiner Pete and Little Will. Packy joined him.

They were both quiet and resting comfortably. Their color was good and the fever seemed to be past. But they talked about projecting their minds all over the planet, seeing huge green lizards in the swamp, and even finding and talking with Waco Whacko's eggs. "The fever was high; it's always high. We've had a number of cases of brain damage." Mange shook his head. "The limited telepathic ability of some of the show kids is something I discussed with Bone Breaker and that Ssendissian, Nhissia. But even the Ssendissians can't release their

thoughts from their bodies, sailing through space and time. The
fever is always very high; the skin hot to the touch. Perhaps
brain damage."

Packy rubbed his chin and looked at the vet. "Waco's snakes
couldn't move things with their thoughts, could they?"

"Telekinesis?" Mange shook his head. "No."

"Little Will can. A bunch of those on the road gang saw
her move a helluva huge rock."

Mange raised his eyebrows. "And how many of those had
the bug?"

"I don't know, but—"

"Did you see her move the rock?"

Packy shook his head.

Mange shook his head again and walked toward the door.
"What I wouldn't give just for a goddamned thermometer."

Although the ice wagons began rolling their sawdust-packed
cargos through the town on their way to Tarzak, The Season
the fourth saw no one from Miira or the Emerald Valley travel
south for the celebration. There were too many new grave
markers; too many down with the bug; the recovered too weak
to travel. Those who could gathered in Miira's tiny square and
observed The Show by watching Packy Dern put Robber
through her routine. A week later Packy was in his bed, down
with the bug.

It was on the thirteenth of Wind, the fifth year since the
crash, that Little Will rose from her bed and hobbled out into
the sunshine. As she felt the warmth of the sun reach to her
bones, she reached her hand inside her robes and felt the way
her ribcage protruded in front of her sunken abdomen. Everyone
in Miira looked as though they were starving to death.

Pete was still in bed; still weak.

She moved slowly down the street until she came to Packy's
house. Cookie Jo was sitting on the stone bench in front of the
house nursing her child, Mort.

"Cookie, how's Packy?"

Cookie Jo nodded toward one end of the bench. "Sit down,
Little Will. You look like a strong wind'd blow you away."

Little Will shook her head. "The sun does me good. Besides,
if I sit down, I don't know how long it would be before I could
get up again." She nodded toward the door. "How's Packy?"

A look came into Cookie Jo's eyes. "I don't know. Mange

says the fever's past. But Packy just stays in bed like he was waiting to die. He won't eat anything."

Little Will held her hand to her forehead as dizzyness whirled the ground. "Maybe I will sit down for a bit." She took the three steps necessary and dropped down upon the bench.

"Are you better now?"

"Better. I'm still a little wobbly on my pins."

Cookie Jo rearranged her baby, then looked at Little Will. "Honey, are you sure you should be up? If you had a mirror right now, you'd scare yourself half to death."

"If I was a bikini queen, I'd be in the ballet."

"How's Pete?"

Little Will shook her head. "Weak. I think he's on the mend, though." She looked into the dark doorway of Packy's house, then back at Cookie Jo. "Is it okay if I go in and see him?"

"He won't talk to anyone. Not even me."

Little Will placed her hand against the wall of the house and pushed herself to her feet. Still holding onto the wall, she entered the room and stopped inside the door. "Packy?"

Hearing no answer, she walked to the window to her right and pulled aside the piece of blanket that covered it. Sunlight flooded the room. "Pull back that curtain."

Little Will looked in the direction of the weak voice and saw Packy's emaciated form in bed. "What are you, Packy, a bat?"

"Pull back the curtain and get out of here."

Little Will hobbled to the next window and opened it to the light. "Packy, you have to have light to put your clothes on."

"Clothes?" The boss elephant man stared at her with sunken eyes. "I'm not putting on any clothes, and if you got any sense, you'd get yourself back to bed."

Little Will folded her arms and looked down at Packy. "I can't go to bed. There's bull to be pushed."

Packy turned his face to the wall. "Just go away, Little Will. Please."

"Just going to curl up and die, huh? You know what Bullhook Willy would've said."

Packy turned on his side, facing the wall. "He's dead. Everybody's dead. Every goddamned body's dead."

Little Will felt the tears spring to her eyes. "He'd say, 'Bullhand, get your narrow ass out of that hay and push some bull!'" She fumed at Packy's back for a moment, then lifted her right leg and kicked the boss elephant man in the soft end.

"Ow!"

Packy rolled over and sat up as Little Will staggered to regain her balance. "Dammit, Little Will, I don't care if you are married! I'm gonna whip your butt till it glows in the goddamned dark!"

She turned toward the door. "First you have to catch me." Little Will stepped outside and leaned against the doorframe. The street seemed to tip and swim in front of her face. "Cookie? Cookie?"

Little Will felt strong hands grip her upper arms. "Are you all right?"

"Get me back to my bed. I can't walk..."

She seemed to fall through a hole in the planet's crust. And the planet was hollow, dark, and cold.

Bullhook Willy was drunk. She remembered that she was nine years old. It was only later that she figured out that her father had been carrying a few snorts under his belt.

They had been in the main sleeping bay of the *Baraboo*. Since he wasn't hitched to anything or anyone, Bullhook Willy slept with the rest of the bullhands. He had taken a long pull from a bottle, then pointed the neck of the bottle at her.

"There's not a goddamned bullhand on this ship who's worth a crap without his bull." He tapped the bottleneck against his chest. "Me too. Especially me." He took another pull, lowered the bottle to his lap, then smiled at her. "Lookit me, kid. Lookit me hard. I'm nothing without those bulls. Not a damned thing."

He rubbed his eyes, then looked above her at something only he could see. "A bullhand, his name was Goober Jones, worked the Snow Show out of Seattle when Poison Jim and I were together. Damn Goober. He turned his bull into an outlaw...killed Poison Jim." He shook his head and looked back up at that nothingness. "You ever find a bullhand who thinks he's something without his rubber mule, you kill that sonofabitch or throw 'im out on the lot. Got no business swinging a bullhook."

Then, with his hand, he waved images from his mind and laughed. He told her a story. It was the one about Kraut Stuka. Kraut was filing his bull's toenails when the show's new vet asked Kraut why the bull was making that "pok-a-ta-pok-a-ta" sound with her trunk.

"'Oh,' says Kraut going back to his bull's pedicure, 'this bull's an outboard.'"

She didn't know what an outboard was. But she laughed, because Bullhook Willy laughed. And Bullhook Willy was boss elephant man for O'Hara's Greater Shows. She laughed because the laughter of giants is infectious. And Bullhook Willy was a giant. He was the man in charge of the care, feeding, performance, training, and procurement of over a hundred of the largest land mammals known anywhere in the universe.

Her father.

NINETEEN

When Little Will opened her eyes, Packy's tired face was looking back at her. It was just like after the crash. She reached out her hand and touched Packy's. The boss elephant man squinted at her. "Little Will?"

Her mouth was dry and she wet her lips with her tongue. "Packy." She squeezed his hand as another face came into view. "Pete."

Shiner Pete knelt on the floor next to the sleeping cushions. "How do you feel?"

Little Will closed her eyes and thought. For some reason, the question wasn't an easy one to answer. Her eyes opened and she smiled. "Hungry. How's Reg?"

Packy nodded. "In the pink."

She frowned first at Packy then at Pete. "You two are up."

Packy snorted and looked at Pete. "I guess you're right, Pete. You got yourself a real fortune teller in this girl."

"The last I remember, I was up and you two were flat in the sack."

Packy raised his eyebrows and looked into her eyes. "You mean the time you struggled out of your sickbed for the sole purpose of kicking poor old Packy's ass?"

Little Will's face grew hot. She nodded.

Shiner Pete took her other hand and held it. "That was five months ago."

"Five months."

"It's Payday, the fifth of Layup."

Little Will pulled upon the hands that held hers until she was in a sitting position. The effort made her stomach swim. "I want to go to the *kraal* and see Reg. Then to the lake. I just want to scrub myself until I bleed, then stretch out in the sun. And food. Mountains of food."

Pete reached back and his hand returned holding a cup of cold broth. Little Will's lips eagerly sought the cups's edge, and she quickly took a large swallow. About to take another, she frowned. "I . . . I think I'm full."

Packy laughed and shook his head. "Your stomach's shrunked down to the size of a pea. You'll be able to eat more later."

She took a tiny sip of the broth, choked it down, then returned the cup to Pete. As Pete replaced the cup, she looked at Packy. "If it's Layup, then there's only a few weeks until The Season."

"That's right. Still nobody's going to Tarzak 'cause of the bug. But we've been building stands here in Miira. By the Boolabong, Little Will, we got us a Great Ring right here in Miira."

Little Will frowned as she tried to remember something. "I had a dream. Ming. I was in Tarzak, and Ming . . . Ming's dead." She looked at Pete.

"We haven't heard anything like that. Goofy Joe was through just yesterday, and he didn't say anything about Ming being exed."

She placed her hands on Packy's and Pete's shoulders. "Help me up. I want to see Reg."

Pete took her hand and reached beneath her left shoulder, pulling her to her feet as he stood. She looked down at the boss elephant man. "Packy?"

He smiled and shrugged. "Pete'll help you up to the *kraal*. My legs; they don't work so good. Cookie Jo'll be by in a bit to help me out."

Horror crossed Little Will's face. "Did it . . . is it because I kicked—"

Packy laughed and shook his head. "Hell no, girl. You were so weak you couldn't't've killed a fly with that kick." He pointed in the direction of the *kraal*. "Robber got spooked by a storm about two months ago and she walked around on me a bit. I always said Robber was a pain in the ass, but . . ." He shrugged and held out his hands.

"Packy, your still boss elephant man?"

He nodded. "You're damned right I am. And you better get your act together fast, snippit, 'cause we got another road to do. We're cutting through to the Miira–Kuumic Road from Porse. It'll take almost three days travel off the trip from White Top Mountain to Tarzak." He frowned. "I suppose Kraut's gonna try and pay us off again with those damned BB's of Mootch's. But I guess as long as they buy things in Tarzak—"

"BB's? The road gang was paid off for the mountain road with BB's?"

Packy sighed as his eyebrows went up. "Like the man once said to me, 'If I was smart, I'd be in the treasury wagon.'"

Little Will shook her head as Pete helped her out of the door. "All that for a handful of BB's."

Pete laughed. "Hey, we got bags of 'em—thousands—for the job. And we've already paid off the Sina fishers with 'em, and iron from Kuumic—"

"BB's!" Little Will glanced at Pete. "Mootch Movill must have billions of those things. I love you, my man, but with your brains you could be a bullhand too. BB's!"

Shiner Pete shook his head and helped his wife up the incline to the *kraal*.

By Put Up of The Season the fifth, Little Will and Pete put on a feed for Waxy and Mange to mark the occasion. Packy and Cookie Jo couldn't be there. Packy was down again with the bug and Cookie Jo was caring for him. There would be a Season in Miira. A lot of people didn't have the bug; but there would be a pall on the event. A lot of people did have the bug; for the third and fourth time. Dot the Pot was also in bed.

As Little Will and Pete brought the food to the table, Waxy and Mange sat upon their cushions. Waxy spoke without looking at Mange. "You looked at Dot yet?"

Mange grinned and nodded his head. "I looked at her."

Waxy's eyebrows went up and he faced the vet. "Well?"

Mange's grin disappeared and he shook his head. "I don't see any way around it, Waxy."

Waxy looked at the table and sighed. "Damn. That woman's

strong as a damned bull!" He shook his head. "Never thought the bug'd get her."

"It didn't."

Waxy frowned at Mange. "Headaches, cramps, dizzyness—if it's not the bug, what is it?"

Mange plucked a tungberry off of a plate and popped it into his mouth. "Dot's pregnant." He chewed on the fruit, swallowed it, then faced Waxy with an impassive expression. "We know what causes that, now."

Waxy stood and ran from the room into the street. Mange looked up at Little Will. "I'm sorry about that. It looks like only dinner for three."

Little Will grinned as she dropped onto her cushion and faced the vet. "Mange, are you sure?"

The vet nodded. "It's nice to hand out news like that once in awhile. I bet Waxy is crowing his way around the planet right now." He chuckled once, then his expression grew somber as Pete took his place at the table. "Everything you two told me has checked out. When Goofy Joe came through Miira last time, he told about them planning to rebuild the Great Ring in Tarzak out of cut stone. That, and Ming is dead. They don't know the cause. Goofy Joe came straight here after he found out, so there's no other way you could have known. This means that you two can use your thoughts the way you said you could. It's not brain damage."

Pete nodded. "Well, that's good news—as far as it goes."

Little Will frowned as she munched upon a tungberry. "When we were both sick, we tried to contact one of those monsters we saw before in the Great Muck Swamp. Pete couldn't get to its thoughts, but I think I did."

Mange's eyebrows went up. "And?"

Little Will shrugged. "I can't explain it. It felt me, and . . . and it was surprised. Just surprised. It was curious in a way, until I spoke to it. Then it just ran off into the swamp screaming like a little kid."

Mange chuckled. "I bet you scared the eggs out of the thing."

Pete and Little Will laughed. Pete pointed toward the door with his thumb. "Where's Butterfingers?"

Mange shook his head. "It looks like he's got the bug, too." Mange snorted. "At least I don't have tungberry pits all over the table."

Pete frowned. "He doesn't like the pits?"

Mange shook his head. "He likes the sweet part, but that sour shot from the pits he hates."

Little Will held her hands to her temples. Pete looked at her. She looked up Mange. "Mange, this is . . . like I told you when I saw the rocks coming down on Pete and the bulls. It's the tungberries."

"What's the tungberries?"

Little Will leaned forward. "Mange, it's the tungberries. That's the cure for the bug!"

Mange smiled and shook his head. "We tried that. A lot of troupers have died who ate tungberries by the bushel."

"The pits, Mange! Did they all eat the pits?"

Mange sat back and rubbed his chin. "I don't know." He held out his hands. "It still doesn't explain why the newborn babies on the Central Continent don't get the bug. They eat tungberries, but I've never seen a kid that liked the pits. It's an acquired taste."

Little Will frowned, then looked back at Mange. "Did you ever see a kid spit out the pits? They don't crack them for the sour taste, but they don't have any teeth, either."

Mange studied Little Will. "So they swallow the pulp and the seeds whole." He looked down at the table top. "And just about everyone has the bug on Midway, including the kids, because . . . they don't have tungberries *at all* over there!" He looked again at Little Will. "Maybe. Just maybe." He picked up the plate of tungberries and began squashing the grape-sized fruit with his hand. Then he picked out the small handfull of pits from the mass of pulp then stood up and grabbed the jug of sapwine.

Little Will looked up at Mange. "How are you going to try them?"

"Butterfingers McGuinea pig."

The vet turned and ran into the street. Shiner Pete looked at his wife. "It looks like our dinner party is playing to an empty house." He broke some cobit. "I sure hope the tungberries are the answer."

Little Will looked down at her food, then turned her head and looked through the doorway at the night. "They'll work." Images danced in the darkness. "I see other things, too, Pete. What are we going to be without the bulls?"

"We'll be man and wife. There are other things you can—"

She faced him. "I mean the *bullhands!* What will they be without the bulls?"

Pete shook his head. "Just like everybody else."

Little Will stood. "You don't understand." She walked out into Miira's dark street and headed toward the *kraal*. She walked the incline, climbed the fence, and studied the shadows.

She whispered to herself. "Without the bulls, we are nothing."

The beginnings of the things Little Will saw that night unfolded as the years passed. By The Season the sixth, the Porse Cutoff had been constructed. The success of the tungberry experiment had everyone eating the things—pits and all—and shipments of fruit and tungberry plants being sent to Midway. By The Season the seventh, the "bug" had been eliminated, and the Momans prepared once again to hold the celebration in the Town of Tarzak. As she rode Reg across the delta bridges, Little Will again saw the roadside watchers counting the bulls. They counted seventeen. Ming had died in Tarzak, the two Emerald Valley bulls had sickened and died from eating the poisonous spring ferns that grew up north, and one of the three bulls in Kuumic had died in a mine accident. There were a total of nineteen bulls left upon Momus.

During Put Up that night, they learned who had survived the bug; who had died. Duckfoot Tarzak, Leadfoot Sina, Fisty Bill Ris, Grabbit Kuumic, Dogface Dick, Cholly Jacoby, Madam Zelda, and many others passed into memory.

That night Spats Skorzini introduced himself as the Master of the Great Ring of Tarzak, and introduced Warts as the Master of the Tarzak Priesthood. The spielers in Tarzak were calling themselves barkers; the candy and fizz butchers were calling themselves merchants; and the canvasmen and razorbacks were calling themselves roustabouts.

The bullhands were still bullhands.

On the way back to Miira, Chilly Ned's bull, General, went outlaw, killing three hostlers and two children, and had to be executed. The only method available to them was an ancient one. They anchored General's back legs to some trees, and then attached a strong team of Perches to a slip-ringed chain around General's neck. To Little Will the strangulation of General seemed to take forever. The execution filled everyone's mind, and no one noticed Chilly Ned walking off alone into the darkness.

Sixteen bulls made parade in Tarzak for The Season the seventh. The two Kuumic bulls still lived, and then there were eighteen bulls upon Momus. Passing onto the Big Lot were

Amazing Ozamund, magician; Packy Dern, boss elephant man; Stretch Dirak, advance car manager; Electric Lips, barker; Ptomaine Tilly, candy butcher; Skinner Suggs, boss hostler; and Chilly Ned, bullhand.

Before they had left Miira, the bullhands elected Little Will boss elephant man—Master of the Miira Bullhands.

On Put Up, the Master of the Tarzak Priesthood disclosed the official religion of the Moman priests. A survey had been conducted, and the priests had agreed in advance to take on the religion of the majority. The majority preference was "no preference." And the Master of the Tarzak Priesthood spake:

"In accordance with our agreement in Porse, then, the priesthood's official religion is the majority's: No Preference. It might be time-saving to take notes on rituals and prayers supplied by those with religious afflictions in case the need of such rituals and prayers pops up in the future."

And Poge Loder stood and spoke from the Miira section of the Great Ring. "I want to know about profanity. A priest shouldn't go about talkin' the way Waxy does."

Warts studied upon the request, then replied to Poge. "Among other complaints, I have pondered the use of the name 'Momus' as an oath, and I see little objection. Momus was an ancient mythical Earthling deity specializing in ridicule. The Governor named this planet after that deity as a joke. Hence, I cannot see how using the name as an oath would constitute blasphemy. Since we are officially No Preferencians, I can't imagine what *would* constitute blasphemy.

"However, along with your complaints, Poge, I have received many complaints concerning the use of certain words by priests, and these complaints do not all come from the religiously distressed. At burials we should have no more send-off phrases such as 'Give 'em hell, you son of a bitch,' 'When you get there, save one with big knockers for me,' 'You were a beautiful bastard,' and 'Death sucks.'

Warts turned to the other members of the Moman Priesthood standing in the ring with him. "I would add that in recording pregnancies and births, the proper word is fetus, not 'watermelon' or 'loaf of bread'; the word for womb is not 'the old patch' or 'oven,' and the process by which this event accrues is not to be referred to by the expression you are currently using."

Waxy placed his arm upon Turtlehead's shell. "Could you *please* go up into the Miira stands and explain the proper pronunciation of our trade to old Poge?"

"Why?"

"He seems to be missing the goddamned point of what the hell it is to be a damned priest. That's why."

"The proper pro—"

"I know. I know. But tell Poge. He needs it."

Turtlehead moved off into the cut-stone steps of the Miira blues.

Warts cleared his throat and addressed the Great Ring. "In answer to the question put to me by many of you, the invention of the telephone has been postponed for lack of interest."

On The Season the eighth, they learned that Jingles McGurk, Goofy Joe, and Mootch Movill had taken on apprentices, and were demanding new job titles. From that day on, loan sharks were to be known as "cashiers," gossips as "newstellers," and liars as "storytellers."

Only twelve bulls made parade that year. Four had to be retired; too weak to make the trip to Tarzak. Little Will had remained in Miira along with Mange Ranger and Shiner Pete. Before the bullhands returned to Miira from The Season, Mange placed into Little Will's arms a baby boy and a baby girl. She named the boy Johnjay, after John J. O'Hara. She named the girl May, after the month that used to begin every show—a long time ago.

Shiner Pete asked his wife if now the future of the bullhands looked so bleak. Little Will did not respond. The baby boy appeared to have mental powers that dwindled hers. She could not imagine what Johnjay would become.

The baby girl, May, was crippled. She would never have the use of her legs. Mange was sorry. Pete accepted it. Little Will stopped probing the future. The answer had come to her long before. For the bullhands there would be no future. The elephant song would die. What, if anything, would replace it, she could not imagine.

But she knew one thing: while the bulls lived, the bullhands lived. She took her gold-tipped bullhook and held it within arm's reach of her baby, Johnjay. He touched its coldness, withdrew his hands, and cried.

Deep in the Great Muck Swamp, Waco Whacko knelt before the mound beneath which were buried the five Ssendissian eggs. As he tested the moisture of the soil, he spoke.

"Hanah will have our baby in a couple of months."

"It is what we have all waited for."

"She should go back to where Number Three went down. There are people there that can help her. And I want to be with her."

"No."

Waco stood and looked down at the mound. "What do you mean, no?"

"The meaning is clear."

"You would not let me go with her?"

"Neither of you will leave us. Hanah shall have the child here."

Waco looked down the hill toward the shack. "This is foolish! What if the child dies?"

"Then you and Hanah will produce another. We cannot risk you leaving us."

He looked back at the mound. "What if they both die? It happens often with human births if the proper help is not available."

The eggs were silent for a moment. *"Waco, if they both die, you will find another female. With her, then, you will produce another child."*

"And if another female doesn't come along?"

"Hanah will stay, Waco. Both of you will stay." The eggs appeared to talk among themselves for a moment. Then they spoke again. *"It is time you were told, Waco."*

"Told what?"

"You will never leave here. Hanah will never leave here. We shall keep your child, and your child's descendants, until we are free of our shells. Don't try to fight this, Waco. We are strong enough now to prevent you from harming us. We can kill Hanah."

Waco walked down the hill toward the shack. When he was midway between the shack and the mound, he turned back. "We have loved you and cared for you night and day for years. Why don't you trust us?"

"We are only babies, Waco." The thought-hiss of Ssendissian laughter came from all sides. *"We do not know any better."*

At the feeling of more laughter, Waco's hands turned into fists. He began storming up the hill. "It's time you were taught better!"

A huge hand of nothingness swatted Waco to the ground. He pushed himself up from the ground, touched his hand to his mouth, then withdrew it and looked with astonishment at the blood upon it. "Damn you!" He looked up at the mound.

"If you do this, it will cost you our love. Don't you understand that?"

"We do not need love, Waco. What we need are keepers. You taught us that."

The huge hand of nothingness swatted Waco's face, bowling him backwards toward the shack. Again and again the force struck until Waco was unconscious.

The eggs called to the shack. *"Hanah Sanagi. Come and collect your mate."*

Dull-eyed and listless, Hanah emerged from the shack. She stumbled at the eggs' direction until she stood over Waco's bleeding form. She looked down at him and half-smiled, half-cried. "I told you. I told you."

The eggs spoke to her. *"You will have the child here, Hanah."*

"I know." She squatted and began cleaning the grass and dirt from Waco's cuts. "I know."

"The child will be a female. Her name is Ssura."

Hanah looked toward the mound, confused. "Her name?"

"Her name is Ssura. It means guardian. And she is ours. We are already in her mind."

Hanah placed her hands upon her swollen abdomen, bowed her head, and was sadly amused to think that the biggest favor she could do for her child would be to kill it.

"We are in your mind, too, Hanah Sanagi."

She sighed and returned to cleaning Waco's cuts. "I know. You never let me forget."

On The Season the eleventh, Little Will brought Johnjay and May to Tarzak. Eleven bulls made parade. By The Season the fifteenth, there were only eight bulls. On The season the twenty-first, there were two bulls in the parade. Seven others were in the Miira *kraal* too old, too weak, to travel to Tarzak. On The Season the twenty-eighth, the only bull to make parade in Tarzak was Reg.

Little Will walked alongside the animal, and they were followed by Johnjay carrying May, and by the remaining bull-hands of Miira.

On The Season the twenty-ninth, the bulls and the bullhands of Miira were absent from the parade.

TWENTY

By The Season the thirty-first, the only remaining bulls upon Momus were the six retired pachyderms in the Miira *kraal*. Few went out of their way to attend Tarzak's celebration. However, more than a few traveled to Miira to see the six old bulls that still lived. For most Momans, it was a trip of privation and hardship. The children and the young adults complained. But the old ones—those who had come down when the *Baraboo* was exed—would listen to no complaints. They went to Miira to see the bulls; that, and to remember a time that had long passed into memory along with many of their friends and loved ones.

The young ones had never seen the show. The sparkle, the joy, the need of the big top, was something foreign to them. The bulls were curiosities—freaks from a storyteller's past.

Those who came would find a young girl seated in the grass of the *kraal* making drawings while a handsome young boy sat upon one of the bulls, or stood by its side. When the girl would leave, the young boy would carry her to the house of Little Will, Master of the Miira Bullhands. Then he would head for The Tusk, Miira's tavern. There at the tavern, the one called Johnjay would amuse his friends, and whoever happened to be within earshot, with loud, drunken lies about telepathic eggs, pachyderms, and a ghost called Bullhook Willy.

If urged, and if plied with sufficient movills and sapwine, the boy would demonstrate his abilities at cards and dice. And he would lament that no one would gamble with him because people believed wrongly that he had inherited his parent's mental gifts. Then a card in the center of the table would flip over by itself. The boy would place his hand upon the card and look as though he were embarrassed. And then he would laugh.

"Bah! But my head is boiled!" Mortify weaved, looked at the closed door of The Tusk, then looked down at his companion sitting in the dust of the Miira Square. He dropped down next to him and looked up at the stars. "When, oh, when shall our rescue from this mudball come?" Mortify laughed. "Look at them. Look at the stars, Johnjay! My mother, Cookie Jo, says we used to live there. Imagine that."

Johnjay looked up, his head swimming. He giggled. "There seems to be an uncommon number of stars out tonight."

Mortify waved a hand at Johnjay. "Your eyes are crossed."

Johnjay picked at his bullhand's robe, belched, and turned toward Mortify. "Does it look as though Cups was in the right, then, to throw us from his door?"

"Foo!" Mortify scratched his head and pointed toward the tavern door. "I am the one studying medicine with old Mange! Not Cups! Who then should know better than I what potions we need?"

"To ward off the evening chill."

"To remove tungberry stains."

Johnjay laughed. "And to remove warts—"

"Shhh!" Mortify looked about the darkened square. "The priests are *everywhere*." They both laughed. Mortify reached inside his robe and withdrew a jug. "Observe. *Medicine!*"

Johnjay sat upright. "By Momus, there is dip in your blood. How did you steal that?"

"Steal?" Mortify looked mortified. "Would you have me put out on the lot? This is my price for carrying Cups's footprint upon my soft end!" He uncapped the jug, drank deeply from it, then handed it to Johnjay. "Here. Time to soften those hard edges of reality."

Johnjay drank from the jug, spilling a small amount upon his robe. He lowered the jug and bobbed his bleary gaze at his companion's shadowed form. "Tell me, Mortify."

"Tell you what?"

"What is your price for this potion?"

Mortify's expression grew somber, and he looked up at the stars. "Tell me how I can get to those other worlds, Johnjay. Where the houses and streets are bright with many lights; where there are wonderful machines and entertainments, rich foods..." He reached for the jug, took it, and drank.

Johnjay shook his head. "Maybe there are no other worlds." He retrieved the jug as Mortify lowered it.

"No other worlds?"

Johnjay drank from the jug, then handed it back to his companion. He waved a hand toward the sky. "What if they are myths? Stories invented in one of old Movill's drunken stupors? He is not Master of the Tarzak Storytellers because of his strict application of truth. What if we have always been here?"

Mortify placed the jug upon the ground between them. "Nonsense. Why would the old people lie?"

"To give us hope? Do they entice us with tales of these other worlds—worlds that have many bulls—to keep the bull-hands with no bulls at their craft?"

Mortify shook his head. "There are too many things. We can see pieces from the cars. And there are the drawings—"

"My sister, May, paints the bulls. But she also paints pictures of things she's never seen."

"There is something else, Johnjay. Old Mange, he can't use three quarters of his knowledge. To use it requires machines and instruments that don't exist to administer powders and potions that no one can make." He leaned forward. "That's why I want to go to those other worlds, Johnjay. To learn."

Johnjay shrugged. "For what purpose?"

"It interests me."

"If it interests you." Johnjay nodded, then drank from the jug, replacing it between them.

"Johnjay, don't you want to know why you can see images from other's heads, or how you can move things and see what will happen with your mind?"

"Not particularly. I find little use for such things in working harness for my father." He shrugged. "Maybe I would like to see a real circus; a circus like we've been told the show was. Someplace that has more than six bulls." He shook his head. "Perhaps not—"

"You two!" A boom came down from above them. "Stop that noise and go home!" The shutters above the tavern door slammed shut.

Johnjay stood. "It is a public square!"

The shutters opened again. "Yes, and you may howl in it the night through if you want to travel to Porse to wet your whistles from now on!"

Mortify pushed himself to his feet and pulled upon Johnjay's arm. "Come! Hush and come! Cups threatens doom!" He pulled harder.

Johnjay staggered against Mortify, then began weaving toward the corner of the square. "Doom, doom, doom."

Mortify laughed. "Doom, da doom, doom."

"Doom diddy boom boom, doom doom!"

They snickered and giggled their way to the corner of the square, then Mortify pushed Johnjay down the road toward the *kraal* and turned to stagger toward his own home. Johnjay turned twice around and stopped to scratch his head. "Gone. Everyone is gone, gone, gone."

He shrugged and began the climb between the dark houses toward the *kraal*. "Ba bum, de dum." He held his robe out and whirled in the center of the street. "Ba bum, ditty bum, de dum." He stumbled, came to a halt, and looked up at the stars.

"Momus, you great fat laughing fool! With all that I drink, you do not even give me pink elephants. Here is a bullhand without a bull, in a circus world that has no show. Am I not funny?" He hung his head, sighed, then headed toward his parents' house. It was a simple affair, four rooms and a porch, situated on the edge of the *kraal*. Johnjay supported himself by one of the porch supports and looked into the darkness for the bulls. He could see nothing, for the night was too dark. Shaking his head, he went through the door curtain, through the eating room, into his tiny sleeping quarters. He dropped upon his sleeping cushions and stretched out. For a moment, he stared at the fuzzy images of stars hanging outside the room's sole window.

"What must it have been like to travel among the stars? What were those other worlds like to walk upon?"

"Johnjay?"

He turned as he heard Little Will's voice. "Yes, Mother?"

She entered the room carrying a small fat-oil lamp. "Johnsay, don't you know how late it is?"

He closed his eyes and placed his hands beneath his head.

"No. But it must be very late. Very, very late." He opened his eyes, then closed them against the brightness of the flame. "Was there something you wanted, Mother?"

Little Will looked down at him and bit her lip. "I wanted to give you something."

He squinted an eye open and saw his mother's arm extending beyond the flame, holding an object. He reached out a hand and took it; then he examined it in the light from the lamp. It was a bullhook. An uncontrollable laughing fit came over him as he dropped the bullhook to the floor. "And now, Mother . . . and now all I need is a bull!" He continued to laugh.

"It's made from angelhair wood."

"Then . . . then I must have an angelhair bull, too!" He laughed and laughed until he slept.

Little Will left the room bringing the light with her.

Days later, Little Will sat in the shade of the porch, watching her daughter, May, in the *kraal*. May sat on a blanket, her thin legs folded beneath her. May held her paper board with her left hand; while her right hand moved rapidly across the paper. Johnjay sat astride Reg's neck; both man and bull were motionless.

A shuffle in the dirt walkway, then a cough. Little Will looked to her right to see Mange Ranger hobbling on his cane. "Mange, what are you doing out in the sun?" She met the veterinarian and led him to her chair.

He lowered himself into the chair, nodding his thanks. He coughed again, then leaned back and sighed. "Little Will, it's been thirty years—no, thirty-one—thirty-one years since I've seen a flake of tobacco. And damned if I'm not hacking away like I was still on the weed." He looked up toward the *kraal* for a moment, then looked down and shook his head. "Time passes."

Little Will placed her hand on Mange's shoulder. "The new extract didn't work."

Mange shook his head sending one of his few remaining wisps of white hair down across his brow. He pushed the hair back with a shaking hand. "Damned stuff didn't do anything." He glanced at Little Will, then looked at the house across the walkway. "I shouldn't have gotten your hopes up." He looked toward the *kraal*. "May's twenty . . . twenty-four, now." Mange snorted. "Twenty *real* years old. But she doesn't look a day older than thirteen or fourteen." He looked up at Little Will. "She's going to be a cripple the rest of her life. I'm sorry."

Little Will shook Mange's shoulder. "May knows that. It doesn't bother her, Mange. She was given a different gift."

"Does drawing and painting make up for not being able to walk?"

Little Will looked toward the *kraal*. "To her it does." She looked back at the old man. "Mange, one day those bulls are going to be all gone." She felt her eyes moisten. "All gone, Mange, but we'll have May's pictures. It's important to the bullhands; it's important to her."

Mange shook his head and sighed. "Bone Breaker and I must have talked it over a hundred times back with the old show. Damned shame he had to die when Number Two went down." He nodded. "And the records." He looked at Little Will. "If we'd been able to save the records I could've kept track of all those kids with the bent genes. Maybe I could've been prepared . . ."

"Did you find another one?"

Mange nodded as he rubbed his eyes. "I think so. Wanna and Jimbo from Tarzak. Know them?"

"No."

"She's a wardrober and he's a cashier. They have a son, Mungo. He's twelve years old and he weighs almost three hundred pounds." Mange shook his head. "And not a scrap of fat on him; he's one big muscle." He tapped the side of his head. "Feeble-minded. He can hardly remember anything from one minute to the next. They brought him for glasses. He can't see very well either. Oh." Mange reached into the pocket of his threadbare white coat. "Speaking of glasses; here's Pete's." He held out a small cloth-wrapped bundle. "Now you tell Pete if these aren't exactly right to send them back. Boxcar Bo over in Kuumic has a complete set of diagnostic lenses made up now, and he's made up the eye charts, too. If these aren't right, Butterfingers can make him an accurate prescription next time."

"I'll tell him." Little Will took the bundle and placed it into the pocket of her robe. She withdrew a small pouch, shook a number of copper beads into her hand, counted them, then dropped them into Mange's hand.

Mange looked at the coppers, chuckled, then dropped them into his coat pocket. He nodded toward the *kraal*. "What about Johnjay? Anything besides telepathy?"

Little Will folded her arms and shook her head. "He can see futures. And he can read minds. He can also move things." She sighed.

"What is it?"

"Mange, he just doesn't do anything with his gifts. Or anything else. When he isn't carrying May around, he's down at the tavern drinking with his friends. He doesn't care about anything else." She held out her arms, then let them drop to her sides. "He can handle the bulls, but he doesn't care. No future, he says." Little Will looked toward the *kraal*. "The only reason he's up on one now is because May needs a model."

Mange pushed himself to his feet. "Johnjay's generation was born on Momus, Little Will. They're not from our universe." He coughed and shook his head. When his lungs calmed down, Mange looked up at the sky. "I wonder what it will be like a hundred years from now." He looked at Little Will and laughed. "I guess that's not going to be my problem."

Little Will motioned toward her door. "Will you be sharing the evening meal with us? Pete'll be back soon."

Mange shook his head. "My appetite's been off lately. I have to be getting back. If I don't sit on top of him, Waxy won't take his medicine. It's a good thing he has Turtlehead to help him, otherwise I'd never get him to stay in bed." He walked out from under the porch roof, waved a hand then began his slow shamble down the walkway.

"Good-bye." Little Will turned and went through the doorway. *"Johnjay."*

"Yes, Mother?"

"Bring May in. She's had enough sun, and it's time for dinner." She smiled as she felt Johnjay search her mind trying to discover what was for dinner. *"I haven't made up my mind yet, Johnjay. Stop playing and bring May in."*

"Yes, Mother."

Little Will moved toward the window and watched as Johnjay slid from Reg's back, patted the bull's cheek, then went over to his sister. May looked up at her brother, quickly drew a few more lines, then tucked away her charcoal and held out her arms. Johnjay wrapped the blanket around May's legs, then placed his arms behind her back and beneath her legs and lifted her.

Little Will's gaze moved from her twins to Reg and the five other remaining bulls. Too old to work the roads or to travel the road to Tarzak for The Season, but without them the bull-hands were nothing.

She looked above the window at the gold and mahogany bullhook hanging there, and the angelhair-wood hook hanging next to it. Perhaps Johnjay had been right when he had said that the bullhands already were nothing. Little Will did not sweep the thought from her mind. She placed the thought aside. It was an old companion.

TWENTY-ONE

It was May 29th, the thirty-second year since The Crash. The sun was bright, and Johnjay sat upon the *kraal* fence. May was in the *kraal* finishing a drawing, and Johnjay was concentrating upon tying knots in the grass with his thoughts.

Forty miles to the southeast, Arnheim's Fault straightened out a kink, flattening approximately a third of the houses in Tarzak. The shockwave rumbled through the towns of Tieras and Porse, then hit the Town of Miira. The vibration was something more to be felt than heard. Johnjay looked toward Miira's square as he felt the *kraal* fence moving beneath him. The few people in the square stood silently, looking upward. The rumble of the ground grew much louder.

"Johnjay!" He turned at the sound of his sister's cry.

"May!" No sooner had he uttered her name, three of the spooked bulls trampled her. "May! May!"

When he reached her side, she was unrecognizable. The blood was in his eyes, hell in his thoughts, as he looked up at the rampaging pachyderms near the edge of the cliff.

That evening Johnjay stood in the center of the Miira Ring. The people of Miira moved silently into the blues, but Johnjay did not see them. He saw only his mother, Little Will. She stood a few paces away, her left side toward him, her arms folded and her head bowed. Beneath her left arm was the mahogany-handled, gold-tipped bullhook. Shiner Pete walked into the Ring and stood silently between mother and son. Pete studied Johnjay until his son turned away and looked at the blues. They were all there: teamsters, bullhands, cashiers, newstellers, riders, merchants. Turtlehead and his three apprentice priests took their places in the blues. Great Waxy would not sit with them, for his job was in the Ring.

Johnjay closed his eyes. *"Mother, what I did was right!"* The thought was sent, but refused. He bit at the inside of his lip until he tasted blood.

The sounds of motion stopped, and Johnjay opened his eyes. He blinked until the scene was no longer distorted by tears. He turned and saw the priest Waxy holding his book. Great Waxy's usually jolly face was hidden by his priest's hood. The shadow cast by the hood made him look headless for a moment—the ghostly dispassionate recorder of the town's judgement. Waxy's deep voice filled the Ring. "Who starts?"

Little Will lifted her head. "I will."

A man wearing the grey and maroon of the bullhands stood in the blues. "You are his mother."

Little Will unfolded her arms and pointed her bullhook at the man. "Lizard Bait, I am also Master of the Bulls. It is my place to speak for the bullhands."

Lizard Bait looked around the Ring for support, but found none. He resumed his seat. Waxy nodded toward Little Will. "Go on. You've got the hall."

She lowered her arms and let the bullhook hang down from her right hand. She turned completely around, looking at the faces in the blues, stopping when she faced Johnjay. She pointed the bullhook at her son. "Johnjay killed the five bulls Gonzo, Twinkie, Peg, Molly, and Lady. If I hadn't been able to control Reg, he would have killed Reg, as well. He drove them over the cliff behind the fence." She turned from Johnjay and faced the blues. "I saw this."

Shiner Pete walked over to his wife and touched her arm. She pulled her arm out of reach and turned her back on her husband. Pete faced the blues. "You all know those bulls killed my daughter, May. Johnjay's sister. You know May was a cripple and couldn't run. What you don't know is what May meant to Johnjay—"

"Bah!" A woman in bullhand's stripes stood in the blues. "Bulls kill bullhands; bullhands don't kill bulls! You're in harness, Shiner. Get out of the Ring!"

"I have a say! He's my son!" Shiner Pete stared down the woman. "Those bulls were too old and you all know it. They were old and mean." He looked around at the people of Miira. "Hell. If I'd been there, I would've killed 'em myself!" The people in the stands rose and shouted in anger. Shiner Pete held up his hands for quiet, but the noise continued until the harness man lowered his arms and stood motionless.

Waxy looked at Johnjay. "Say something, Johnjay."

Johnjay looked at Waxy. The priest's face looked very old. Johnjay looked down at the sawdust, then up at his mother. Her back was toward him. He talked to her mind. *"Mother, I am your son."*

This time she answered. *"No son of mine kills bulls."*

Johnjay looked at the bullhands in the blues. "Look at you. You call yourselves bullhands, yet when was the last time you worked a bull?" He pulled at his own gray and maroon striped robe. "This rag says I'm a bullhand. But I work harness with my father. My sister . . . May wore one of these robes, and she painted pictures. That was what she was doing in the *kraal*. She was painting pictures of those damned bulls so you and your children wouldn't forget what a bull looked like. That was when those damned animals killed her!" He spat on the sawdust. "Then I killed them. And if I could do it over again, I would!" He folded his arms.

Waxy sighed, bowed his head for a moment, then roared at the blues. "Spit it out, troupers! What does the Town of Miira say?"

A voice. "Put his trunk on the lot!" And more voices—all saying the same thing.

"On the lot! Put his trunk on the lot!"

Waxy looked at Little Will. "You brought the charge. You're Master of the Bulls. Can Johnjay pay off the bullhands?"

Johnjay's mother shook her head. "There is no price that can be set." Her back was still toward her son. "Let his trunk be put on the lot."

Waxy's voice faltered. "For . . . for how long?"

Little Will turned and pointed her bullhook at her son. "Let Johnjay not be within sight of the Town of Miira until . . . until the last bull dies." The mother looked at her son. "When Reg dies, Johnjay may return."

Waxy turned to the blues. "What about the rest of you?"

A roar of assent from the blues washed the Ring. Waxy made the entry as Johnjay turned and walked from the ring.

He went to his house, gathered his things, then began walking north on the road toward the Emerald Valley. As he reached the incline to the Snake Mountain Gap, he heard the people of Miira singing "Black Diamond."

He sent his thought. *"Good-bye Father."*

There were tears staining the answer. *"Good-bye, Johnjay. It won't be forever."*

"Good-bye, Father."

"Good-bye, Johnjay."

Johnjay looked over the houses of the Town of Miira. *"Mother?"* There was no answer. *"Good-bye, Mother."* Johnjay began to climb the incline.

TWENTY-TWO

It was at night at the peak of the Snake Mountain Gap. Tarzaka the fortune teller prepared her fire and set out her cobit cakes. She sat alone watching the flames from her fire fight back the gap's dark, when a stranger wearing the bullhand's gray and maroon paused by her fire. His hair was black and his frame was gaunt. Hell was in his eyes. She motioned toward her fire. "Come and join me, bullhand. It is a lonely road we travel."

The man studied her for an instant, then shook his head. He turned and continued down the road.

Tarzaka held up her hand. "Wait."

He looked at her. "What do you want?"

She shrugged. "What do you want?"

He almost smiled. "To be alone."

"It is a strange person who wishes to be alone at night in the Snake Mountain Gap. It is said that many ghosts walk these walls." She pointed toward him. "One who wears the bull-hand's stripes should know these things."

He laughed. It was a laugh of pain, not humor. He faced away from the fire, toward the night-blackened chasm. He

raised a fist. "Damn ghosts! *Damn* you, ghosts! If you have
any power, come to me and use it!"

Tarzaka gasped. *"Don't!"*

The stranger turned toward her, his face displaying none of
the humor of his voice. "You fear ghosts, fortune teller?"

Tarzaka shrugged. "Who does not? Does it pay to tempt
fate?"

The bullhand laughed. Still the laugh was a cry of pain. He
stopped laughing and pointed at her. "Fate does not kiss the
hand of those who pay homage to it, fortune teller. It is just
there."

Tarzaka trembled at the bullhand's words. "These are hard
things you say. What is your name?"

The bullhand studied the fortune teller for a long time. Then
he tossed his wrap of belongings next to the fire. "My
name . . . my name is No One. That is my name." He moved
to the fire and squatted next to it. His eyes studied the woman
in blue. "Your name, fortune teller?"

She wet her lips. "I am called Tarzaka." She studied the
bullhand for a few moments. "Your name is a strange one."

He pulled cobit dough from his wrap and placed it by the
fire. When he had finished, he looked at the fortune teller.
"No One is my name." He again gave a humorless grin. "Would
you share my cobit in exchange for a fortune, Tarzaka?"

She studied the bullhand. "You, No One, do not believe in
fortunes."

"I thought it might be amusing." He shook his head. "I
believe in them, Tarzaka; I do not believe in yours."

Her eyebrows raised. "And why not?"

"You play games with cards, balls, and wishes, Tarzaka.
You do not tell fortunes."

"And did Momus himself whisper this in your ear?"

"I need no advice from myths." The bullhand drew back
the left side of his mouth into a half-smile. "Instead, Tarzaka,
why don't I tell you your fortune?"

The fortune teller laughed. "There would be no more point
in doing so than if I asked you to watch me handle bulls."

The person called No One laughed, stood, and walked to
the wall of the road cut. As he scraped mud from the rocks,
he called back to the fortune teller. "Then my fortune has no
value, Tarzaka." He returned to the fire, packing and shaping
the mud with his hands. "And a fortune that has no value, you
may have for nothing."

Tarzaka snorted. "Perhaps you should pay me."

No One sat cross-legged across the fire from the fortune teller and placed a ball of mud upon one of the fire's rocks. After he had done so, he motioned with a muddy hand toward his cooking cobit. "I think you might find a bullhand's predictions amusing, but of course you are right. Take your price."

The fortune teller leaned forward, picked up the hot cobit bread, broke it in half, and returned one half to the rock. She felt the other half with her fingers. "It is done. You should take yours before it burns." She looked at No One. The light from the fire danced upon his face, showing it to be painted with stripes of mud. She swallowed. "Your bread, No One. It burns."

No One grinned. "When the spirits are upon me, Tarzaka, I may only eat cinders." He closed his eyes and spoke as he passed his hands over the mudball. "Hugga Bugga, Mumbo Jumbo, and Razzamatazz, come to me that I might see what is to be——"

Tarzaka spat a mouthful of cobit into the fire. "You make free with the friendship of the fire, bullhand! I will not sit still and hear you ridicule my profession!"

No One bowed his head. "I meant no disrespect, Tarzaka. Take the rest of the cobit as my apology."

She took the remaining bread and pointed it at the mudball. "What is the purpose of that?"

"It my crystal ball; my door to the future." The fortune teller opened her mouth to speak. No One held up his muddy palms. "Wait!" His eyes looked up, toward the dark. "I see them. Yes! Now I see them!" He lowered his glance and looked at the fortune teller. "Your name is Tarzaka."

The fortune teller shook her head. "I told you that."

"True. True." He closed his eyes. "And . . . you come from Tarzak."

She snorted. "You are being foolish!"

No One smiled. "Did I speak truly?"

"That is my name!"

He nodded. "Ah, yes. I see. Please excuse my pitiful performance. I will try to do better." He studied the fortune teller for a long moment. "And there in Tarzak you studied under Shirly Smith, the Great Madam Zelda."

Tarzaka sighed. "Since the Great Zelda was the only fortune teller with the Old Show——"

"I know. I know." Again No One smiled. "The apologies

I owe you mount so high I may never be able to repay them."

Tarzaka stretched out by the fire, leaned an elbow against the ground, and propped her head upon her open palm. "You are becoming quite tiresome, No One."

His shoulders slumped in exaggerated despair as his hands fell into his lap. "Ah, me." He cocked his head to one side, and smiled. "And there in Tarzak you live in secret with a roustabout named—"

Tarzaka sat bolt upright. "It is a lie! How—"

"It is no lie, Tarzaka." No One stared at his mudball. "And his name is Ahngarus. He is quite handsome, isn't he? Tall, strong, tanned skin, black hair and gleaming teeth. And his arms. So strong. And his body . . ."

The fortune teller looked at the mudball, then back at No One. "You cannot know this."

No One smiled. "Your parents would have you marry Vidar the cashier from Sina. He is wealthy; a good catch. But in the secret of the night you and Ahngarus slip away—"

"Enough!" The fortune teller's wonder turned to anger as she placed her palms to her burning face. "You are quite a trickster, No One. But gossip is not fortune telling."

No One grinned. "I see that I fail again. Shall I tell you how he kisses you, or—"

"I am tired of this, No One!"

The bullhand studied the fortune teller. "In your mind you call yourself sham. The lines on hands you know to be nothing more than wrinkles; your cards nothing but paper; your crystal nothing but polished quartz to focus a point of light to keep your customer's mind off of your knees rattling the table."

She stared at him. In her eyes the hate of being discovered was burning.

"But when you were a little girl, the Great Zelda told you many times that bunking the rubes is the entire art of fortune telling. You, of course, remember your first time with a customer. You held his attention while Zelda went through the man's belongings, signaling to you the things that were there."

Tarzaka's color drained from her face. "How many coppers did my fortune bring?"

No One shook his head. "No coppers. He paid you in tung-berries. As your master Zelda took half. You exchanged your berries for coppers in the Tarzak market that afternoon. In exchange for the berries, you were paid twenty-one Movills. The Great Zelda ate her berries." No One stared into the fortune teller's eyes. "Is my performance improving, Tarzaka?" He did not wait for an answer. "No? Then let me try again. When you were fourteen, traveling with your father down the Blowdown Cliff Cut, you fell from your horse and were injured. Ever since you have had sharp pains in your belly. You are here tonight because you are returning south from Dirak where you had heard that a healer . . ."

Tarzaka stood, her eyes wide. She slowly backed away from No One.

He raised his brows. "Am I not improving?"

"You are a *devil!*"

He held out his hands. "I see that I am not improving." He reached out and picked up the mudball. "Poor Tarzaka." He looked up at her. "There was nothing the healer could do, was there?" He looked back at the mudball. "There is a future for you in my crystal ball, Tarzaka. Do you wish to hear it?"

"A future?" Her voice was rough; her back was against the rock wall of the roadcut.

No One looked back at his mudball. "Of course a good future will take the surprise and wonder out of your life; a bad one will hang a pall of doom over whatever breaths remain to you." He looked up at her. "Shall I tell you your future, fortune teller?"

She turned and ran from the fire, into the darkness of the road toward Miira. She heard No One scream at her back. "Do not stop, fortune teller! The ghosts of Snake Mountain are at your back! *Run! Run! Run!*"

At the fire, No One looked into the dark, then down at the mudball in his hand. He flung the ball against the rocks and watched it splatter. He sat next to the fire, wrapped his arms around his knees, rested his forehead against his arms, and wept.

The dawnlight had tinted the sky above his head, but it would be almost noon before the rays of sunlight would creep down the eastern wall, warming the bottom of Snake Mountain Gap. No One's head rose from his arms, and he looked at the slit of sky above the gap. Dark clouds were building to the north. He looked at the clouds, finding in them a sense of identity—a reflection of his soul. He looked down at the black wall of the gap opposite the fire. "There, too, is a reflection of my soul!"

He spat into the fire and turned his head to pick up some

wood for the dying fire. He saw the fortune teller's pack. Next to the pack was a sling-mounted jug of sapwine. He picked up a few pieces of wood, tossed them on the fire, then reached out his right hand and pulled the jug by its sling until it was next to his leg. He spoke to the jug.

"Shall I now become thief as well as exile?" He placed the jug between his knees and pulled the wooden stopper. Lifting the jug, he placed the opening in the neck to his lips and drank deeply. He lowered the container to the ground. "No." He shook his head. "The exile is Johnjay. And he . . . is dead. I am No One." He took another drink. "And Tarzaka did not give me fair exchange for my performance."

He stood, holding the jug up by its neck, then he shouted at the opposite wall of the gap. "No One is a thief!" He drank again, and giggled. "And if No One is a thief, then no one can be held accountable."

He laughed at his joke as thunder from the north rumbled through the gap. "Bang! Boom! Bang!" He sang with the thunder, laughed, and drank again. As he lowered the jug from his lips, he walked to the edge of the road and looked down the chasm at the water far below. He felt splatters of rain on the back of his neck and he looked up at the sky. The drops fell on his face, then the deluge began. His eyes closed, and he stood there feeling the chill wetness reaching his skin. The full impact of the wine reached his head. He held out his arms and began to sway to the sounds of the rain, his feet dancing slowly in the mud of the roadbed. "No One is a thief; No One is a thief."

A flash of lightening followed immediately by a crash of thunder made him shy from the edge of the chasm. Suddenly he felt very cold. He looked back at the still-burning fire. Far above it a rocky overhang protected the place below. He took another swallow from the jug, then weaved his way to the dry place. The fire was hot and he tried to dry his gray and maroon striped robe by rotating in front of the flames. On one of his turns, he paused to drink again. As he lowered the jug, he saw the fortune teller's pack. He staggered next to it, squatted, and placed the jug at his side. He studied the pack for a moment, then laughed. "No One's thievery knows no limits."

He reached, undid the pack's ties, and opened the flap. At the top were folds of heavy blue cloth. He pulled it from the pack. It was a fortune teller's robe. And it was dry. "And why not? Am I not a great teller of fortunes?"

He pulled his own robe over his head, and dropped it to the ground. Stooping over, he picked up the dry robe and put it on. He stood by the fire until the chill left his bones, then he picked up his own robe, wrung it out, then began drying it by waving it over the fire.

"Ah, yes, here is No One: bullhand, fortune teller, and laundry man." He laughed, picked up the jug, and took another swallow. He lowered the jug and looked into the flames. "Thief. Exile." He heard the splashes of approaching footsteps. He looked not toward the sound, but continued drying his robe. "I see you have returned, Tarzaka."

The splashing stopped. He turned and looked into the rain.

Tarzaka's trembling voice spoke out of the deluge. "How do you know these things, No One? You cannot see me."

He shrugged and turned back to the fire. "I am a great teller of fortunes."

She walked out of the rain, pushing the hood back from her face. She studied him for a moment, then squatted by the fire, still looking at his face. "You are wearing my robe, bullhand."

He laughed. "It's a dirty job, Tarzaka, but someone must do it." He laughed again as he took his steaming robe from the fire and felt it with his fingers. He looked down at Tarzaka then felt the blood rushing to his cheeks. "I . . . I apologize. I will return your robe at once."

Tarzaka shook her head. "No."

"No?"

She pushed herself to her feet, walked over to her pack, and squatted down again. From the pack she pulled a red blouse, black skirt, and multi-colored shawl. "This is my performing costume." She whirled her hand at him. "Turn around."

He turned his back to her and hung his head as he remembered the severely depleted jug of sapwine. "How can I repay you, Tarzaka? I meant no—"

"To begin, Johnjay, you can keep still."

His flush deepened as he listened to the fortune teller change. "How do you know my name?"

"Last night I fled toward Miira. On the road I met the Great Goofy Joe and his two apprentice newstellers fresh from Miira. It will not be long before your deed is known all over the face of Momus." She paused. "You may turn back now."

He turned and saw her dressed in her costume. She was bent over, squeezing what water she could from her long black hair. She stood and looked at him. "You are the son of Little Will."

He stared at her for a moment, then looked back at the fire. "If I am?"

"Then you know things that I do not. Things that I want to know."

"I am No One. You may call me No One." He squatted next to the flames. "Since you know who I am, why do you associate with me?"

She squatted across the fire from him. "I want you to teach me to read minds and to see the future."

Johnjay laughed. "Tarzaka, you are *older* than I am! You would make a strange apprentice."

The fortune teller's eyes narrowed. "I still want you to teach me."

He sat on the ground, picked up the sapwine jug, and took another deep swallow. The jug lowered to his lap, he raised his eyebrows. "What if I cannot teach you? It is said that those who can speak to minds are born with this ability. I do not know if it can be learned."

"You must try. That is my price for the robe and the wine."

Johnjay tried to push himself to his feet, but fell back upon the ground. He looked at Tarzaka. "Anything else?"

Her face went pale. "I want . . . I want to know what fortune you saw for me in your mudball."

Johnjay stretched out on the ground and laughed until the wine darkened his mind and put his demons to sleep.

Before it happened, Johnjay saw what was to be. The bulls curling their trunks under, the wild-eyed charge, May crushed—

"May!" He stood at the kraal *fence watching his sister put the finishing touches on a drawing. He leaped from the fence and ran toward her. "May!" She turned and looked at him.*

Was it the vibration of the soil? Gonzo reared her head, then curled under her trunk. The others followed, ponderous legs thundering against the ground, tusks scything at the grass . . .

His right sandal caught on a half-buried root, sending him sprawling on his face. "May!"

She disappeared in a cloud of dust, her brief scream cut short. Without thinking, Johnjay's mind attacked the bulls with

images of legendary Earth beasts: lions, tigers, panthers, leop-
ards. The images panicked the bulls away from May's broken
body. The bulls trumpeted and ran around the fence as Johnjay
looked down at his sister. He covered his face and sank to his
knees. "Oh, oh. She . . . she hasn't any head!"

He lowered his hands, and looked at the bulls. They were
quieting down. The sky and landscape turned red before his
eyes as he sent the images of big cats once more against the
bulls. The elephants screamed, fled this way and that, each
time seeing the path filled with slathering, fanged fury. But
there was one path open, and they took it. They came to the
cliff. But to them it was a stretch of open grass.

Five plunged over the edge before Little Will's thoughts
caused him to black out—

"No One. Wake up." He felt a hand roughly shaking his
shoulder. "Wake up."

He opened his eyes and saw Tarzaka's frowning face framed
by the ornate edges of her shawl. "What?" He looked at the
opposite wall of the cut and saw the sunlight upon it. "Afternoon. the rain's stopped." He looked back at the fortune teller,
then sat up, rubbing his temples. "Why did you wake me?"

Tarzaka pointed down the road toward Miira. "Listen."

He listened. Footsteps. Voices. He pushed himself to his
feet. "Who is it?" He looked at the fortune teller. "Who is it?"

She gathered her things and stuffed them into her pack.
"Goofy Joe, his apprentices, and those who travel with them."
She shook the sapwine jug, glared at No One, then tossed the
jug aside. She stood and pointed at a bundle she had made out
of the gray and maroon bullhand's robe. "Your things are there.
Come. We must leave."

"Leave?" He frowned at the fortune teller. "Why should I
leave, Tarzaka?" He pointed at his chest. "I have as much right
to the road as anyone."

She looked down for a moment, then elevated her gaze until
her dark eyes fixed him with a hateful look. "Do you want to
hear the news from Miira, bull killer? Goofy Joe was with the
old show. Do you *really* want to hear what he has to say?"

He looked down the road toward Miira, his stomach heaving. Far down the road, from around a turn, walked a figure
wearing the clown's orange. Then came two in newsteller's
black supporting a third in similar garb. "What will he say?"

Her eyebrows went up. "Is that future blind to you? Can you not see that future, bull killer?"

He stared at the figures on the road for a moment, then turned, picked up his bundle, and began walking rapidly down the road toward Dirak. Tarzaka shouldered her pack and followed.

TWENTY-THREE

They walked in silence until the sunlight left the Snake Mountain Gap. As the road darkened and the sky paled to gray, the fortune teller touched No One's arm. He stopped and looked at her as though a trance had been broken. "What is it?"

Tarzaka pointed at a smoke-blackened circle of flat rocks by the roadside. "It is time to stop for the night."

No One looked back at the stretch of road they had just traveled.

The fortune teller laughed. "Be brave, No One. The news of your shame is far behind us. Goofy Joe will not travel at night." She walked to the circle of rocks, lowered her pack, and lowered herself to the ground. "Gather some wood."

He frowned at her. "I don't want to stop here."

She opened her pack and withdrew her leaf-wrapped package of cobit dough. "But here is where we shall stop, No one. Gather some wood."

He paused for a moment, then tossed his bundle next to the rocks and began picking up the dead wood that the storm had shaken from the trees above the gap. When his arms were full, he carried the wood to the ring of stones and dropped it. Squat-

162

ting next to the stones, he felt the bed of the last fire. "It is cold. We must start our own fire."

"Do you have flint and steel?"

"No." He stood and walked to the rock wall of the cut and tore off a piece of crisp drymoss.

She turned to her pack and began feeling the objects within it with her hand. "Only fools travel without flint and steel." While she rummaged within her pack, No One returned and placed the drymoss in the center of the ring of stones. He sat back and looked at the ever darkening walls of the gap. The air was still. Something jabbed his arm. He looked and saw Tarzaka's extended arm, her hand holding a small, cloth-wrapped bundle. He took the bundle, opened it, and withdrew the flint and steel.

He held up the steel wedge. "From what car did this come?"

"How should I know? I purchased it in Tarzak." She waved her hand toward the drymoss. "Make the fire; I am getting chilly."

He struck several times, causing heavy, hot sparks to fall in and around the highly flammable moss. The moss began to smoke, a patch glowed, then blue-yellow flames sprang from its surface. No One placed small sticks upon the burning moss, and then larger sticks on top of the smaller. In moments a yellow oasis of light held the darkness at bay. He sat cross-legged, staring into the flames. "It will take some time to heat the rocks."

Tarzaka placed her wrap of cobit dough upon her pack and turned back to the fire. "It is time for you to meet your part of the bargain, No One."

He frowned. "What bargain?"

"In exchange for the robe and the sapwine."

He looked at her and then shrugged. "I remember making no bargain. What did I say?"

"That you would teach me the things I must know to read minds and to tell fortunes. And what is the fortune you saw for me?"

Johnjay shook his head. "I saw no fortune for you. I cannot tell fortunes."

"When I returned, No One, you knew who I was without turning to look."

"You had left your things behind. The chance was fair that you would be the only one returning for them. Anyone else would have had sense enough to stay out of the rain." He looked into the growing darkness down the road to Miira, then turned back to the fire. "Tarzaka, sometimes I see what is to happen before it happens." He motioned toward the fire with his hand. "But it is nothing more than you looking at the fire and seeing that wood will be added to it and that cobit shall be cooked there."

The fortune teller studied No One's face for a long moment. "I have heard the song of Little Will, and the stories. It is more."

No One shrugged. "Not in kind; only by degree." He looked at her. "I saw the bulls kill my sister before it happened. But I knew the bulls, knew my sister, and knew the Miira *kraal*." He returned his gaze to the flames. "I saw no future. I saw what would *probably* happen. As has happened before, something about which I knew nothing could have interfered, making my entire vision false."

"But nothing did."

He shook his head. "No. Not this time."

"What, then, did you see for me?"

"I saw nothing for you."

Tarzaka held her hands to her breast. "Nothing?"

No One laughed. "I meant only that your future is hidden to me. I do not know enough about you, your illness, or anything. I must . . . see enough, know enough, before these things can come together in my head and give me visions."

"But you knew things that you could not have known."

He shook his head, added another stick to the fire, then looked at the fortune teller. "I only took the images that you gave off. All I can know is what you know. Before I could see the probable outcome of an illness, I would need to know much more. How the body works; how this disease works—things such as that."

"It is said that your mother can move things with her mind. Do you have this power?"

"A little." He shrugged. "There are endless training exercises one must do to develop these powers." He picked up a small twig, broke it, and tossed the pieces into the flames. "Other things interested me."

"You knew you possessed these gifts, yet did nothing to develop them?" Tarzaka shook her head. "You are a fool, No One."

"What does a bullhand need with such skills, fortune teller?"

Her eyes narrowed and she opened her mouth to speak, but stopped. No One looked at her. "What were you about to say?"

She snickered. "Read my mind."

His eyes closed slowly, then reopened with a start. "Yes." He looked back at the fire, the flames blurring as his eyes filled with tears. "Yes, I could have saved May's life had I trained my power to move things." He wiped his eyes with the sleeve of his robe. "Thank you, Tarzarka."

"For what?"

"For turning my pain into Hell."

She leaned forward, placed the cobit upon one of the rocks, then sat back. "Will you teach me, No One?"

He stared at the flames for a moment, then pushed himself to his feet, and walked toward the chasm. He halted at the edge and stared into the blackness below. The waters at the bottom roared from the earlier rainfall. No One looked back at the fortune teller. "I will teach you." He lifted an arm and pointed across the chasm. "But we must travel. Across the gap, up into the Snake Mountains, and from there across the Great Muck Swamp." He looked in the direction in which he pointed. "There we will search for the children of my mother's teachers. My mother told me that they have the knowledge of their parents." He lowered his arm and looked back at the fortune teller. "And by using your mind, they can kill you, drive you insane, and would do so for the humor to be found in watching you squirm. Do you still want to learn, Tarzaka?"

The fortune teller tested the cobit with her fingers, then sat back and looked at No One. "Yes." She frowned. "But why take this route through the mountains. Why do we not turn back and go through Miira?"

He returned to the fire and stood next to it. "Was Goofy Joe's news so poor? I am not to come within sight of the town of Miira until the last bull dies."

"I will still come."

No One looked down at her. "Why?"

"I am a fortune teller. I would be a better fortune teller. It is important to the show."

"The *show!* The *show!* The show is dead! *Dead!*" He looked at the flames. "Dead." No One shook his head and looked up at the sky. The brightest of the stars were coming out. "All my life I have had the show spieled at me. Preserve the show." He barked out a bitter laugh. "Miira has almost two hundred bullhands, and only one bull. The horses are all at timbering and road building; there is no *audience!*" He looked back at the flames. "The show is dead."

She tested the cobit once more. "In your heart it is." She took the bread from the rock, broke it, and handed half to No One. "Why will you make the trip, No One? I don't think you feel all that much obligation for the use of my robe and wine."

No One glanced at the cobit in his hand, turned his head, and looked across the chasm. "I may not return home until the last bull, Reg, is dead. I am going to learn how to kill a bull."

Tarzaka's mouth opened in shock. "Before you were horrified at the death of your sister. That is *some* excuse, No One. But what you plan now is *murder!*"

He nodded, still looking into the darkness. "Yes."

"I will stop you."

He turned, looked down at her, and smiled. The fortune teller held her hands to her chest and gasped. "My powers are not developed, Tarzaka; but there are things I can move. Small things, true. But a blood vessel is not very large." He turned away and the fortune teller collapsed to the ground, gulping at the air. "Mind your tongue unless you wish me to pinch you again."

He squatted next to the fire and gnawed at his bread.

The western side of the Snake Mountain Gap could be reached by crossing the Table Lake River before it flows through the Snake Mountains, just north of the Town of Miira. The next crossing was on the north end of the gap in the Town of Dirak. Three nights later, in Dirak's square, the people of the town gathered around a large fire. Hoes, plows, scythes, and saws had been placed aside, and the chores of daily existence forgotten, for the Great Goofy Joe of Tarzak was to play the square. No One and Tarzaka were lost at the back of the crowd, their hoods up.

Tarzaka whispered, her voice trembling. "We have our provisions, No One. We should be going."

Slowly he shook his head. "I must do this."

"Do what?"

"I must hear what Goofy Joe has to say. I want to hear what the people of Momus will hear about me and about what I did."

"What if you are recognized?"

No One looked at the robes surrounding him until he found

an orange one. He reached out his hand and tapped the figure's shoulder. "Clown."

The figure turned. "Yes, fortune teller?"

"Have you any clown white in your kit?"

She raised her eyebrows. "Of course."

"Sell it to me."

The clown shrugged her shoulders, and reached into a pack suspended at her side by a strap that crossed her breast. Her hand came out of the pack holding a cloth-wrapped stick. She looked at No One. "I have half a stick."

"Five movills for it, then."

The clown laughed. "It cost me twenty for the stick."

"Ten then."

"There would be no profit in that, fortune teller."

No One studied the clown's face. "Fifteen."

The clown slapped the stick into No One's hand. "Done!" No One counted out the coppers then handed them to the clown. "Tell me, fortune teller, for what does a seer of fortunes need face paint?"

No One replaced his purse, then faced the clown. "What value do you place on my answer? I warn you that it is expensive."

The clown pocketed her coppers and turned back to face the square.

Tarzaka shook No One's arm. "What are you doing?"

He unwrapped the stick, then began to smear the white paint on his face. "I am hiding." In moments, No One's face was a stark white image broken only by his dark eyes.

"Laydeeeez and gentlemen!" All eyes turned toward the center of the square. A master of the ring was conducting the performance. "Tonight the Great Goofy Joe brings us important news from the town of Miira. Great Tackhammer, the master of the Dirak priests, and the singers of Dirak will assist."

A figure wearing the black and white diamonds of the priests replaced the master of the ring in the center of the square. He began in a quiet voice, and the crowd hushed. "It is written in the books of all of the priesthoods, that to have a circus, there must be bulls. Bulls are the circus's special animal; and bullhands are the keepers of a special trust."

Great Tackhammer removed a document from his robe and unrolled it. "This is copied from the archives of the Tarzak Priesthood. It is a letter written by the Great John J. O'Hara to the officials of World Eco-Watch—" Tackhammer was interrupted by loud hissing from the crowd. "The letter's date is March Fifth, Twenty-One and Twenty-Seven." Great Tackhammer began reading by the light of the fire.

"'My Dear Mister Chappin, I have pondered it ever since I was notified that your bunch filed for a restraining order to prevent my show from taking possession of the two bulls I ordered. We have done all of the forms, appeared at all the hearings, and have all of the permits and licenses required by the laws of three nations. There's enough paper hanging on each one of those pachyderms to supply my advance with bills for two seasons. And now you want to change the rules. As I said, I've pondered it. I figure there must be something in the water down your way.

"'The application for the restraining order says that your action is being taken "in the interests of the animals, and the heritage we hold in trust for future generations." If whoever wrote that is ever at liberty, I have a straw hat and cane waiting for him. Thanks to your brilliant management, the bull populations in both African and Indian preserves are crowded to where you hire hunters to go in and kill them. Then you cut them up for cat meat. But you don't even do that very well. Last summer over a hundred African bulls starved to death in the drought.

"'I don't suppose that any of you simps have figured out yet that those bulls are part of *this* generation's heritage, and that maybe *this* generation would like to get a peek at a bull. Now maybe getting shot and cut up for cat meat is better than being in a show. When times are lean, there are plenty of troupers that'd agree with you. But we care for the bulls; because without them, we wouldn't be a show. I've seen a lot of bullhands die to protect their animals; and I wonder just how many puzzle wizards in your paper factory ever died for an elephant? Hmmm?

"'To hell with it. Thanks to you people, it has taken me close to two years to close this deal, and I'll be damned if you're going ex it now. Either withdraw that application for a restraining order, or I'll dump one of *my* problems in *your* lap. You see, our snake charmer has a bunch of cobras and coral snakes, and I'm kind of concerned about their welfare. I just might send him and his poison hose collection over to your house and have you check into it.'"

Great Tackhammer lowered the letter. "This comes from The Great Patch Wellington's collection of letters he never allowed John J. O'Hara to send."

As Tackhammer moved from the square, the cashiers from Dirak collected the coppers from the crowd. A cashier paused in front of No One and held out her hand. "Coppers for the priest?"

No One glanced at her, then reached into his purse and handed her two movills. The cashier continued moving through the spectators as a figure in black newsteller's robes was helped by two apprentice newstellers to the center of the square. It was the Great Goofy Joe Master of the Tarzak Newstellers. He shrugged off the helping hands, and the apprentices retired. The newsteller spoke.

"Five days ago in the town of Miira, Johnjay, Little Will's son, killed five of the last six bulls on Momus." Not even the sounds of breathing broke the stillness. "May, Johnjay's sister, was trampled underfoot by the bulls, then Johnjay went and exed 'em." Goofy Joe looked around at the crowd, then held up his arms. "The town put Johnjay's trunk on the lot until Reg, the last bull, dies." Goofy lowered his arms, looked down, then back up at the crowd. "That's the long and the short of it."

The Great Goofy Joe looked around at the faces surrounding him. "May was a bullhand! Her mother is a bullhand! Her granddad, Bullhook Willy, was a bullhand. He was boss elephant man with the old show. Bullhook learned to handle bulls from Poison Jim Bolger with the Snow Show out of Spokane. Poison Jim died trying to calm an outlaw bull. People Bullhook knew and loved—Buns Bunyoro, Siren Sally Fong, Black Kate, and more—died working their bulls for the old show."

No One turned and began walking from the square. His pace quickened, but Goofy Joe's voice was not to be left so easily behind: "Bullhook Willy died after Number Three went down 'cause he went into the main carrousel when no one else would. He's the one who opened the doors. He died doing that."

Tarzaka caught up to No One, Goofy Joe's words still at his back.

"A lot of you are young. Never seen a show. You don't know what the bulls mean to the show. We only got one bull left, now. When Reg dies, the show dies."

No One began running. The Great Goofy Joe's voice covered the Town of Dirak. "Miira put Johnjay's trunk on the lot. What are you people going to do?"

The words screamed by the crowd moved his feet even faster. "Blackball! Blackball! Blackball!" As he left the edge of Dirak and ran along a timber road into the northern foot hills of the Snake Mountains, No One could hear the voices of the people of Dirak raised in song.

> *Black Diamond, old Black Diamond, you was a killer true;*
> *But nothin' can forgive what them Rangers done to you.*

TWENTY-FOUR

The news traveled quickly. From Anoki, Ikona, Dirak, and Ris in the Emerald Valley, south through Arcadia to Kuumic, and east through Tarzak and Sina across the Sea of Baraboo to Mbwebwe, the people listened in horror, then blackballed Johnjay, son of Little Will, no longer of the Town of Miira.

No One stood in the sparse trees at the crest of the Snake Mountains looking far down at the dense, distant expanse of jungle called the Great Muck Swamp. Tarzaka, breathing in gasps and dragging her pack by its strap, stopped several paces behind him, and leaned against the rocky wall of a ledge. She dropped the pack, rested her head against the ledge, and gulped at the air. After a moment, she squinted at their surroundings, then pushed away from the ledge. "We are at the top." She closed her eyes, sank back against the rocky wall, and slid down it until she was seated.

No One turned and walked back toward her. "The Great Muck is huge. I never realized how huge."

Tarzaka placed a hand across her middle and drew up her knees. "Are we to stop here for the night?"

No One looked at the sky, then frowned at the fortune teller.

"We have four hours of daylight left. We can put considerable distance between us and this place before night." He looked toward the swamp. "The sooner we make the swamp, the sooner we can find what we both seek." Tarzaka issued a brief, involuntary moan. No One studied her, then sat down upon the ground. "Is your belly after you again, fortune teller?"

The left side of her mouth drew into a bitter smile. "I have kept up so far, No One."

He glanced at her, then wrapped his arms around his knees. "Is there something you want to say?"

"I do not enjoy having my blood vessels pinched, No One. Therefore, I mind my tongue."

He studied her. "Yet you stay with me." He looked at her harder, seeing her pain for the first time. "What is wrong?"

The fortune teller shook her head, laughed, then winced with pain. "You are alone in your shell. So alone." She laughed again. "I have been groaning behind you for days. For days." She nodded. "And now you notice."

"I did not ask you to come along."

She shook her head, winced, and drew up her knees even further. "It was part of my price." She turned her head and stared at him from beneath her hood. "And you have yet to live up to your part of the bargain."

"I told you that I cannot tell fortunes. I can only see that which is likely to happen." He held out his hands. "Even then there are conditions."

"No One, you can also read minds. And you can move things. I would know how to do these."

No One pushed himself to his feet. "I don't know how to teach these things! Besides, why does a fortune teller need to know how to move objects?"

Tarzaka closed her eyes. "You might need that power soon."

He turned his back on her and stared out over the mountaintops. "Don't speak nonsense. If you are rested, let us be off. If we leave now, we can make the edge of the swamp in two days."

"I cannot move, No One."

He glanced back at her, then shrugged and looked back toward the swamp. "Then I shall leave you behind." He glanced over his shoulder at the fortune teller. "Are you coming?"

"You won't leave me behind, No One. I am your only audience."

He turned slowly, glaring at her, his face contorted in anger.

"What do you *mean?*" No One walked quickly to the fortune teller's side and shouted down at her. "What do you *mean?*" He stared at her for a moment, looking for her meaning in images; then staggered back a step as waves of pain assaulted his mind. He squatted next to her. "What can I do?"

Tarzaka shook her head. "Nothing right now. I must rest." Her eyes fluttered open, then closed in pain. "But you must think, No One, about what you must do. If you can pinch a blood vessel, then you can at least move small things. After I have rested, I want you to reach inside me with your mind and find the thing that makes me ill."

"Tarzaka, what if there is nothing I can do?"

"Then there is nothing you can do. But remember, No One, we have a bargain; you must try. Help me down. I must sleep."

No One helped her to lie down and adjusted her pack beneath her head for a pillow. She was on her side, wrapped into a tight ball. He felt the skin of her cheek and found it hot and dry. No One placed his hands upon his own face and found it hot and wet. Wiping his hands on his robe, he stood and began preparing their camp.

As evening's shadows chilled the mountaintop, No One rose from the fire he had built and spread his bullhand's robe over Tarzaka's still form. He tucked the robe around her body, sat next to her, and glanced at his unopened jug of sapwine. Shaking his head, he looked at the woman's face. "What do expect of me, Tarzaka?" he whispered.

Her lips barely moved. "To try."

His breath caught. "I didn't mean to awaken you."

"You didn't." She winced, then let her face relax. "We should begin, No One."

He nervously wet his lips, then pushed the fingers of his right hand through his damp hair. "I still don't know what to do—how I should go about it."

"No One, you said that you can see what may happen; that your image of what is to be is the clearer the more you know."

He closed his eyes and nodded. "Yes. But about this, I know so little."

"Then you must learn more." She pushed herself up upon an elbow. "Help me to my back, No One, then begin."

"Begin? Begin what?"

"Begin to learn. Reach inside me with your mind and learn."

He rose to his knees and helped the fortune teller to her

back. Once there, she began to stretch out her legs, then quickly drew them back as she issued a cry. "It...it hurts too much to lower my knees." She nodded. "Begin."

No One swallowed, wiped his face with his hands, then concentrated on Tarzaka's middle as he dried his hands upon his robe. Waves of pain washed over him, and he forced himself to blot it from his mind. Sensation by sensation, the sounds of the wind, the fire, the fortune teller's breathing, the beating of his own heart; he shut them out. The feeling of the rough soil beneath his knees, the wetness trickling down his back, the chill of the coming night; he shut them out. The taste of his own saliva, the smell of the burning wood, all thought of life, exile, and revenge; he shut them out, leaving only the fingers of his mind.

He moved those fingers forward until they reached Tarzaka's hot, rigid skin. "Deeper," he whispered. "Deeper." Heat. Wet heat. Slippery wet heat. The fortune teller moaned, and he quickly withdrew. "I'm sorry. I'm sorry." Again he wiped his face. "I cannot do this."

Tarzaka breathed deeply several times, then she nodded. "You must. Continue and use my cries for information. You must learn if you would see how to cure me. Go ahead."

No One dried his hands upon his robe, then again shut his mind to all but the fingers of his mind. The fingers again entered the fortune teller's body, and again she moaned. He moved the fingers gently to the left, gently up, gently down. Breathing heavily, he pressed the fingers deeper. Tarzaka moaned. "Do you feel them?"

"Yes. It is strange."

"Am I closer to the pain?"

"I cannot tell, No One. Everything hurts so."

No One wet his lips, nodded, then drew his fingers back slightly through the slippery wetness. He moved the fingers slightly to the right, and Tarzaka screamed. He started to withdraw but forced his fingers to remain in place. "Tarzaka. I see this much. This will hurt."

She snickered. "And you say you cannot tell fortunes."

"Quiet."

He moved the fingers first in one direction, then the next, trying to feel the outlines of the hardness beneath his touch. Tarzaka cried out loud several times. No One shook the cries from his mind and made his fingers travel around the object. They met resistance. He searched again, feeling the object sharply bending in upon itself. *Mange, Butterfingers, and their students in Candyjane Miira's horse barn, the dead animal on its back on the barn floor, it's stiff legs straight up, held by ropes. The students were laughing at Surenuff, one of the students, as he ran outside to empty his stomach. The belly of the horse was open, and Johnjay watched as Mange helped Mortify pull out the great shining coils of intestines.*

No One felt the coils and loops again and again, registering the shapes, the textures, the cries of the fortune teller. At a place on one of the coils, he wrapped his fingers around and squeezed. He felt the walls of the tube collapse until his fingers pressed against each other. "Does that hurt, Tarzaka?"

"No. I can feel it, but it doesn't hurt."

He nodded, then moved his fingers and squeezed again. "Now?"

"No."

He moved his fingers, squeezed, and met resistance as the fortune teller screamed and drew up her knees closer to her chest. He released the pressure on the coil, but kept his fingers in place. "Tarzaka. Your knees. Why did you draw them up?"

She gasped at the air. "It lessens the pain."

He moved his fingers along the coil until he met resistance. He frowned, then held his breath as he forced his fingers between the coil and the resistance. Again the fortune teller screamed. "Stretch out your legs."

"I cannot! The pain!"

"Stretch them out!"

The fortune teller cried out, then began lowering her knees. No One felt the pinch against his fingers just as she screamed and brought up her knees again. With her knees up, the pressure against his fingers was reduced. With an effort, he withdrew his fingers, then began feeling the outlines of the resistance.

"No One, what is it?"

"I am not certain. There is a loop of gut here. And it seems that there is . . . yes! Another loop of gut around the first!" He opened his eyes and looked at Tarzaka. "It is almost as though your gut is tied into a knot. It winds tightly about itself and it tightens when your legs straighten out. It loosens when you draw up your knees." He shook his head. "What do I do now?"

"Untie it."

Again he shook his head. "I cannot. I don't have the strength."

Tarzaka reached out a hand and placed it upon No One's

arm. "You must try. That was our bargain."

No One swallowed, shook his head, and swallowed again. "Even if I could, what would happen? Would your gut be like that if it wasn't supposed to be like that? What if I injured something, or released some terrible poison? I just don't know." He waved his hand at her middle. "The loop at the point within the twist—it is very hard. It is full of something."

"That is what is making me sick."

He nodded. "Yes, but it also makes the gut stiff..." No One pursed his lips as he studied his memory. "Perhaps."

"What is it?"

He rose on his knees until he hovered over her. "Stretch out your legs as far as you can." Gingerly, she lowered her knees until she cried out. No One sucked in and bit his upper lip as he closed his eyes and made his fingers enter the fortune teller's body. More rapidly this time, he located the loop. Keeping his fingers in the same area, he felt around the location. He felt more loops, a hardness. "Where is that?"

"It is deep—I don't know—a bone? Yes. The top of my hip."

He nodded and drew the fingers forward and up. He reached out his left hand, put it beneath the robe that covered the fortune teller, then moved the fingers of his hand between the folds of her robe until his fingers rested on Tarzaka's hot, rigid skin. He placed his hand, fingers extended, flat upon her belly. He took a deep breath, then tried to press the fingers of his mind against his hand through the fortune teller's skin. He grunted with the exertion, but felt a tiny pressure against the heel of his palm. Moving his hand until his fingers were where the heel of his hand had been, he pressed again. The pressure went against his index finger. "The fingers of my mind—so tiny. Didn't realize."

"Perhaps you should rest, No One."

He shook his head. "No." He breathed heavily for a few moments, then opened his eyes and looked at her. "When I tell you to, raise your knees toward your breast as far as you can. Understand?"

"Yes."

Again he closed his eyes. He grunted as he again checked the position of the pressure against his index finger. With the fingers of his mind, he reached toward the loop and located it immediately beneath the fingers of his hand. His mind-fingers felt their way along the loop until they came to where the gut

looped and crossed itself. The position of the knot was left,
and he moved to the draw end of the slip knot. Carefully he
wrapped the fingers of his mind around the gut and took several
deep breaths.

He nodded. "Now."

Tarzaka drew up her knees, trapping No One's left hand
between her thighs and belly. No One set his jaw, grimaced,
and pulled. They both screamed. "Your knees! Draw them up
farther!"

"I . . . can't—" Again she screamed.

No One felt the gut loosen, then move slightly, then stop
as the fortune teller's legs slumped to the ground. "Tarzaka!"
He looked at her face to find her unconscious. "By damn,
woman! Wake up!" His breath came hard. No One paused for
a moment, then reached down with his right hand and placed
it beneath the fortune teller's knees, keeping his left hand in
place. He lifted her knees toward her breast, bent over, then
placed the weight of his chest upon her knees.

The fingers of his mind renewed their grip, and pulled again.
"Almost . . . almost." He eased off, took several breaths, then
pulled again, pressing down against her belly with his left index
finger with all of his strength. His words came out in strained
gasps. "Now! . . . Move, damn you, move . . ." The veins stood
out on his neck and temples, his face became bright red.
". . . Moving. *Moving!*" He screamed with the effort, and
screamed again. Before the echoes of his last scream died, No
One was face down in the dirt, unconscious.

*It swims. It all swims. My feet flying over my head; the
world in chaos. . . . What is it down there. Mother. Mother! It's
me! It's me, Mother! Johnjay!*

*. . . until the last bull dies. They were silent as he walked
from the ring. Silent! Damn their silence! Damn them their
bulls! Damn them Reg! Reg! Reg! . . .*

His eyes opened to find himself looking up at a clear sky
colored with evening's dying orange. No One tried to sit, but
he winced with the effort. "I feel as if I had been whipped with
bull chains."

"No One?"

He pushed himself to a sitting position and looked at the
fortune teller. She was on her side, facing him. No One cocked
his head to one side. "Well? How are you feeling?"

"Pain. But different pain; good pain."

No One again looked at the sky. "A day. We have lost an entire day."

"Two days. You slept all through yesterday and last night."

He pushed himself to his feet, letting an involuntary groan escape from his lips. He moved to the site of the campfire, squatted down, and spread the fingers of his right hand above the bed of ashes. He nodded. "Umm. It is still hot." He blew at the ashes, exposing a few glowing coals, then he picked up a twig and gathered the coals together. He added twigs and sticks, blew air at the coals, and in moments the flames lit his face as they crackled the wood. No One glanced around, located the jug of sapwine, and picked it up. He drank deeply, letting the liquid ease his aching head and muscles. He drank again, then sat next to the fire.

Tarzaka got up, moved next to the fire, and sat down across it from No One. "Upon what are you thinking?"

He shook his head. "Nothing." His hand held up the jug. "A friend of mine from Miira—" He paused, then lowered the jug, shaking his head. "—a former friend. He calls this medicine." No One felt the tears tempting his eyes. "He is called Mortify, and he is an apprentice to old Mange." No One drank again.

"Mortify is no longer your friend?"

The jug came down. "I have no friends! Those I thought to be friends abandoned me before the town." He stabbed a finger at his chest. "Not one spoke for me. Not one offered me aid. Friends, bah!" He drank again, then stretched out his legs. "Ah, the aches ease. I never believed I could be so exhausted."

The fortune teller nodded. "It took much from you, No One." She reached into No One's pack and withdrew a wrap of cobit dough, then began shaping the cakes. She kept her gaze upon the cobit cakes as she spoke again. "You killed five bulls. Can any friendship be expected to withstand such a crime?"

No One looked down at the flames. "They killed my sister. I was right to do what I did."

"And what would your sister think of your deed, No One?" The fortune teller looked up at him. "If you could ask her now, what would she say to you?"

No One's eyes widened with horror, then he stood and flung the sapwine jug behind him where it shattered upon the rocks. "Damn you!" He held his fingers to his temples as his face twisted with unshed tears. "Damn you," he whispered. The hands came down and he turned from the fire. "Gather your things. We leave now."

"It is almost night."

"Gather your things!" He stooped, picked up his pack, and went to where Tarzaka had been sleeping. Bending over, he retrieved his bullhand's robe and stuffed it into his pack.

The fortune teller called to him. "We both need to rest, No One."

He slung the pack over his shoulder, then glanced at her. "If you are going with me, hurry." He walked into the growing darkness toward the mountain slope that would bring them down to the Great Muck Swamp.

Tarzaka quickly assembled her kit, shouldered it, then stumbled off into the dark after No One.

TWENTY-FIVE

Little Will sat upon the *kraal* fence, staring at the isolated grove of angelhair trees among whose roots Shiner Pete's body now rested. She swung the gold and mahogany bullhook by its handle, absent-mindedly tapping the hook and goad first against one sandal, then the other. The angelhair hung from the trees in long, lazy swirls, stirring themselves only slightly in the heat of the afternoon. Around the small grove was the lowgrass growing between the rotting stumps of the timbered out forest that once surrounded Miira. In time, thought Little Will, even the evidence of the stumps will be gone.

She heard a snort and turned to see Reg pulling up trunkfuls of dried lowgrass as the bull rested from her morning's workout with Standby. Young Bigfoot would show for her turn in a few minutes. Little Will sighed. It would be another two months before her turn with Reg. She turned back to look at the angelhair grove. A figure wearing the bullhand's striped robe moved from beneath the trees. Little Will frowned and shielded her eyes from the sun. It was Dorthidear, the daughter of Great Waxy and Great Dot.

Little Will nodded. Sometimes she forgot that Shiner Pete's father was also buried in the angelhair tree grove, as well as several others—Mange, Butterfingers, Packy, Cowboy, Snag-gletooth, Skinner, more.

After Dorthidear had walked out of sight, between the houses of Miira's newly named Mange Street, Little Will came down from the fence and began walking toward the grove. Halfway down the hill, she turned toward the town and looked at the barn in which, at her instruction, a crew of bullhands attempted to clean and assemble the skeleton of the bull Gonzo. Of the five bulls Johnjay had stampeded from the cliff's edge almost a year before, Gonzo's skeleton had the least broken bones. Reg would die—some day. Then the bullhands would have nothing but May's pictures, Gonzo's skeleton, and their memories to pass down to their children.

Little Will smacked the bullhook against her leg and con-tinued downhill until she came to the edge of the grove. Once into the shade, she noticed a figure in bullhand's robe seated by Great Waxy's grave marker.

"Dot?"

The figure turned toward her, then opened her mouth in an almost toothless grin. "Little Will? Come closer. It is you."

Little Will walked more deeply into the grove and stopped next to the old woman. "You're not well, Dot. You should be in bed."

Great Dot shook her head as she reached out a shaking hand to pluck weeds from her husband's grave. "I won't get any sicker being here. Besides the fresh air and sun's probably good for my bones." She glanced back at Little Will. "Dor-thidear'll be back to haul me to my bed in a couple of hours. Can't reason with that girl."

"She has more sense than you." Little Will sat next to the old woman. She looked across Waxy's grave and saw the fresh-turned soil that covered Shiner Pete. New blades of lowgrass were already springing from it. The paint on the wooden marker at one end of the grave was already beginning to crack. Its words read: Shiner Pete Adnelli, Master of the Miira Har-nessmen, Born June 16th, 2135; Died Winter 20th, YSC 32nd. Little Will felt Dot's hand on her arm.

"Child, child. Don't worry. Dusty has the rock for the headstones quarried. He promised to begin very soon."

Little Will smiled and shook her head. "That isn't it. I just can't believe Shiner Pete's gone. He was so young."

Dot withdrew her hand and resumed plucking away at the weeds. "Child, did you and Shiner talk much?"

"Of course." Little Will shrugged. "Well, we used to talk. Before Johnjay's trunk was put on the lot. Not much since then, I guess."

The old woman nodded, then sat up and rested her hands in her lap. "He would come to me and talk."

"You?"

"I was his stepmother."

"What would he say to you that he couldn't say to me?"

Great Dot leaned forward and straightened her husband's weathered grave marker. The letters were illegible. "Losing Johnjay ate out Shiner Pete's heart, Little Will. That's what killed him. The fall from the horse was his excuse."

"He didn't want to live? I don't believe that."

Dot shook her head and laughed—a laugh of sympathy, not of scorn. "Child, at times you're as thick as your old man was. I can't count the number of women in the old show that would've married that man in a second. But he just didn't know. Didn't even imagine that anyone but the Lion Lady could love him."

"You?"

Dot shook her head. "No. Not me. I had my bull." She looked at Little Will. "Do you remember Siren Sally?"

"No. The name, but I can't remember her face."

"She was one." Dot looked across the clearing at an over-grown pile of rocks that served as a grave marker for the original troupers buried in the trench cut by Number Three. Beneath that pile was Bullhook Willy. "Maybe I was one. I can't really remember." She looked back at Little Will. "From the day Shiner Pete saw Johnjay's trunk put on the lot, he was a dying man. It just took him a while and a fall to make him lie down."

Little Will shook her head as the tears began to fall from her cheeks. "I had to do what I did. *Johnjay killed the bulls!*"

Dot nodded, then gestured with her head up the hill toward the *kraal*. "I know what bulls mean, Little Will. I pushed bull long before you were born. I was there when Bullhook Willy got his name with the old show. But Johnjay was more important to Shiner Pete. He didn't have anything else."

"He had me."

"Did he?" Dot studied Little Will.

Little Will stared for a moment at her husband's grave, then she closed her eyes. "I thought . . . I thought he did." She slowly shook her head. "I don't know. I just don't know." Dot lifted her arm and put it around Little Will's shoulders, drawing Little Will's head against her breast. "Dot, I shut him out. I felt he blamed me, and I shut him out!"

Dot stroked Little Will's hair. "Honey, now listen to me. You were right in what you did. Shiner Pete was right in how he felt, but you were right in what you did."

"Was I wrong when I asked the town today to let me bring Johnjay back?"

"No. Not in your heart, Little Will. Shiner Pete is gone, and someday Reg will be gone. Now that you have to share Reg with all of the other bullhands, she might as well be gone now. You need someone, and you want your son. There's nothing wrong with that. It's just a damned shame the town voted you down."

"Shiner Pete needed someone, and I shut him out."

"He had me." Dot put her hand beneath Little Will's chin and lifted her head. Then, with the same hand, she wiped the tears from Little Will's face. "That's all in the past, now. You must think about the future."

"Dot, what should I do?"

"What do you want, child?"

Little Will collapsed against Dot's breast. "I want my son! I want Johnjay!" Her shoulders heaved as she freshened her cheeks with new tears. "Where is he, Dot? All the towns have blackballed him. He's been in the wild for almost a year. I don't know if he's even alive. I couldn't live if I found that he's dead." She looked up at Dot, the old woman's image blurred by her tears. "How can I get the town to change its vote."

"You can't. Little Will, no one can forgive what Johnjay did. Don't expect them to. But you can tell your son that you love him. Send your mind across the face of this planet, find him, and then tell him."

"What if he won't forgive me? I couldn't bear it, Dot. What if I can find him and he won't forgive me?"

"Still he must know. And you must tell him. Remember your father."

Little Will sat up and sniffed. "My father?"

"Bullhook fought with his dying breaths to be with you. To let you know that your father loved you. I was there and saw him. He didn't make it, but he tried." Dot held Little Will's chin, forcing the Master of the Miira Bullhands to look into her eyes. "And you hated him for dying—for leaving you. Didn't you?"

Little Will pulled away from the old woman's grasp, but continued to stare at her. She stood, wiped the tears from her face, then looked toward the *kraal*. Bigfoot was making her way up the hill for her turn at the bull. "For a while." She looked at the woman. "Am I so awful, Dot?"

"No." The old woman resumed plucking the weeds from her husband's grave. "You are not bad. Just human."

Little Will looked down at Great Dot, then turned and looked at the overgrown pile of rocks that covered the dead from Number Three. She walked to the grave, squatted down, then began pulling the weeds from it. "I'm sorry, Daddy. I'm so sorry."

Far west of Miira, No One stood on a highgrass-covered rise looking up at the tall trees that rose straight from the mud and water of the Great Muck Swamp. The high leaf cover darkened the swamp, making the air still and dank. Here and there a slender shaft of sunlight would break through briefly illuminating the dust, vapor, dancing waterwasps and punks-quitoes before the wind at the top of the trees shifted the leaves, cutting off the beam.

He brought his gaze down and looked for sweetwater bub-bles among the death-white bulb lillies floating close to the spongy rise upon which he stood. "Bah! The sweetwater comes up everywhere except at a convenient place." He looked back at the trail his steps had made through the highgrass. "I've come far enough, and spent enough time. I hope that woman has sense enough to stay at the camp."

He looked back at the water, grimaced, then put down the water jug, shucked his robe and kicked off his sandals. Picking up the jug again, he stepped off of the rise and sank up to his chest in the swamp's rot-smelling ooze, and half-paddled, half-walked his way through the bulb lillies to the nearest of the ripples marking the sweetwater. As he reached it, his skin was chilled by the sweetwater's lower temperature. He uncapped the water jug, lowered it into the water, and stood quietly waiting for it to fill.

"Magoo, magoo."

No One frowned at the sound of the deep-pitched words; then he heard more sounds—muck being sloshed, small trees and brush being broken and crushed. He glanced back at his robe, then turned in the direction of the sounds and lowered himself until the water covered his shoulders.

"Mm, borg borg, da magoo."

The sounds of sloshing and crashing grew louder; and No One sank further into the water until the surface was just beneath his nose. Between the distant trees, he could see movement. Whatever it was had to be enormous. *By Momus,* thought No One, *it is one of the swamp monsters!* Smaller trees were pushed aside, then a beam of sunlight illuminated the thing's massive head for a second. It was green and scaled, the mouth lined with many sharp-looking teeth.

"Dorry borry, bung bung, foo magoo."

No One caught a snootful as the creature swung its great tail around, then planted its fàt behind into a sitting position. It had arms and hands, and the creature placed its hands upon its knees and looked around. "Stooba dooba, de da ma," Its tongue whipped out, bringing down probably several water-wasps. "—goo."

It reached down a hand, plucked a bulb lilly from the water, then popped the ball-shaped flower into its mouth, severed the plant's long stem and root, and tossed it aside. After eating several of the bulb lillies, the creature belched, then began gathering a number of the bulbs in the crook of its huge left arm.

"Mm borg borg, mm borg borg, da da magoo."

No One frowned as he realized the monster was singing. He frowned more deeply as the creature's harvesting operation caused its huge hand to begin plucking bulbs closer and closer to No One's head. No One was torn between diving and breaking for the highgrass; hence, he did nothing. The creature's hand reached out, the scaled fingers grabbed No One's head, then No One began kicking and shouting as he was pulled by his head from the water.

"Oz?"

The creature's eyes widened as its mouth fell open. The monster bellowed a scream, dropped No One, then threw up its arms and fled in a shower of scattered bulb lillies. By the time No One had surfaced, coughed the water from his lungs and cleared his eyes, the monster was gone. No One retrieved his water jug, shivered, and began making his way toward the highgrass.

Back at their camp that evening, Tarzaka cooked the cobit and watched No One's preoccupied stare into the fire's flames. The light from the fire made the shadows of the swamp trees dance as though they were alive. "You have been very quiet since you brought back the water."

"Yes." No One looked up at the fortune teller, then back at the flames. "I met one of the swamp monsters. I never thought they were real." He slowly shook his head. "Huge. As big as two bulls."

Tarzaka held her hand to her mouth. "What . . . what should we do?" She leaned forward. "Are you certain?"

"Hah! The thing picked me up by my head! A closer look I can do without."

"What should we do? How do we cross the swamp to the Arcadia–Miira Road?"

He clasped his hands together and shrugged. "We walk, as before." He again looked at the fortune teller. "A strange thing . . . I felt that it was not dangerous—at least not by intention. It sang."

"Sang? The monster?"

"It sang. At least it sang until it discovered that this bulb," he pointed at his head, "is attached to something more lively than a lilly stem." He shook his head. "I think the thing was more frightened of me than I was of it. I cannot imagine why something that large would ever be frightened."

"It is said that bulls can be frightened by small things: a noise, a gust of wind, the flash of a piece of paper."

No One nodded. "True. Still, the thing was so huge." He turned and looked over his shoulder at the shadows. Were great slitted eyes looking back? He looked back at the fortune teller. "My father used to tell me of the time he and my mother sent their minds into the swamp. My mother said she actually touched one of the creature's minds." He looked down at the fire.

"Well, what happened?"

"The monster fled. She had frightened it."

The fortune teller cocked her head to one side and frowned. "No One, do you have this power? Can you send your mind?"

He shrugged. "I suppose. I haven't done it since May . . . since my sister and I were children. The feeling is unpleasant."

Tarzaka stared at No One. "Unpleasant," she repeated. She spat into the fire. "What a waste, you are, No One! What a terrible waste you are!" She stood and turned to go to her sleeping place.

"Mind your tongue!"

She faced him. "What will you do, No One? What will you do, bull killer? Will you hurt me again? Is that all you can do with your wonderful gifts: kill bulls and hurt people?"

She stood next to the fire. "What I could do if I but had *one* of your gifts! What I could do!" She shook her fist at him. "For all the use you make of your gifts, it would have been no loss had that monster torn off your head!" She lowered her arm to her side, turned, went to her sleeping place, and stretched out in the highgrass, her back toward No One.

"It is good that you paint your face, No One. You are truly more clown than fortune teller."

No One glared at the fortune teller's back. A score of excuses rushed to his mouth, but he stopped them and looked down into the flames.

I will develop my powers, Tarzaka. A bull named Reg and I have a date.

He turned and faced the shadows, closing his eyes. It had been so long. Slowly the feelings of his body dropped away, one by one. Then he could again see the shadows.

The mind alone is so lonely.

He let his mind drift upwards, above the light and shadows, above the trees, far, far above the swamp. He looked up at the sky.

Can I fly to those other worlds? Do I have the power?

Up he went, faster and faster. The stars became very bright, their twinkle ceased, then the full light of the sun washed him. Still the stars remained visible. He looked down. The edge of the planet toward the sun was brightly lit. Beyond that edge, where the Great Muck should have been, was nothing but darkness. *Lost! Lost!* He began toppling down toward the darkness, a fall that he could not control. Down and down, a sickness called fear opened his mouth and forced out a child's scream of terror at the unknown.

No One opened his eyes to find himself back at the fire. He glanced at the fortune teller, but her back was still toward him. The scream, he guessed, had been in his mind. He stretched out and watched the flames until the sleep drifted over him.

"Johnjay. Johnjay. Can you hear me?"

He floated in gray aether, the threads of the voice speaking at him, a breath against his mind. "Who . . . Mother?"

"I've been searching for you, Johnjay. For so long—"

His gray turned to black. "You have nothing to say to me."

"Wait!" A ghostly white swirl ate at one edge of his blackness. "Johnjay, wait!"

"Is Reg dead?"

"...No."

"Call for me when Reg is dead. Until then, you have nothing to say to me." He began forcing the white swirl from his blackness.

"Johnjay, it's your father."

He paused. "What ... what about him?"

"Johnjay, he's dead. He's—"

"Then you are alone, too." That which should have been grief glittered before him—a shining altar of hate. "Good."

"John—"

"Call me when Reg is dead, Mother. That's all I want to hear."

"Johnjay, I lo—"

"Call me when the bull is dead."

His eyes opened. He sat up and looked at the fire's smoking embers, then up at the few stars that had yet to be washed from the sky by the morning's light. He felt something touching the outlines of his thoughts. He placed a wall of coldness against the something, then looked down at the fortune teller. "Tarzaka." He shouted. "Tarzaka!"

She turned over and looked at No One. "What is it?"

He pushed himself to his feet. "Get ready. We are going now."

She looked at the sky, then back at No One. "Now?"

"Now!" He hefted his pack. "We have a lot of swamp to search. The sooner we start, the sooner we find Waco's eggs."

TWENTY-SIX

Little Will sat in Turtlehead's house as the shelled priest held up a paper. "This is the letter of which I spoke, Little Will. I think it may be a clue as to the location of Johnjay. But I cannot be certain."

"Please. Go ahead and read it."

Turtlehead's tiny red eyes scanned the paper as he spoke. "It is from my first apprentice, Noodlebrain.

"'I am writing this to you from the town of Porse, enroute to Tarzak to learn spieling from Great Motor Mouth, as you instructed. To be frank, I hold little hope that the addition of patter will increase the fees priestly acts receive when performing. It is not that our acts cannot stand improvement. Instead, perhaps it is that the average Moman priest does not have enough grifter in his soul.

"'For example, as I was returning from Miira to join the other apprentice priests from Arcadia at the Porse Cutoff, I made camp upon the road for the night. There I was joined by Trouble, an exiled magician from Dirak. He is on the road attempting to earn suffcent funds to replace those that he stole, causing his exile. Trouble did not look like he was a very interesting magician, but out of sympathy for his plight, I bought a performance from him for five movills. The trick he did was mildly interesting; however, in turn he purchased nothing from me! Instead he presumed to lecture me on the fundamentals of separating a fool from his coppers!

"'Whilst this gratuitous palaver was being endured, two fortune tellers—named No One and Tarzaka—entered the camp and exchanged cobit. The one called No One was male and had his face curiously made up in clown white. Tarzaka appeared to be much older than No One; and she remained silent and cross during their entire stay in camp. Both of their robes were torn and soiled from the swamp.

"'I inquired into No One's strange make up, and learned that his answer would beggar the Great Mootch Movill himself! He wanted a *thousand coppers* for his answer! My curiosity regarding No One's paint rapidly cooled.

"'Trouble, the magician, then asked the fortune tellers if they wished to see some magic. Tarzaka shook her head, but No One agreed to a performance and requested the trick Trouble had just performed for me. I cannot imagine how No One could have known what trick I had just seen; but what angered me was that, had I waited, I could have witnessed the trick for *nothing!* At least, that was what I thought.

"'When Trouble attempted the trick, however, it was almost as though unseen hands kept rearranging his cards. He tried the trick four times, each time failing. Tarzaka watched this sorry spectacle without once registering surprise. Exasperated, Trouble gave up and No One kept his coppers.'"

Little Will held out her hand. Turtlehead, let me read the rest for myself."

The priest paused for a moment, then handed her the paper. Little Will eagerly took the paper and began reading.

I asked No One if he would like me to recite history for him, explaining that I am becoming known for my "Epic of the *City of Baraboo*." He wanted to hear no lengthy recitations. But No One did offer me ten movills for the answers to three questions a Moman priest should be able to answer. However, to obtain the amount, or any part of the amount, I must be able to answer correctly all three questions. I agreed.

"You have recently returned from the town of Miira?"

I nodded. "Yes."

"Then, Noodlebrain, does Shiner Pete of the Miira Harnessmen still live?"

I smiled, for I had made the entry in the Miira Book myself. Since it was no longer news, but history, I could answer. "No. Shiner Pete was killed by a horse the 20th of last month." I sensed, rather than saw, an enigmatic emotion go through the fortune teller's body.

Then he asked: "Does the bull, Reg, still live?"

This was easy, as well, for I had seen the bull myself. "Yes, Reg is alive. The bullhands guard her day and night in case the bull-killer, Johnjay, should return to finish his evil deed."

No One glanced at the fire's flames, then looked up at me. "And the third question, Noodlebrain: Exactly where did the Great Waco Whacko hide the Ssendissian eggs?"

I felt my belly go sour. "No one knows that—I mean, No One, the priests do not know that."

"Then you do not get paid." He leaned forward. "Can I sell you a fortune?"

Curse the cage in which he sleeps! "No!"

He nodded once, then smiled at me. His smile was a cruel thing mounted upon that ghastly white mask.

"Your performance was of some small value to me. I shall answer the question you think the most important." His eyes studied me for a moment, then he bowed his head and laughed. He got to his feet, shouldered his pack, and motioned to Tarzaka to do the same. Then he looked down at me. "You will die copperless, Noodlebrain. Wealth is not in your future."

Tarzaka stood, then the pair walked off into the night. Shortly after, Trouble the magician bid me a good night's sleep, and then ran after the two fortune tellers, leaving me alone at the fire, as well as five coppers poorer.

Little Will placed the paper upon Turtlehead's table. "It is Johnjay. I am certain of it. The one called No One is my son."

Turtlehead looked at the sheet. "Why does he search for the eggs?"

She turned and looked into the brightly lit street. "I do not know."

No One and Tarzaka walked the road by starlight. When they were well away from the apprentice priest's camp, she spoke to her white-faced companion. "You saw your father's death?"

He shook his head. "No. I was told in a dream."

"The death of the bull?"

"That was, I fear, little more than wishful thinking, Tarzaka."

They walked in silence for a time, then Tarzaka looked at No One. "When will you again try to put pictures in my mind? It has been a week since you last tried."

"I have tried a hundred times, Tarzaka." No One shook his head. "I cannot find the threads that I must arrange to place an image into your head. Even something as small as a word."

"No One, you *must* try again."

"It is no use!" He switched his pack from his right shoulder to his left. "That is why we must find the eggs. If there is any chance for you, they—" He stopped and stood motionless.

"No One—"

He cut off her words by holding up his hand. "Be still," he whispered. "We are being followed."

Tarzaka held her hands to her mouth, turned and tried to look into the blackness of the road. The swamp insects gnawed at them both as they stood as statues in the dark. "I hear nothing."

"He is not walking."

"He?"

No One nodded. "It is Trouble, the magician we left at Noodlebrain's camp."

"What does he want of us?"

No One stood silent for a few heartbeats, then he laughed. "Trouble!" he shouted. "Come out, come out, wherever you are!" No One pointed down the road toward a shadow moving from the darkness. "There he is."

"What does he want?"

No One shook his head. "He wants to know how I ruined his card trick, but . . ."

"But?"

"I cannot read the rest, Tarzaka. There is a wall around his mind." No One looked at Tarzaka. "Be on your guard."

They watched the shadow grow until Trouble stood before them. His teeth were visible in the starlight. "Greetings, Johnjay." He nodded toward the woman. "Tarzaka."

No One studied the figure's form. "My name is No One."

Trouble shook his head. "You are Johnjay. The bull-killer from Miira. The one who has been blackballed in every town on Momus—"

"How do you *know* this?"

The figure stood quietly for a moment, then Trouble shook his head. "I am not certain. I just know. The news of your deed extends even into the swamp, and the questions you asked, the apprentice priest's answers, the things you did to my cards." Trouble shrugged. "They put themselves together and told me you were Johnjay—"

"By Momus's great fat pratt!" Tarzaka cut the magician short, then she turned, went to the side of the road, and began preparing a fire.

Trouble pointed toward her and spoke to No One. "What is *her* complaint?"

No One glanced after Tarzaka, then turned back to look at Trouble. "Of the three of us, she is the only one who apprenticed as a fortune teller. And of the three of us, she is the only one who cannot tell fortunes."

Trouble chuckled as he saw Tarzaka's head turn toward them for a moment, then turn back toward her preparations. "Again Momus's sense of humor inflicts itself upon his children."

"Will you join us in our camp? The fire is free."

Trouble studied No One. "Why would you invite me?"

"I prefer having you in the light—where I can keep an eye on you."

"I think we might be of profit to each other." Trouble nodded. "Very well, Johnjay."

"I am called No One."

"If you prefer."

"I prefer."

As they walked toward Tarzaka, she began striking her flint and steel, causing hot fat sparks to shower upon the tinder.

Trouble washed down his final mouthful of cobit with sap-wine, brushed the crumbs from his robe, and smiled at Tarzaka. "Fortune teller, your cobit grows cold."

Tarzaka tossed her bread into the fire. "I am not hungry."

No One frowned at her. "You needn't have thrown it away."

"It was mine. I do with my own what I choose." She stood, turned her back upon the two men, and walked from the fire into the night.

Trouble laughed at her, then turned to face No One. "It certainly galls her, doesn't it?" When No One failed to answer, Trouble looked at the fire, his face growing somber. "No One?"

"Yes?"

"Tell me how you ruined my trick."

No One adjusted his pack and stretched out before the fire, his head propped up upon one arm. "What profit is there for me?"

The magician's large frame shook as he again laughed. Trouble wiped imaginary tears from his eyes, sighed, and nodded at No One. "Profit." He made a slight gesture with his hand in a northeasterly direction. "You asked that idiot apprentice priest about Waco's eggs."

No One's eyes narrowed. "Do you know where they might be found?"

"No. Not yet." He shrugged. "I am not certain that they even exist—or ever did exist." He raised an eyebrow in No One's direction.

"I know that they exist, Trouble."

"We live in an age that prides itself in the art of lying."

"Nevertheless." No One's head lolled back. "But then, Trouble, how can your ignorance be of profit to me?"

Trouble looked back at the flames. "I have wandered the Great Muck for almost four years. My ignorance will be of no use, but the things I know speak differently."

No One shrugged. "Such as?"

"Did you know that toward the Upland Mountains there is one of the great swamp lizards that talks?"

No One sat up. "Talks, you say?"

Trouble nodded. "I have heard him speak myself. And there is more. There are other exiles in this swamp, and I have heard some of them speak of a strange swamp woman. It is claimed that all the creatures of the swamp serve and obey her."

No One lowered his head to his pack. "These are curious fantasies, but what do they have to do with Waco's eggs?"

The magician shrugged. "Where else would one get the power to control the monsters of the swamp?" He looked at No One. "To make them speak?" Trouble looked back at the flames. "I cannot see it all, but I see enough to know that these things need to be investigated—if one is interested in finding Waco's eggs."

"And all you want in return is to know how I ruined your trick?"

Trouble shook his head. "Not how; I want to know how to do it. I want to move things with my mind, as can you."

No One smiled. "How do you know I have this power?"

"I am able to do that simple trick in my sleep!" The magician snorted. "It was either you or ghosts!" Trouble grinned. "And I do not believe in ghosts."

"What if I cannot teach you what you wish to know? You might not be able to learn."

Trouble gestured with his head toward where Tarzaka had disappeared in the darkness. "You have a similar arrangement with the woman, do you not?"

No One studied the magician for a long time. Then he shrugged and looked at the flames. "I was already in her debt. But I have no reason to believe that she can ever learn the things that she wants to learn."

"Yet she travels with you."

"She hopes that the eggs can teach her the things she wants to know."

"Perhaps they can do the same for me." Trouble wet his lips. "And I might have something else that could interest you, No One."

"What is that?"

"I think you want to know how I cloak my mind against your thoughts. Do I speak the truth?"

No One sat up, studied the magician, then pushed himself to his feet. "You read minds?"

Trouble shook his head. "No. I cannot. But I can prevent others from reading mine. My younger brother, Tribulation, can read minds. I had to learn how to prevent him from reading mine if I was ever to have a thought of my own. I learned to stop him." He looked at No One. "As I stopped you."

No One looked into the darkness, then turned back to the magician. "Once we come to the eggs, I will do what I can if you have been useful in finding the eggs."

"The other?"

No One shrugged. "I have had little occasion where protecting my mind was necessary." He frowned and, for a moment, pondered the reach of his mother's thoughts. He slowly nodded. "Yes. I would learn the other, as well. But we must find the eggs, and you must help. That is the price."

Trouble held out his hands. "We strike a bargain."

"Wait here. I'd best find out what's happened to Tarzaka."

The magician shrugged. "She is off whining someplace. Why bother?"

"She might be injured."

"What is that to you?"

No One looked from the darkness to the flames, then from

the flames to the magician. No One frowned, shook his head, and looked into the darkness once more. "Wait here." He left the fire and walked after the fortune teller.

He found her, far from the camp, sitting atop a roadside stump. "What are you doing?"

She sat huddled in the darkness. "Go back to the fire, No One. You cannot understand what I think with your crippled head."

"Make yourself plain."

Her dark form shook its head. "Nothing. I meant nothing. Go back to the fire."

"Then come along."

"No." Her head lifted and her eyes looked at the stars. "It is unfair. It is *so* unfair."

"That Trouble and I can see the probable and you cannot?"

Her head snapped in No One's direction. "Yes!" She stabbed a finger at her breast. "I am the fortune teller! *I* am!" She looked back at the stars. "I am the only one of us who wants to be a teller of fortunes. What force is it that chooses who is to receive these things? What sarcasms occupy its mind?"

No One laughed. "You would look for fairness in a world created at the hands of a madman? You look for justice within Arnheim's perverted legacy? What would you call fairness, Tarzaka? That if I desired it I would be granted the skin, face, or form of a freak? That if I wanted to make others laugh, I would be granted the skills of the clowns?" Again he laughed. "You ask nonsense questions, and are full of fantasy." No One looked toward the camp, then back at Tarzaka. "Trouble has agreed to help us find the eggs. Are you coming?"

She issued a brief, bitter laugh. "And now a loutish thief joins our little band." Tarzaka shook her head. "Trouble can be your audience now. Why do you need me?"

"I *don't* need you! I never did!" No One stared at the dark figure for a long moment. "Tarzaka, what do you mean about my audience? When you say that, what do you mean?"

She turned toward him, the shadow of her hood making her faceless in the starlight. "You can do so much—so much that I want to do—yet you know so little, No One. So little." She waved her hand in the direction of the camp. "Go back to your new disciple, No One. I will be along later. For now, leave me alone."

"Tarzaka—"

"Just go, bull-killer. Go!" Her hand dropped to her lap, and No One could hear her crying. "Just go."

He paused, then turned and walked toward the camp with slow steps.

TWENTY-SEVEN

For all of the next day the trio walked southwest on the road to Arcadia. That night they halted next to a large lake and built their fire at a place where the stars reflected from the lake's still waters, placing the limits of the sky in that direction beneath their feet. As Tarzaka prepared the cobit, and Trouble attempted to regale her with nonsense tales of the swamp, No One stood on the lake's shore looking out across its surface. In the dark, the far shore was invisible between the stars of the sky and the stars of the water.

What must it be, he thought, to leave the hopelessness of this prison behind? What would it be to move among those many suns?

He studied the constellation called the Big Lot; four extremely bright stars forming a rectangle. It was said that the two stars forming the Forty-ninth Street side pointed to the place from which O'Hara's Greater Shows originated. But the sun being pointed at was not bright enough to appear in the sky. Other constellations contained or pointed at the suns of other stands the old show had played. It was said that the dim tip of the right tusk of the constellation of Ming was the sun around which orbited the planet Ahngar. Ahngar, one of the old show's wintering grounds. Ahngar, the home of Sergeant Spook Tieras, retired bullhand. "At least old Spook can see his homestar," No One said to the night air.

He turned and walked up the slight rise to where Trouble and Tarzaka were sitting before the fire. Tarzaka looked up at him as he came within the light from the fire. "The cobit is done."

After No One sat down and was finishing his cobit, Trouble held out his arms. "Such silence! Here we have a fire, a pleasant night, fortune tellers and a magician. We should have entertainment."

No One's face remained impassive. "After your endless jabbering upon the road today, I welcome the silence."

The magician shrugged. "My talk might not be worth a storyteller's copper, but we do have a bargain. Show me how you ruined my trick. How do you move things with your thoughts?"

No One leaned upon his pack. "And for this, you show me how you cloak your mind?"

"Yes."

"Very well. Take out your cards and perform your trick."

Trouble reached into his robe and withdrew his worn deck of cards. He handed the deck to Tarzaka. "Go through the deck and choose a card, then show the card to No One." The magician spread a thick cloth upon the ground before him.

The fortune teller flipped through the deck, showed the Boss of Animals to No One, then looked at Trouble. "And now?"

"Shuffle the cards and hand them to No One." Tarzaka did as she was instructed. Trouble nodded at No One. "Shuffle them again." No One shuffled the cards. When he was finished, he returned them to the magician. Trouble took the cards and spread the deck faces down upon the cloth. Once, twice his hand passed over the cards, and then he reached down, picked up a card, and held its face out toward Tarzaka and No One. The card was the Boss of Animals.

No One nodded. "Well done. Now perform the trick again."

Trouble gathered up the cards, shuffled them, then handed the deck to Tarzaka. This time the fortune teller picked the Four of Shovels, showed it to No One, then shuffled the cards and handed the deck to No One who also shuffled them. No One handed the deck to Trouble. The magician spread the cards as before, pulled out a card, and faced it toward his two companions. It was the Nine of Wheels. Trouble raised his eyebrows. "And?"

Tarzaka smiled. "It is the wrong card, Trouble." She leaned to her right and flipped over cards until she came to the Four of Shovels. She tapped the card with her finger. "That was the one I selected."

The magician looked at No One. "Well? How do you do it?"

No One gestured with his hand toward the cards. "Do the trick again, but slowly."

Trouble gathered the cards, shuffled them, then handed the deck to the fortune teller. Tarzaka selected the Deuce of Flags and showed the card to No One.

No One sat up and looked at the fortune teller. "And now, Tarzaka, you shall see fortune telling at work. Do you see the deck in your hand?"

"Of course."

"Replace the card you picked." He turned toward Trouble. "It is the Deuce of Flags." He looked back at Tarzaka. "Do you see where you placed the card?"

"Yes."

"Our magician also sees. Shuffle them. As you shuffle them, Trouble will be watching. And he will watch as I shuffle them. When he spreads them out, something will tell him which card is the most likely to be the proper one. Not magic, but the same sight you call fortune telling in me."

Tarzaka studied the deck, then shuffled the cards, and handed them to No One. No One handed the deck to Trouble without shuffling them. "Go ahead; but once you see the card that you want, pick it up very slowly."

Trouble spread the deck upon the cloth. He studied the cards, then his eyes widened for a moment, then he reached out his hand. As his hand came close to the card he had selected, its edge disappeared beneath the card that covered it. "Hah!" Trouble brought up his hand as though it had been burned; then he brought his hand down and turned over the top card. It was the Seven of Flags. He turned over the card immediately beneath it and exposed the Deuce of Flags. He looked at No One. "How do you move the card?"

"I reach for it. As though I had another set of hands. I just reach for it, feel its touch, then I push. That is all."

Trouble snorted. "That is no answer!"

No One looked at the magician through half-closed eyes.

"Can you explain to Tarzaka how you know which card to choose?"

"Certainly. It... well, I just do. I have studied the cards many times, people's hands, and the way they shuffle cards."

"Still, Trouble, how do you know which is the right one?"

The magician's shoulders went up. "I just do. It's a feeling—as though the card announced itself to me. I can do the actual selection with my eyes shut, just using my touch."

No One shrugged. "That is no better than my explanation. I did have to train this power. My mother started me with little things, and when I could handle them with ease, bigger things. They were children's games and I soon lost interest. But the mechanism I use is no more understood by me than is the power to see the probable."

Tarzaka clasped her hands and rested her chin upon them. "Did she also train you to see the probable?"

"More games. She used to toss a wooden ball into the air, and I would have to guess where it would come to rest." His eyes became haunted. "She tried to teach these things to my sister; but May's gift was a set of crippled legs. May could not learn."

Tarzaka turned toward Trouble. "May I borrow your cards?"

Trouble gathered the cards and held them out. "In exchange for the cobit?"

She nodded and took the cards. She fanned them and studied the faces of the cards. "On its own the mind can see fast enough to make judgements as to order, place..." She nodded again.

Trouble threw her his cloth. "Here. It will keep the cards clean."

As Tarzaka spread the cloth and began spreading, arranging, and studying the cards, Trouble turned to No One. "Still, I want to know how to move things."

"I told you. Practice. Enough practice will tell you if you have the ability. But I cannot give you the ability."

"Mmm." Trouble shook his head, studied the ashes in the fire, then grunted. "Bah!" He grunted again, then let out a breath as he looked up at No One. "Can anything be lighter than ash?"

"Trouble, you must sort what you wish to move from everything else. I began with but a single piece of dust."

"Hunh! Dust, eh?" He scratched his chin and shook his head. "If I could but move things, my fortune as a magician..." He looked at the fire, then back at No One. "I could pay off

Gluey, my victim, and buy back my place in Dirak town. By Momus! I could even become Master of the Dirak Magicians!" He nodded vigorously and rubbed his hands together.

No One looked at the fortune teller, saw her studying the cards, and looked back at the magician. "How do you cloak your mind, Trouble?"

Trouble pursed his lips, shrugged, and held out his hands. "It's much the same sort of thing, No One. I think it and it is done." He scratched his head. "I had to try thinking of many things before I could keep Tribulation from seeing my thoughts—he saw them as pictures before his eyes." He shook his head. "Many things. Then one day Tribulation was angry with me. He could not see my thoughts. Instead he saw a blackness that seemed to cover me in his pictures."

No One studied Trouble's face. "A blackness..." He sat up. "What were you thinking of?"

"Nothing." He raised his eyebrows. "I was trying to think of nothing so that there would be nothing for my brother to see." The magician shrugged. "But it is impossible to think about nothing. If you are thinking you have to think about something."

"Trouble, you said, *'If* you are thinking.'"

"Yes. That is what I was trying to do—to stop my mind altogether—" Trouble leaned forward, his face angry. "I tell you my brother was near to driving me madder than Arnheim's bedbugs! I was willing to try anything!" He sat back. "I couldn't stop thinking." He pointed a finger at No One. "But in *trying* to stop, I did something." He shook his head. "A dullness. I felt as though there were a pressure upon the tops of my eyeballs. My eyes are a bit out of focus, but I can still think when I do that. And no one can get into my mind to see what is there. Is that enough?"

No One studied the flames, then looked up at Trouble. "I think so. Yes. I think so." No One reached behind himself, picked up two sticks, and added them to the fire. "Trouble?"

"Yes?"

"What of the swamp woman you told us about?"

Trouble stretched out, placed the back of his head upon his pack, and looked up at the stars. "I have heard of her. She is supposed to live near this lake."

"What powers does she have?"

Trouble lifted his hands and let them fall upon his chest.

"To hear some of the exiles tell of them, she can crumble mountains with the mere snap of her fingers. Others say she is mad." He turned his head to look at No One. "Twice I have heard the rumor that she is the daughter of Great Waco himself." He looked back at the stars. "Who knows what is truth and what is legend?"

Tarzaka looked up from the cards. "The priests say that all legend is rooted in fact."

Trouble drew down the corners of his mouth. "The Noodlebrains of Momus." The magician continued looking at the stars. "The priests also tell us that the old show's route man, the Great Ratman, is up among those stars someplace trying to find us. And someday he will return and put us upon the star road once again." He closed his eyes and clasped his hands upon his chest. "It has been thirty-three years since the Crash. If he has not found us now, he never will. I see that much of the future."

No One looked up at the stars, then down at the magician. "How do we find the swamp woman?"

Trouble shrugged and settled himself more comfortably. "I imagine that we start searching the shores of the lake."

Tarzaka looked toward the star-spangled expanse of water. "It is a very large lake."

Trouble snickered and turned his back upon the fire. "Ah, Tarzaka, and you say that there is no fortune teller in your blood." He snickered again and then was still.

Tarzaka, her face flushed, returned to studying the cards, while No One pushed himself to his feet and returned to the lake's shore. He sat for a long time staring at the stars reflected in the water. The swamp was unusually quiet. He frowned as he noticed that the stars before his eyes were moving—ripples upon the water.

He stood as he heard the soft singing of a deep voice coming from a great distance. The words were strange, but somehow familiar. It was the tune and how the words fit the tune:

> Dee bazin da gungal dee id lathered fo doo zup,
> An ellyfunk, uh lizun, da munnies, zanna bup.
> "Mizens," zed de lizun, "Wheezall gizzard dere da zee
> "Hif zeecan mazzerfac da zound firozopee."

Little Will had sung the children's song to him many times.

She had learned it from her father. Little Will had said that the song was taught to her father by Waco Whacko the snake charmer.

> *Deep within the jungle there did gather for to sup,*
> *An elephant, a lion, a monkey, and a pup.*
> *"My friends," said the lion, "We are gathered here to see*
> *"If we can manufacture a sound philosophy."*

The singing stopped and No One strained his eyes trying to see the singer. He searched for a long time, but eventually even the ripples were gone. He turned and went back to the fire.

With his head upon his pack, his eyes staring at the flames, No One's mind put together the things that he had seen, heard, and learned. He knew the swamp woman to be Waco's daughter, and where they had to search to find her. He closed his eyes and frowned, because his mind had not disclosed the extent of the swamp woman's powers.

An image floated in front of his face. A woman, no. A girl. A woman. Her face glowed, her almond-shaped eyes gazed lovingly at him from a swirling mist of black hair. His breath caught as she turned and offered her bare body to him—

No One bolted upright and looked around. Trouble and Tarzaka were both asleep, the wind and lake water undisturbed. He rubbed his hand across his mouth and shook his head. He looked again toward the water. *Who are you?*

Nervously his tongue moistened his lips. He looked back at the fire, lowered his head to his pack, and waited for sleep to come.

TWENTY-EIGHT

They were awakened just before dawn by the deep rumblings of a storm coming from the west. Flashes of lightning illuminated the sky as they quickly cooked the morning's cobit while a fire could still be made. Before they had finished their cakes, the heavy rain began to fall. "Bah!" Trouble hooded his head and hefted his pack as he glanced up at the sky. "It is still as dark as a cashier's conscience." He turned to No One. "We should lay up until the blowdown has passed."

No One looked at the western sky, then across the choppy waters of the lake. He faced Trouble. "This could go on all day. I don't want to lose a day."

The magician placed his hands upon his hips. "The fate of the Universe will not be changed if we take a little longer. I have just as much reason as you for learning from the eggs—"

"No." No One shouldered his pack. "No, you don't."

Tarzaka turned from No One and looked at the magician. "No One has a bull to kill." She looked back at No One. "True?"

No One began walking down the road. Tarzaka pulled her

pack strap over her shoulder. "Trouble, we cannot get any wetter than we are now."

"Bah!" Trouble held out his arms. "Where to, then, No One?"

No One looked back over his shoulder. "We follow the road toward Arcadia until it leaves the shore of the lake. Then we follow the shore."

They walked against the driving rain for hours, the chill numbing both thought and bone. While his mind thought upon Reg's death, No One's eyes were concentrating upon stepping around the large puddles and maintaining his footing upon the road's greasy surface. Just then a feeling of warmth filled him. He stopped. Trouble and Tarzaka stopped a few steps beyond.

Trouble looked around at the dripping green trees that bordered the road, his eyes wide with fear. "What is this, No One?"

"Do you feel it?"

Trouble nodded. "Aye."

No One looked at Tarzaka. "And you?"

Tarzaka's eyes were dulled, her face slack. Ignoring No One's question, she turned to her left and began walking toward the lake's jungle-lined shore. No One placed his hand upon her arm. "Wait, Tarzaka. Where—"

She pulled her arm free and continued into the trees. Trouble grabbed No One's shoulder. "We must follow her."

No One looked at the narrow strip of trees between the road and the lake. "This cannot be the place. There is nothing there."

Trouble glared at No One. "Place or not—" He waved a hand in impatient disgust at No One. "Bah!"

The magician hurried to follow the fortune teller. No One frowned at Trouble's back until it disappeared into the trees. He hesitated, then turned to follow them. As he approached the edge of the road, he heard a voice as it filled his mind.

Come, Johnjay. Come to me.

He stumbled and fell to the road. The voice—its strength— never before had No One experienced its like.

Come to me, Johnjay.

He crawled to the nearest tree and used its trunk to pull himself to his feet. His breath came in harsh, short gasps. "Who? Who are you?" He closed his eyes and forced his thoughts to form. *"Who Are You?"*

Come to me.

No One sagged against the tree and tried to make his thoughts ask the question again. But before he could ask, the answer came.

Come to me, Johnjay. I am your wife.

No One recoiled from the tree, anger driving the warmth, the thoughts, from his head. He screamed at the sky. "I will be damned if you are! Damned, I say!" His head filled with the pain of cruel laughter.

Then you are damned. Come to me, Johnjay.

The laughter left him, and he looked at the trail in the highgrass made by Tarzaka and Trouble. He studied the bent blades of grass as though by force of will he could make them refuse his steps. His feet moved forward and he entered the trail.

For hours he unwillingly lurched and stumbled through the dense vegetation. At times the trail would be invisible to his eyes, but his feet never failed to find it again. Twice he called out Trouble's name and received no answer. In time the rain stopped, followed an hour later by the sun. Minutes later the swamp steamed under the heat. No One's head swam from the effort and from the hot, thick air. When the power left his legs, he fell face down into the highgrass.

When his breath returned, he rolled over onto his back and stared without sight at the branches, leaves, and vines above. He shook his head at the ache in his legs. "What moves me against my will?" He rested quietly for a long moment, then pushed himself up to a sitting position, and looked down the trail. He was a long way from the road. No One cupped his hands around his mouth and called out. "Trouble! Trouble! Tarzaka!"

He lowered his hands and listened but could hear nothing but the buzzing of the insects. He hung his head as he took his hands and began massaging his tired legs to keep them from cramping. He paused, frowned, and looked at his surroundings. "Why did she let me rest?" He thought again. Did she? What did Trouble say about the cloaking of his mind? It appears as a blackness to the mind reader when . . . he was trying to think of nothing. No One nodded. "I dropped from exhaustion, my mind went blank, and she *lost* me! Yes." He held his hands to his head. How does one think about nothing?

His hands fell to his lap as an edge of warmth touched him and left. He pushed himself to his feet. "She is after me again!"

How to think about nothing? No One closed his eyes. *Whiteness. A white wall, large enough to fill my entire vision, no matter in which direction I turn. The texture of the wall— eliminate it. Whiteness. Just whiteness.*

The edge of warmth covered him again, but his legs did not move. *Whiteness. And now, take away the white.* He felt the edges of his mind grow dull, a pressure as though someone's thumbs were pressing upon his eyeballs. All about the outside of his skull, it was as if great avians were flapping their wings and screaming in frustration. But they were outside; not inside.

He looked down the trail, his eyes slightly out of focus. He spoke out loud. "Swamp woman? Can you hear me, swamp woman?"

The flapping and screaming about his head increased to a frenzy, then suddenly died. No One waited, then allowed a small patch of whitness to return. "Swamp woman?"

You fight me, yet you call to me?

No One wet his lips and nodded. "Swamp woman, I will come to you, and on my own. But I will not be forced. On my own. You have what I want."

I have your friends as well.

"They are nothing to me, swamp woman."

The laughter threatened to break down his barrier for a moment, then it eased. *Very well, Johnjay. Come to me. Follow the trail. I will have them teach you how to kill the bull. I am waiting, my husband.*

"By damn! Woman, I am not your husband!"

The laughter returned, then No One was left alone with nothing but the gnaw of fear for company. He studied the trail for a long moment, then began to walk it with shaking steps. "Is it fear?" He asked himself. "Is it tiredness or fear that shakes my legs?" The answer was not clear and No One refused to risk removing the cloak from his mind to clarify it. He already knew that the fear was in his heart. Along the way, he saw Tarzaka's pack by the trailside. A few steps beyond was Trouble's pack. He hefted them both, placing their straps over his left shoulder, and continued down the trail.

Just before the darkness came over the swamp, No One reached the edge of a clearing. He eased the packs from his shoulders and studied the open place. It was a gentle rise grown deep with highgrass. At it's top appeared to be a mound or monument of some kind. He looked around at the clearing's treeline, but could see nothing. Looking again to the front, he saw the trails of Tarzaka and Trouble through the highgrass leading toward the mound at the top of the rise.

He squatted and rubbed his temples with the tips of his fingers. Cloaking his mind for so long had produced a center-pole splintering pain through his eyes. He studied the mound and decided against removing his mind-cloak. The swamp woman had not attacked his mind for hours, but No One was convinced that she was waiting for him—waiting for him to show the slightest weakness.

He quickly looked again at the clearing's treeline, then he hid the three packs beneath some brush. Standing, he turned into the jungle to the left of the trail and began quietly working his way around the clearing. After an hour of this, he went again to the clearing's edge and tried to make out what could be seen. The darkness was fully upon the swamp, but far to No One's left was the light of a torch—two. No, a torch and a cooking fire.

He crept farther into the clearing, squinting his eyes, trying to compensate for his cloak's effect upon his focus. Behind the cooking fire was a thatched shack. To the right of the shack, a torch was mounted upon a tall pole driven into the ground.

No One studied the scene, then he looked up the rise toward the mound. The mound appeared much larger now, and there seemed to be a dark-robed figure seated before it facing the shack. He studied the figure for a long time, but it remained motionless. He moved even further into the clearing, stopped, and squatted. The figure did not move its head; did not appear even to move its chest.

As the sound of voices came from the shack, Johnjay leaned forward and lowered himself upon his hands until his eyes were just above the tops of the highgrass. He turned his head but saw nothing stir at the shack. Looking back at the motionless figure, No One began crawling up the gentle slope toward the mound. The figure's left side was toward him, its face shrouded by the hood of its dark robe. When No One came close enough, he saw that the figure was seated in a roughly made wooden chair. Ten steps from the figure, No One turned and began crawling to his left, watching the shack. He could see inside the shack's door and he recognized Tarzaka—or at least some-one wearing a fortune teller's robe—seated just inside. He moved further around the top of the rise, then turned his head to his right and looked at the figure.

In the dim light from the shack's cooking fire, he could
make out a face, stark white with large dark eyes. He moved
closer and closer until his breath caught. It was the grinning
face of a death's head, the large dark eyes nothing but empty
sockets. He leaped up, turned away, and ran downhill, his
imagination hot upon his heels. In his panic, he let the cloak
fall from his mind. An instant later, he was thundered into
darkness.

*The naked woman, the almond eyes laughing at him from
that mist of long, black hair. "You are mine, Johnjay! Now
you are mine."*

*Images of skulls, great swamp monsters, shining lengths of
gut, the five bulls charging over the edge of the cliff, the
judgement of the Miira Ring, Goofy Joe demanding that the
town of Dirak blackball him...*

"You are mine, Johnjay. You are mine..."

He opened his eyes in the dark to see Tarzaka looking down
at him, her face lit only by the flames of the cooking fire
coming through the doorway. The only other light in the shack
was a small oil lamp. Tarzaka looked across his chest and
nodded. "He is awake."

No One looked to his right and saw Trouble sitting cross-
legged beside him. "Trouble, what is happening?"

The magician looked out of the doorway, then back at No
One. "The swamp woman has us." Trouble again looked out
of the doorway. "She is gone right now."

No One tried to sit. "We must run while we can." Both
Tarzaka and Trouble forced him to his back. "What are you
doing?"

Tarzaka looked at No One steadily, her face rigid. "We go
nowhere. It is time for you to live up to your part of the
bargain."

"Bargain?"

"No One, you said you would take me to learn from the
eggs. They are close by. All that we must do to learn from
them is for you to give Ssura what she wants. Ssura is the
creature's name."

No One frowned, then looked at Trouble. "And you?"

Trouble slowly nodded his head. "I have seen what the eggs
can do, No One. If I can learn but a bit of it, I can go back
to my town. You understand that? Isn't that why you've come

here? Isn't that why you want to kill the bull? Give Ssura what she wants."

No One shrugged off their hands and sat upright. "And you two would have me do this thing?"

The left side of Trouble's mouth drew back in a half-smile. "It would seem to be a pleasant enough task."

"And what would that be?"

Tarzaka grabbed No One's arm with a surprisingly strong grip. "Understand, No One, that unless you do this thing, none of us get what we want. Including you!"

"Can I not get a straight answer from either of you? By the gray beard of Momus, what must I—" No One turned his head toward the door as he saw a figure standing high upon the incline. It was the creature he had seen in his vision; just as naked, just as beautiful. She just stood there facing the shack.

Trouble nodded toward the figure. "No One, Ssura is the daughter of Waco Whacko and Fireball Hanah Sanagi. I cannot tell when, but I can see that she has been without her parents a very long time. Perhaps since she was five or six years old." Trouble looked at No One. "She has been reared for the most part by the eggs. She protects them at their command."

No One frowned as he studied the figure of the swamp woman. "We mean no harm to the eggs."

Tarzaka adjusted her robe and looked at the figure standing upon the opposite side of the fire. "The eggs would strike a bargain with us."

"What bargain?"

The fortune teller nodded toward the door. "Up there, in that mound behind the skeleton, is where the eggs rest. They will still be eggs when the three of us have turned to dust, and they must be cared for if they are to survive. This is Ssura's mission handed down to her by her father. But she will not live forever. She needs a child."

No One's eyebrows went up as his jaw fell down. "She *what!?*"

Trouble nodded. "She wants a child from you, No One. As I said: a pleasant enough task."

"Bah!" No One looked from Trouble to Tarzaka, then back at Trouble. "Why not you? You were here first."

"Through Ssura the eggs have seen your mind. They know of you. Ssura spoke to us of Little Will and your grandfather, Bullhook Willy. They want you, not me." Trouble held out his hands. "And the eggs will not teach us unless you agree."

No One snorted. "Then they will not teach us! I will have lost nothing but time. There are other ways to kill bulls. You two have this great desire to learn from the eggs—"

Tarzaka held up her hand. "As do you."

"—let Trouble perform this service!" He pushed himself to his feet. "I am leaving!" As he approached the door of the shack, the jungle around them wailed with cries, screams, and growls. "By damn, does she control the creatures of the swamp?"

Trouble nodded. "She cannot get through to my mind when it is cloaked, but this clearing is guarded by uncounted numbers of those swamp monsters. They reach me with a most impressive argument." The magician looked at Ssura. "I do not doubt that she will kill us if you do not give her what she wants."

No One looked out of the door and saw Ssura's arms rise. The howling from the jungle ceased. He stared at the swamp woman. "How long?"

Tarzaka spoke softly. "Until a live child is born."

No One turned slowly toward his two companions, his head hung down. "A *year*. Almost an entire *year*." He turned and looked out of the door, toward the figure seated before the mound. "The skeleton."

Tarzaka's voice trembled. "It is Waco. She said he once told her that he would never rest until there was a child to carry on the watch after her. She seems to have taken her father's words quite literally."

Trouble pushed himself to his feet and placed a gentle hand upon No One's shoulder. "No One, look at her. She has beauty enough to shame a ballet girl. Besides, we haven't any choice. It's that or all of us either die or remain prisoners the rest of our lives."

No One moved slowly from beneath Trouble's hand. This time the jungle did not scream. Trouble and Tarzaka watched as No One came abreast of the fire. The swamp woman screamed, laughed hysterically, then ran toward the skeleton. No One looked back at his two companions briefly, then turned and continued up the incline until he was swallowed by the dark.

Tarzaka faced Trouble. "Do you think he will be all right?"

Trouble shook his head and placed his arm around the fortune teller's shoulders. "I do not know. What I do know is that the swamp woman is crazier than Arnheim's cuckoo clock."

Again he shook his head. "I only hope that No One can, er, perform adequately under the current circumstances."

Tarzaka looked past the fire into the darkness. "Could you?"

Trouble snorted. "No. That lady scares the salt from me. She is straight from the white rubber lot."

TWENTY-NINE

As he entered the darkness, suddenly No One could see nothing. The dim reflection from Waco's laughing skull was gone, as were the stars. He tried to turn and see the fire, but he could not move. "Ssura!" The echoes returned with ten times the strength of his call. But the echoes were in his mind, not against his ears. "Ssura!"

Laughter. Loud, raucous, laughter. The ground fell away from beneath his feet, and he turned and tumbled in the blackness, the laughter growing louder. He held his hands to his ears, but could not feel his hands touch his head. Then, first his right leg, his nose, his left eye, were assaulted with stabbing pains, and from there every scrap of his body was filled with agony. No One screamed, flailing his non-existent arms and legs at the nothingness.

"*Mother! Help me, Mother!*"

Knives of searing white light split the dark, and he felt himself being sucked into a mire of tentacled, slime-covered horror. He screamed and screamed until the blackness covered his mind.

• • •

Little Will sat up on her sleeping cushions, torn from her sleep by the screams in her head. *"Johnjay? Johnjay, where are you?"*

She drove everything from her mind, listening for her son's thoughts. Minutes later, her shoulders slumped, and she sighed. Nothing but a stronger version of the same nightmare? She shook her head.

She pushed herself up from the floor cushions and walked to her window. That evening there had been a cold wetness in the air, and the window was shut. She propped it open, looked into the darkness toward the *kraal,* and listened. On the still air she could hear distant yells and laughter coming from the direction of the tavern. From the *kraal* came a snort and the sound of heavy footsteps.

"Reg!"

She turned, grabbed her bullhook, and rushed from her room, through the eating room, out into the night. As she came to the fence, she stopped, then listened to her mind as she spread a net of thought over the *kraal*. There could be nothing inside the net, and she would have felt it if something was attacking from outside. *"Johnjay? Are you here, Johnjay?"*

She wet her lips with the tip of her tongue as a sickness filled her stomach. Looking into the darkness of the *kraal*, she wondered aloud. "Have you already done your terrible deed, Johnjay? Have you killed the last bull?"

Little Will climbed the fence and came down inside. "Reg? Reg? Come, Reg!"

She heard a snort, then the pachyderm's great feet thundering against the lowgrass. In the dimness of the cloud-shrouded night, she saw the shadow of a mountain coming at her. "Reg—"

First she felt the slam of a great weight against her face and chest; an instant later, her upper left arm being crushed, thrust into the soil by a foot weighted with six tons of stampeding flesh.

. . . Bullhook Willy had told her the story of Black Diamond when she was only eight. It was an old, old story, and only one of a thousand such stories that had the same moral: bulls only mind one bullhand at a time. Curley Prichett used to be Black Diamond's bullhand, years before; but at the stand in

*Corsicana, Texas, Black Diamond's handler was Jack O'Grady.
Curley had made his home in Corsicana, and he had asked
Jack O'Grady if he could lead Diamond from the loading runs
to the lot. He wanted to impress his neighbors.*

*On the way to the lot, the street lined with spectators, Curley
assumed Diamond knew him and would obey him. That was
why, when the baggage nags held up everything, Curley gave
the spectator, Eva Donohoe, permission to pet Black Diamond.
But Curley used to be Diamond's bullhand, and wasn't any
longer. Not the way Diamond saw it. Diamond caught Curley
with one of his tusks and flung the retired bullhand over the
nearest car. Then Diamond knocked Eva Donohoe to the side-
walk and ran his tusks through her body . . .*

*All of the bullhands of Miira, in turn, had been handling
Reg. How else were they to maintain their skills? How else
were their children to learn them? But bulls only mind one
bullhand at a time. Little Will used to be Reg's handler, but
no longer. Reg had been under the hooks of hundreds of different bullhands, and was confused, angry, desperate, old.
Little Will understood this as her mind went blank.*

It is said by those who traveled the road between Arcadia
and the Porse Cutoff that for two years the swamp rocked with
the pained screams and frightened footsteps of the creatures
that lived there. Great scars appeared in the surface of the road,
cutting the road clean through in places. The trees, highgrass,
and brush surrounding the body of water they called Nightmare
Lake turned black and were swept with fires. Trade along the
route halted, and whatever ice or cast iron that made it to
Tarzak came south through Kuumic and then across the Great
Desert. The towns north of Tieras, as well as the entire Emerald
Valley, could bring in trade goods only at prohibitive prices.

It became so bad that talk was begun among the peoples of
the Central Continent towns. At The Season the thirty-fourth,
in Tarzak's Great Ring, the talk led to the possibility of constructing a road north from the White Top Mountain Road,
west of the Great Muck, to the base of the Snake Mountain
Range, and from there, east to the town of Miira. The route
would avoid the swamp altogether.

But the only bull left was Reg, and Reg was old. The
proposed road could be constructed with horses, wagons, and
Steengrease, but it would take at least another two years. Also,
the cost would be measured in lives as well as movills. The

Season ended with no plans agreed upon, no contracts awarded.

Soon after, in May of the thirty-fifth Year Since The Crash, lone travelers that braved the cursed route reported that all was quiet in the Great Muck. The vegetation around Waco's Lake was again green. The story was confirmed by others, and soon the gashes in the road were repaired and trade resumed as though nothing had happened. Everyone, save the Great Mootch Movill, was at a loss to explain what had occurred. Mootch's story involved the landing of the great treasure ship *Caddywampus*, with its holds laden with jewels, spices, fine fabrics, and a potion he called "real whiskey." But Mootch was a storyteller, and was known as such. It was a fine story; but for answers that could be relied upon, there was no supplier. However, by The Season the thirty-fifth, the only memory of the event was lost deep within the scriptorium of the Tarzak Priesthood; on the road all that was remembered was Mootch's tale of the *Caddywampus*.

No One placed the final rock upon Waco's grave, stood, and walked the few steps to the fresh water pool at the edge of the clearing. He pushed back his hood and knelt to sip from the pool. Just before his lips touched the water, he saw his own image in the water backgrounded by an angry black sky. His hair was as white as his clown-whited face. He reached his left hand up and touched it to his hair. When had it turned white?

More rocks.

No One looked away from the water to see Ssura standing behind her father's grave. He turned back to the water, took a drink, then sat back upon his heels.

More rocks!

He shook his head. "No more rocks. Enough." He looked again at Ssura. She stood, naked as always, her fists upon her hips. "Ssura, where is my child?"

She shook her head. *Not yours.* She pointed toward the edge of the clearing closest to the road. *You go now.*

No One looked up toward the mound on the top of the rise. He shook his head. "No. First the eggs must speak to the others. Tarzaka and Trouble."

Ssura laughed, her voice at a wild pitch that assaulted No One's ear drums. *No want. Eggs no want. No need them; no want them.* She presented her back to him and ran away; presumably toward whatever she used for a shelter.

No One shook his head, trying to remember the hateful,

clawing, repeated acts that eventually produced the child. It could not be called the making of love. It was the cold, unfeeling manufacture of a child. No One's eyes narrowed as he again saw his image in the pool. He had not been able to perform. Alone with a crazy-strong wild woman in the dark of the jungle screaming at you—who could? The eggs—the eggs *made* him perform. He clenched his jaws against the indignity—the exploitation—the shame.

And the child? No name. No One's child had no name. He didn't even know if the child was male or female. It had been a year, alone among the trees of the swamp, since Ssura had lost her stomach. And No One had no claim to the child. Both the swamp woman and the eggs had made that very clear. The week before, the eggs had nothing more to teach him; but they refused to teach Tarzaka and Trouble. They had what they wanted from No One; the bargain was off.

No One pushed himself to his feet and began walking up the rise to the mound. Tarzaka and Trouble could roast themselves as far as he was concerned. But the eggs. Those damned, cursed eggs. They had made a bargain.

Come no closer, No One!

No One felt the feeble thoughts of the eggs working upon him. *You are small,* he said to the eggs. *You are too small and too weak. We have made a bargain. I have done what you wanted; now you shall do what I want.*

The feeling of scorn washed from the mound down the rise toward No One. *We do what we choose, stud beast. And we need you no longer. Have we not given you full command of your powers? Have we not shown you the two great visions you will someday have? Go away unless you want us to make you give yourself a child.*

No One's mind reached out and placed its fingers around the eggs within the mound. *I can crush you, now. I will, unless you live up to your part of the bargain.*

The eggs cried out: *Ssura! Kill! Ssura! Kill!*

No One laughed. *Your thoughts cannot get beyond me, now.* His fingers reached within one of the shells. They wrapped around the head of a cold, slime-covered creature. *How does it feel? All I must do is to close my fingers and your head will be crushed!*

We agree! We agree, No One. Whatever you want! We agree! We agree!

No One released his mental grip upon the Ssendissian infant, and then studied the mound. *Are all of you listening to me?*

They all answered: *Yes*.

Then hear this. Any time I choose, no matter where I am on this planet, I can reach out and destroy the lot of you. This is the power you helped me to achieve. Do you all understand this?

The eggs answered in unison. *Yes*.

No One nodded. *Then you shall meet your side of the bargain that we made. There is now a child that is doomed to spend its life in twisted horror, caring for you. I have done my part. Now you must teach Tarzaka and Trouble all that you can teach them. If you do not, I shall reach out and smash your shells! If I now have the power to kill a bull with my mind, your insignificant lives are in even greater peril.*

No One looked down from the mound at the shack where Trouble and Tarzaka stood in the doorway looking back at him. He held his hands to his mouth. "It is settled . . ."

He laughed, then lowered his hands and spoke to the pair with his mind. *I have talked with them. Now your school begins. Do you understand?*

The pair waved back. Tarzaka began running after him. She shouted. "No One, wait! You must not do what you are planning. Wait!"

He lifted his hand and the fortune teller stopped as though she had run into a masonry wall. No One studied them for a moment. *Good-bye.* He turned and faced the edge of the clearing nearest the road. Within a few moments he had located his pack, now rotten and crumbled with age. He set his jaw and continued moving his feet through the trees and highgrass toward the Arcadia–Miira Road.

Little Will sat upright against the litter's raised back. Clutched in her right hand and resting upon her lap was the gold-and-mahogany bullhook. The bullhands of Miira were gathered behind her and at her sides, and all watched as Bigfoot, new Master of the Miira Bullhands, entered the *kraal* and approached Reg.

Little Will studied Bigfoot as the young woman approached the old bull. Her motions were sure, unhurried. To look at her from the outside, fear was not in Bigfoot's vocabulary. But the bullhands knew the things Bigfoot's guts were telling her. *Run. Run and don't look back. This bull is a killer. Run!*

After crushing Little Will's arm to a useless stump and

shattering the bones in her left leg so badly that two years later she still did not have the use of it, Reg had broken through the *kraal* fence and had headed into town. Reg's trumpeting had brought the sleeping Miirans out of their beds into the street just as the bull entered it. They fought to get out of the bull's way, but by the time Reg was brought under control, six broken bodies lay in the dust.

Since then Reg had killed two more bullhands and had crippled a third. Little Will sat forward as Bigfoot stopped directly in front of Reg. The bull snorted and, with her long trunk, took a swipe at the bullhand. As the trunk came around, Bigfoot smacked it with her bullhook. Reg's head reared up and the bull's massive feet shuffled uncertainly in the lowgrass.

As Reg settled down, and Bigfoot held her hand out toward the beast, Little Will leaned back and closed her eyes. She listened as Bigfoot spoke gentle words to the elephant, and let her mind's image rise from her body. Little Will's image sailed upward, then rolled among the clouds. This image had two good arms and two good legs. She turned and looked far below at the scene in the *kraal*. Reg's trunk was wrapped around Bigfoot's left wrist. The young woman's bullhook was in her right hand, in conspicuous view of the elephant. The bull's trunk crept up Bigfoot's arm and shoulder, sniffed at Bigfoot's hair, then slithered off. Bigfoot held out a raw cobit root, and Reg took it.

Little Will watched the scene, a touch of jealousy in her heart, when blackness began crowding the edge of her vision. She rolled until she faced the blackness. It extended up from the horizon until it blotted out the sun. She looked down but none of the bullhands seemed to notice anything different. She again faced the blackness, startled at how much it had grown.

What are you?

She moved toward the black, again shouting at it. *What are you?*

The voice came from the center of the darkness. *Get out of my way, Mother.*

Johnjay?

Get out of my way. I am here to finish the job that I started.

Johnjay! No! I'll stop you!

You cannot.

The blackness swept her from the sky and she opened her eyes to find herself in her litter. She looked up at the sky but could see nothing but cloud-dotted blue. She closed her eyes tightly. *Johnjay, don't do it. Don't do it, Johnjay.*

Wind rustled the tops of the trees, and the clouds began to darken. Bigfoot had Reg kneeling. She climbed upon the beast, sat astride its neck, then the beast stood. Bigfoot said something, and Reg began walking. Straight, then left, then right, then the bull stopped and reared up upon its hind legs and stood there. The bullhands surrounding Little Will applauded, cried, cheered.

The tears trickled down Little Will's cheeks. *Can't you see what you would be destroying, Johnjay? Can't you see that, even now?*

You, Mother! You and all of those sanctimonious people! You . . . you shall see the powers I now have.

The sky darkened and thunder began rumbling from the west. The bullhands surrounding the *kraal* looked up at the sky. Little Will closed her eyes, forced her image from her body, and flew up at the dark clouds. *Johnjay, stop! Stop!*

The darkness before her shaped itself into an enormous black and green dragon. Tongues of fire leaped from its mouth, its talons, each one the size of a tree, reached down toward the *kraal. Nothing can stop me. I have a debt to pay to this bull and to all of my good, good friends and neighbors.*

He swatted her from the sky, and as she tumbled toward the ground, she screamed. *Look at them, Johnjay! Look at their minds! Look at what you are doing! Look at their minds!* Blackness covered everything, and Little Will collapsed unconscious upon her litter.

She awakened in her room, screaming. Mortify knelt next to her. "Be calm! Calm yourself!"

Little Will shook her head. "Johnjay, the blackness, the . . . dragon . . ."

Mortify patted her hand. "Everything is all right, Great Little Will. Please believe me. You've simply had a bad nightmare."

"Reg? Is Reg all right?"

Mortify nodded. "Reg is fine; as is Bigfoot. That girl has that bull minding her manners."

"The blackness . . . the dark."

"It was just a little sour weather. That and you're tired. Get some rest, and you'll see that everything will be just fine."

Little Will pointed at her room's window. "Help me up and bring me there."

"Well, I don't know if I should. I mean—"

"I *said* help me up!"

"Very well." Mortify took Little Will's hand and pulled until she was standing upon her wobbly legs. Placing an arm around her waist, he helped her to her window. She looked out toward the *kraal* and saw Bigfoot still working Reg, the bullhands of Miira still watching the pair. Mortify held a hand out toward the scene. "See? Did I tell you?"

She examined the scene again and again. Then she faced Mortify. "Help me to my bed."

After he had done as he had been requested, Mortify bade farewell and left. Little Will stared for a long time through her window at the sky. The strength of the thing she had felt; Johnjay could have razed the entire town of Miira if he had wanted to. And the hate. His hate of Reg was a malignant thing that had seemed to engulf her. But Reg still lived. "Reg is still alive, and the bullhands still have a bull."

And, she thought, Johnjay is still an exile. He could have killed the bull, but didn't. "My poor son. Is it because you only now see the terribleness of your deed? If you have just learned that, how you must be suffering."

She closed her eyes and let her image float freely. *Johnjay! Johnjay! Let me come to you. Let me come to you now. Johnjay?* As she called, she drifted off to sleep.

THIRTY

No One stood upon the crest of the Upland Mountain Range. Far below to the north was the Great Muck and Waco's Lake. In the far distance, a pure white cloud covered the peak of White Top Mountain. The thread of the White Top Mountain Road writhed down from the frozen lakes until it was almost lost in the jungle below. There, at the town of Arcadia, it joined the great road that stretched from Miira southwest through the Great Muck until it reached Arcadia, then turned south and went over the Upland Range, and down to the Great Desert where it ended in the Town of Kuumic.

Twin columns of white smoke rose from the iron furnace in Arcadia. Where the columns became one, the river of smoke bent and pointed northeast in a straight line toward Miira. No One turned his back on the Great Muck and walked the crest until the Great Desert spread before him. Tears filled his eyes and he raised his open hands toward the sky.

"Momus! Momus, you great fat laughing fool! Momus, look at me! Look at me . . ."

He whirled about, and the direction of the smoke changed. His palms faced White Top Mountain, and seconds later its cover of clouds was gone. He looked at a boulder upon the

ground and watched with unblinking eyes as it exploded into
a thousand pieces.

He looked back at the sky, his arms still raised. "But I
cannot alter the past, you great joker. The past is set for all
time, and I damn the laws of your universe!"

He lowered his arms to his sides, then hung his head as a
breeze, heated and dusted by the desert sands, washed his
clown-whited face. "Momus, how does the one called No One
live with himself?" He nodded, his tears falling to the ground.

He had seen them in Miira gathered around the *kraal*. Little
Will, torn and broken in her carrying litter; Tokyoso, crippled;
the families of the eight bullhands Reg had killed since the one
called Johnjay had his trunk put on the lot. All of them watching
Bigfoot. All of them finding their meaning, vicariously filling
their existence, through the actions of the new Master of the
Miira Bullhands as Bigfoot put Reg through her paces. He had
visited their minds and had gone away ashamed.

But it was more than the bullhands. The others. The hostlers,
riders, harness men, barkers, priests, newstellers, roustabouts—he had visited their minds as well. Reg was their tie
to the stars, to the old show. Even for those who were not
bullhands, the bull was their special animal. The bull was the
show; and the show still lived in the hearts of those who had
been watching Bigfoot and Reg. The old troupers, and those
who had been born on Momus, as well.

But it had been the vision of reverence—ecstasy—that he
saw when he visited Bigfoot's mind that had driven his power
from Miira. It was the same vision he remembered when he
had once read his sister's mind as May sat on the grass with
her brushes and paints. It was a private, savage joy mixed from
pride and belonging.

It was the joy he once witnessed as a child in Tarzak during
The Season the twenty-first when he was but thirteen years
old. The peculiar-looking Master of the Tarzak Priests, Warts,
read from the old route book of the great clem on the planet
Wallabee. O'Hara's Greater Shows and the Arnheim & Boon
Circus did battle there, and as Warts told the tale, the young
Johnjay crept into the old priest's head to see what the priest
saw as he spoke.

No One looked again at the sky. "Arnheim. Did you see
them, too? Neither you nor I, no matter what we do, can kill
the show. The immortal cannot be killed, and the show is
immortal."

For a moment he entertained thoughts of sending his thoughts to Miira, to his mother's house, to seek her comfort, to ask her forgiveness. He shook his head as the heat of shame filled his chest and face.

He looked again at the Great Desert. "What shall I do?"

The years of Ssura's, the painful lessons from the eggs bought at the price of enslaving a helpless infant—for nothing. All for nothing.

"If I want, I could be the greatest magician or fortune teller this world would ever see. If I want, I could rule this entire planet with the fear of my powers." He issued a bitter laugh, then spat upon the ground.

Dark thoughts crossed his mind; thoughts of flinging himself over the edge of a convenient cliff, as he had caused the five bulls to do. A calm crept into his soul. He nodded.

"Yes. There is that."

He searched his own mind for an opposing argument, but could find nothing save a slight curiosity. The eggs had seen something in his mind. Two great puzzles resided in his head; two visions the eggs had called them. All that was needed for the puzzles to come together—for him to see the visions— were a few pieces. He shrugged. It was something to do; a mission; a thread of purpose; a scrap of meaning.

"Two great visions." He nodded, wiped the tears from his cheeks, and began his trek down the mountain toward the road to Kuumic. "The cliffs will be there if and when I need them."

It was two years later at the Miira Ring, The Thirty-seventh Year Since The Crash. As always, when newly arrived news- tellers or priests played the Ring, the one called Little Will sat in the blues, hoping for some news of Johnjay. That night there was the new Master of the Arcadia Newstellers, Tamborine by name, playing the Ring. Tamborine had unusual events to re- late.

"There is a magician I met," she said, "whose magic is more wonder than tricks. His name is Trouble, and I swear he had the power to alter the spots upon his cards. He travels with a fortune teller named Tarzaka, who is no mere peeker of mitts. She can tell *fortunes*. She knows all that has been and can see that which is to be."

Tamborine remained silent for a moment, then continued. "The strangest thing, however, is a happening I witnessed at the eleventh fire from Kuumic on the Road to Tarzak in the

Great Desert. There were fourteen gathered at the fire the night of which I speak, and the performances exceptional, even though there was a preponderance of priests. Three clowns, one each from Tarzak, Sina, and Porse, contested, and then in turn the priests began.

"Badnews, apprentice priest from Tarzak, recited the epic 'The *City of Baraboo*,' relating the adventures of the old show, and Badnews was in fine voice, indeed. Then Noodlebrain, apprentice from Arcadia, recited his recently completed saga 'The Road,' in which is told the history of the bulls on Momus. Great Teena, Master of the Mbwebwe Priesthood, recited her epic 'Car Number Two' relating the history of the settlement and development of the Continent of Midway.

"Three other priests rose, each one speaking his favorite work. Oilum, one of the fisher-priests of Sina, recited his epic of the old show, 'Edition Twenty-One and Thirty-Five.' Toldus, second apprentice from Ikona, performed his history, 'The Season The First.' Finally Great Muggsy, first priest under Great Warts of the Tarzak Priesthood, stood and spoke to us 'The Saga of Bullhook Willy.'

"The exchange of movills was substantial, and no one paid more than a strange fortune teller named No One. His face was painted in clown white and his robe was ragged and torn. Great Muggsy asked No One for a fortune. At first No One studied the dark priest, then the fortune teller nodded and stood.

"At first he looked down at Great Muggsy and asked, 'Do you know me, Great Muggsy?'

"The dark priest nodded his head. 'Yes. I know you.'

"The fortune teller looked around at our faces, then looked above the fire at the night sky. Then spoke. 'Once, long ago, I was promised two great visions. These visions, I was told, would come upon me once I had seen and learned enough. And for the past two years I have been across the face of this planet, looking and learning.

"'Four months ago I met Great Mareseadoats and his wife, the singer Ieada, upon the Miira–Arcadia Road. There I purchased a history and Ieada's show songs. The visions almost came upon me. But something was still missing.' He held out his hands. 'The priests at the fire tonight have supplied me with the missing pieces.'

"Great Muggsy looked up at the fortune teller. 'Is this to be a fortune for one of us?'

"'For all of you,' No One answered. 'My first great vision

is of the planet Momus and its people. There will be dark times ahead, as the show has always seen dark times.'

"We whispered among ourselves, for surely the fortune teller was mad. The show had been dead for the past thirty-seven years. Great Muggsy hushed us to silence, then he again faced No One. 'And with the dark times?' he asked.

"'There will be the good as well.' He held his hands up to the night sky. 'The show lives now and will live forever. I see it again flying among the stars, playing once again under canvas to the many races of many worlds, its name once again a thing to thrill the hearts of old and young alike.' He lowered his hands and looked at the faces around the fire. 'And there will be bulls. More bulls than the old show had. All this I saw in my vision.'

"Great Muggsy's eyes were wet with tears as he smiled and nodded. 'And, fortune teller, does your vision say when this will take place?'

"'No,' the fortune teller answered.

"Then the strangest thing happened. Great Muggsy asked another question. 'And your second vision, No One?'

"No One stared steadily at the priest, and then he spoke. 'My second vision is for me alone. It is my own fortune.' He looked around at those seated at the fire. 'In exchange for supplying me with the missing pieces to my puzzles, I give the fortune of Momus to you to play as you will.'"

Tamborine held out her arms. "Then the white-faced fortune teller turned from the fire and walked out into the night. He walked not toward Kuumic nor toward Tarzak. Instead he walked north straight into the desert toward the Upland Mountains." The newsteller lowered her hands and looked at those seated in the blues of the Miira Ring. "Was the fortune teller mad?" She shrugged. "Who knows? The things he said, the paint upon his face, his walk into the waterless desert in the middle of the night, all speak of madness. But his fortune speaks to my heart.

"We all thought the fortune teller to be mad; but we talked among ourselves, and thought long and hard about No One's vision. As I said, I had only weeks before seen a magician do real magic and another fortune teller who used no cards, crystal balls, or mumbo jumbo. Instead that fortune teller told real fortunes. If one such fortune teller exists, another can."

The newsteller held her hands to her breast. "In here I know that the strange fortune teller spoke.the truth. In here the show is not dead. It is not dead in the hearts of those who listened that night to No One. And you should not let the show die in your hearts." Tamborine pointed toward the night sky. "One day the show will again fly among the stars; the show will go on."

Little Will cried silently as the cashiers moved into the blues to collect Tamborine's movills.

THIRTY-ONE

Twenty days after leaving the desert fire, No One once again stood upon the shore of Waco's Lake, his robe caked with the dust of the desert. He looked through the trees toward the clearing and saw the mound-capped rise within it. He blanketed the clearing with his mind. *I am back.*

He sensed first shock, then anger coming from the eggs. Then there loomed next to him a black cloud that twisted within itself. *Why are you here? Go away!*

Ssura, I have come for my child.

Leave! She is not your child!

No One nodded and smiled. *Then my child is my daughter.*

Ssura's cloud whirled with a fury sufficient to tear trees from the soil. *She is not yours! Leave! Leave, or I will kill you!*

No One heard the eggs join in. *Kill him, Ssura! Kill him! Kill him!*

The black cloud moved closer. No One reached out the fingers of his mind and evaporated the cloud. The trees and underbrush that had been sucked up in the draft caused by the cloud fell to the ground. Ssura was in the clearing, staggering toward the mound.

No One entered the clearing and headed toward the mound. *Where is she, Ssura? Where is my daughter?*

The naked woman fell against the mound, then rolled over until she was facing No One. She screamed a hysterical laugh, then stood up and held out her arms. The creatures of the jungle rose as a single entity and descended upon No One. The great swamp lizards fought with mud snakes, insects, and dragon parrots to destroy him. He was thrown to the ground, a dragon parrot thrust its beak at No One's head, then blood gushed from his cheek. He felt the foot of one of the great swamp monsters on his back, crushing him. With his mind he rapidly constructed a clear shell of force about his body. The pressure of the foot left his back, and he got to his feet as the creatures threw themselves against the shell in helpless fury.

He moved toward the mound, and even more creatures were thrown against him; so many that he could not see. His mind rose above the fighting, slavering beasts, to see Ssura calling and directing still more things against him. The frenzy of claws, fangs, wings, and talons moved closer and closer to the mound until Ssura was covered in a blur of animals and blood. Then the creatures stopped. One by one they walked, flew, or slithered away leaving behind their dead and Ssura's blood-streaked body, her breast heaving for air.

No One let the wall of force dissolve as his mind returned to his aching body. The pain of his injuries drove him to his knees, and he cried out. After a moment, he struggled to his feet, hobbled over to Ssura, and knelt beside her.

"Ssura. Can you hear me?"

Her mouth barely opened and she coughed blood from it. "Kill you! Kill—"

No One faced the mound. *Release her! Release her, or I will crush each and every one of you!"*

He looked at Ssura's face. It stared at him blankly, the eyes wide and dull, the jaw slack. "Ssura?"

The eggs spoke. *There is nothing there, Johnjay. All she had was what we gave her.*

He grabbed her by her shoulders and shook her. "Ssura! Where is my daughter? Ssura!"

The woman's eyes turned toward him, seemed to focus for a second, then the light in them went out. Her head fell limply to one side. He lowered her gently to the ground and wiped some of the filth and blood from her lips.

"What would have been, lovely Ssura, had you been free?"

No One pushed himself to his feet. The clearing was deathly quiet except for a tiny whimper. He limped around the mound until he could see the opposite side of the clearing. Near its edge, just beneath the trees, No One could see the crooked wooden bars of a crude pen. He walked toward it, and as he approached it, he felt the thoughts of the eggs at the back of his head.

She is ours, No One! She is ours! Leave us be! We need her to live!"

No One shut out the voices. He reached the pen and looked between the bars. Huddled in the corner was a small, frightened black-haired creature so crust-covered in filth it was barely recognizable as human. Johnjay placed a wall of thought surrounding both himself and the child.

"Child?"

The girl winced and cowered against the far wall of the pen. From her mouth came a high, weak wail. No One walked around the cage, the girl crawling in the muck to stay against the opposite side, until he came to the lashed-down door. He pointed the edge of his hand at the lashings, and they parted.

He opened the door, bent down, and entered the pen. The girl screamed and held her fingers before her as though they were claws. No One squatted before her and held out his hand. The girl swiped at the hand, then drew her arms against her famished breast and wailed, hiding her face in her hands. No One reached his hand out even further and touched the girl's filthy matted hair, stroking it.

"It's going to be all right, child. All right."

The girl shuddered beneath each touch of his hand. No One formed his thoughts and placed them in the girl's head. The thoughts were of warmth, hugging, love. She opened her fingers slightly and peeked at No One through her fingers.

He felt images of fear, pain, anger, and loneliness coming from the girl. She had but one word: Girl; her name. No One placed the palm of his hand against her cheek.

"Everything will be all right, child. I am your father. I've come for you."

THIRTY-TWO

Six years passed, and it was late in Thunder, the Forty-third Year Since The Crash. Two figures dressed in new bullhand's robes, a white-haired young man and a young girl, walked the Miira–Arcadia Road through the heavy downpour. Johnjay looked down at her. "Girl, are you getting tired?"

She nodded. "And cold, Father."

They stopped and Johnjay released the girl's hand and swung his pack from his shoulder. From the pack he withdrew a ragged blue robe and wrapped the girl in it. He replaced the pack, then picked up the girl and kissed her. "It won't be long now."

She put her arms around the man's neck and rested her head upon his shoulder. Johnjay continued walking through the rain.

In the distance he could just make out the shape of a figure riding a horse in his direction. The horse was walking very slowly, its head and neck down against the rain. Johnjay patted the girl's back and continued walking.

His mind studied the past six years. He had buried the eggs deep in the mud of the swamp, and little by little Girl grew to trust him. In time she learned to talk, and then cry. Soon after, she learned how to laugh. As No One, the man had gone forth upon the road exchanging fortunes for food and goods. The

232

bullhand's robes he had obtained from a Kuumic wardrober to be worn on this day that he had seen so clearly one night at a fire near the Kuumic–Tarzak Road.

The figure upon the horse was slumped, its bullhand's hood pulled over its head. As Johnjay came abreast of the horse's head, he reached out and gently took the bridle in his hand. The horse stopped, but the figure upon its back did not move. Johnjay walked to the figure's side and shook its arm. "Mother? Mother?"

The figure sat up, rubbed the sleep from its eyes, and looked down. "Johnjay!" She bent over and reached out her arm, placing it around Johnjay's neck. Her legs slipped from the horse's back and flopped lifeless in the mud. Johnjay's strong arm wrapped around Little Will's waist, holding her upright. She looked up into Johnjay's face. "Reg is dead. She went night before last."

Johnjay nodded. "I know. I am very sorry."

Little Will nodded, then placed her forehead against Johnjay's chest as her hand clenched at his robe. "I missed you. I missed you so."

Johnjay kissed his mother and held her tightly. "Mother, there's someone I want you to meet."

Little Will sniffed, looked to the bundle still sleeping upon her son's right shoulder. She reached over and lifted the blue cloth from the child's face. "How beautiful she is."

"She's your granddaughter. Her name is Girl."

"That is no proper name. Girl."

The child opened her eyes and started at the sight of the stranger. Johnjay laughed. "Girl, meet your grandmother."

The child looked at her father, then she smiled at Little Will and extended her arms for a hug. After a moment she released her grandmother and turned to Johnjay. "You can put me down, Father."

Johnjay lowered her to the muddy road then straightened up and looked at his mother. Her eyes were brimming with tears. "You can come home now." He held her close and nodded.

"It will be good to be home."

"What will you do, Johnjay? I know of the great powers you possess."

"Mother, I'm going to study with Mortify. I am going to doctor. I will be a very good doctor."

Little Will pushed back a little and glanced up at the sky.

"We should be going. People will be saying we don't have sense enough to come in out of the rain."

Johnjay lifted her to the back of her horse and laughed. "When did bullhands ever have sense enough to come in out of the rain?"

As he turned the horse around, Little Will reached to the kit tied behind her on the horse's saddle. She reached out her hand toward her son. In it was a gold and mahogany bullhook. He stared at it.

"Take it. It's yours now."

He shook his head as he took the object in his hands and studied it. He looked up at Little Will. "Thank you, but I can't take it." He turned and held the bullhook out to Girl. "Do you know what this is?"

The girl took it and nodded. "It's a steering wheel. You tell the bull what to do with it."

Johnjay looked at his mother, and she nodded back. He squatted next to Girl. "That bullhook is yours now. Take good care of it."

Girl hugged the bullhook to her chest and nodded, her face in smiles.

Johnjay stood, placed his right hand upon Girl's shoulder and took the horse's bridle with his left hand. He began walking toward Miira. "Let's go home. It looks like the rain is letting up."

Little Will wiped the tears from her eyes as she nodded. "It'll rain again. It always does."

Girl waved the bullhook in the air. "Life with a circus is just one long uninterrupted dee-light!"

In moments the rain had closed behind them.